THE ELIXIR OF LIFE

THE ELIXIR OF LIFE

ARTHUR RANSOME

With an Introduction by S. T. Joshi

Hippocampus Press

New York

Published by Hippocampus Press
P.O. Box 641, New York, NY 10156.
http://www.hippocampuspress.com

Cover art by Sir William Fettes Douglas (1822–1891), detail from *The Al-chemist.* Cover design and Lovecraft series logo by Barbara Briggs Silbert.
Hippocampus Press logo designed by Anastasia Damianakos.

First Edition
1 3 5 7 9 8 6 4 2

ISBN-13: 978-0-9814888-9-9

To My Mother

Introduction

Arthur Ransome's *The Elixir of Life* (1915) is one of the rarest works of twentieth-century supernatural literature. It is not cited in E. F. Bleiler's otherwise exhaustive *Guide to Supernatural Fiction* (1983); no entry on Ransome or his book appear in such works as Jack Sullivan's *Penguin Encyclopedia of Horror and the Supernatural* (1986), David Pringle's *Horror, Ghost, and Gothic Writers* (1998), or even Donald H. Tuck's *Encyclopedia of Science Fiction and Fantasy through 1968* (1974–82).[1] Published only in England by Methuen, the book apparently received no substantive reviews in the United States, and it is currently found in only six libraries in the United States; the British Library in London has only a microfilm of it.

Ransome himself (1884–1967) is, of course, a presence in the literary history of England. He attained celebrity by a series of children's books—including *Old Peter's Russian Tales* (1916), *Swallows and Amazons* (1930), and *Peter Duck* (1932)—that featured liberal doses of fantasy. He wrote a number of books on fishing and sailing, and these retain their interest and popularity today. During the 1910s he spent several years in Russia, witnessing the Soviet revolution of 1917 at first hand; he subsequently wrote three stirring books on the Russian political situation. As a literary critic he attained prominence with such works as *Edgar Allan Poe: A Critical Study* (1910) and *Oscar Wilde: A Critical Study* (1912); the latter book inspired a lawsuit against Ransome by Lord Alfred Douglas, but Ransome prevailed in the litigation. He translated Rémy de Gourmont's languid philosophical treatise *A Night in the Luxembourg* in 1912—a work Lovecraft read in 1923. Ransome's *Autobiography* was published in 1976.

The Elixir of Life is Ransome's only novel for adult readers. An earlier work, *The Hoofmarks of the Faun* (1911), is collection of stories; I have not seen this volume, but one review suggests that it contains some horror/fantasy content.[2] Ransome wrote *Elixir* in a period of a few

---

1. I wrote a brief entry on Ransome and *The Elixir of Life* in *Supernatural Literature of the World: An Encyclopedia* (Greenwood Press, 2005).
2. "They [the stories] are fantasy; but they are fantasy in which some symbolic meaning is evidently intended. And they are put forward, not as vague pictures of mood, in the manner of most prose-poems, but with the definite imaginary logic which the relation of an event requires. Poe has done things of the kind; and the influence of Poe is in some of Mr. Ransome's stories pretty clear." [Lascelles Abercrombie], Review of *The Hoofmarks of the Faun*, *Times Literary*

weeks during early 1915, while on one of his earliest visits to Russia. He engagingly describes the process of writing in a letter to Dora Colling-wood:

> I am having the most exciting adventure of my life. I am . . . writing a ro-mance. The idea got stuck in my head, and would not get out. I ought, as you know, to be doing serious work, and there is plenty to do, but this wretched tale kept dangling itself in front of my eyes, until at last I made a bargain with it. I said, 'If you will let me write you in three weeks, I'll do it', and the tale, humble beggar, said, 'Fire away', so I chucked all other work and fired away. This is the end of the first week, and behold six chapters, 20,000 words are written, and the rest is still seething. The whole book will be sixty thousand, . . . and if I really do get the whole thing into rough draft in the three weeks it will be a record, for me at any rate. You can have no conception of the excitement of the performance. I start out each day at nine sharp, and go it all day, knocking off finally at seven. Then in the eve-ning I smoke pipes and gossip with my heroes and heroine, and discuss next day's business. Then I sleep. Then up, wallop down two glasses of cof-fee and a whack of bread, and off again.[3]

Lovecraft would have approved of this frenetic manner of writing under the spur of inspiration, for he felt that this was the only way that genu-inely meritorious literature could be produced: a work should be written when it insists, in the face of all obstacles, on being written. In his auto-biography Ransome speaks of his work in considerably greater detail. He begins by noting:

> Then, one day when I was thinking about something quite different, I saw the faint glimmer of a story, somehow growing out of a long dialogue be-tween a philosopher and a homunculus. It was a discussion of the elixir of life, with a few roots still clinging to a book I had read about Paracelsus. This was something very unlike [Hugh] Walpole's novels, and I did not tell him about it in detail in case he should by seeing the weak points of the story make it impossible for me not to see them myself. I did not want to see them. I wanted to write the whole story, if only to prove to myself that I could.[4]

Supplement No. 488 (18 May 1911): 192.

3. Ransome, Letter to Dora Collingwood (27 February 1915), *Signalling from Mars: The Letters of Arthur Ransome*, ed. Hugh Brogan (London: Jonathan Cape, 1997), p. 22.

4. *The Autobiography of Arthur Ransome*, ed. Rupert Hart-Davis (London: Jona-than Cape, 1976), p. 175.

Ransome goes on discuss the rapid progress of the work: 19,500 words by February 27; 34,000 a week later; 46,800 a week after that; and, on March 20, "I had 58,500 words in typescript and I had stuck." (By "stuck" Ransome appears to mean that he not yet finished writing the book—specifically, what he terms the "missing vital chapter of the book, 'An Invitation to Eternity.'") Still unsure whether the work was publishable, he solicited the opinion of his friend Hugh Walpole, who "laughed at the idea that I should have any difficulty in finding a pub-lisher for it, [and] urged me to do the revision at once, to send the book back to England in time for publication in the autumn."[5] Ransome fin-ished his revisions on April 17 and a few weeks later sent the ms. to Methuen, which did indeed bring out the book that autumn.

Reviews of the work were few, but one of the more interesting ones appeared in the *Times Literary Supplement*—a review written (as the online edition of that periodical now identifies) by Walter de la Mare. De la Mare concludes his review by observing:

> There are some horrific moments in Mr. Ransome's romance—unusually sudden exits of his characters from this world into another place. He "hath an art to make dust of them" with a rapidity uncommon in mortal experi-ence, whereby they instantaneously "fall into indistinction, and make but one blot with infants." The Elixir may not be a novelty, and though Mr. Ransome introduces certain ingenious features into its decoction and indulges in curi-ous and speculative thinking about it, he might have indulged himself still more without complicating or impoverishing his story. It is his own ingenu-ousness and jollification of high spirits that keeps it bubbling—unflavoured by this black modern world, a story "Slipt in the black space 'twixt an idiot's gabble And a mad lover's ditty."[6]

De la Mare's reference to the fact that the tale "may not be a novelty" refers to the antiquity of the elixir of life theme in supernatural litera-ture, extending back to the Gothic novel at least to William Godwin's *St. Leon* (1799), if not earlier. And yet, it cannot be said that the theme has been treated with notable effectiveness in prior supernatural work; certainly, Edward Bulwer-Lytton's drearily prolix novel *A Strange Story* (1862), in spite of Lovecraft's charitable discussion of it in "Supernatu-ral Horror in Literature," cannot be said to utilise the motif successfully. Indeed, aside from Ransome's novel, one of the more substantial treat-

---

5. Ibid., pp. 175–76.
6. [Walter de la Mare], "New Novels," *Times Literary Supplement* No. 714 (23 September 1915): 321.

ments of the idea can be found in . . . Lovecraft's *The Case of Charles Dexter Ward* (1927).

It is unfortunate, then, that Lovecraft—who inserted a brief discussion of the Ransome novel in the revised version of "Supernatural Horror in Literature" ("In *The Elixir of Life* Arthur Ransome attains some darkly excellent effects despite a general naiveté of plot")—read *The Elixir of Life* only after writing *The Case of Charles Dexter Ward* in a less than two months in January–March 1927. He borrowed a copy of the novel from W. Paul Cook and read it in August 1928.[7] There can be no doubt that Lovecraft was struck, perhaps even a bit taken aback, by the parallels between his novel (which remained unpublished until after his death) and Ransome's. Some of the parallels are understandable in works addressing the elixir of life theme, such as the citation of the alchemists Paracelsus, Raymond Lully, and Cornelius Agrippa; even the fact that Ransome's baleful hero-villain, Killigrew, withdraws from society for a time and then comes back as his own son after he has taken the elixir—just as Simon Orne came back to Salem posing as his son Jedediah—is to be expected. But some other passages in the two novels are striking in their similarities. Killigrew's diary speaks poignantly of his gradual moral corruption as he continues to seek eternal youth—something that can only be achieved by murder—and remarks of his initial fascination with the elixir: "My desires were pure. I did not ask for youth that I might garland my head with flowers and gorge myself with sin. I cared for knowledge only, and for that end alone I hoped for eternal life." How could Lovecraft not have recalled an analogous passage in his own novel, when Charles Dexter Ward writes a harried letter to Dr. Willett and speaks in extenuation of his own involvement with Joseph Curwen: "I have brought to light a monstrous abnormality, but I did it for the sake of knowledge. Now for the sake of all life and Nature you must help me thrust it back into the dark again." And Killigrew's final dissolution in a cloud of "light grey dust" echoes Willett's destruction of Joseph Curwen, whose remains "now lay scattered on the floor as a thin coating of fine bluish-grey dust."

---

7. "Just now I am reading 'The Elixir of Life', by Arthur Ransome, one of several books lent me by W. Paul Cook. While there is considerable vapid romanticism in it, a pall of genuine horror hangs over the setting; & I do not hesitate in pronouncing it distinctly worth perusal." H. P. Lovecraft to August Derleth, 20 August 1928; *Essential Solitude: The Letters of H. P. Lovecraft and August Derleth*, ed. David E. Schultz and S. T. Joshi (New York: Hippocampus Press, 2008), 1:153.

I have elsewhere conjectured[8] that Lovecraft's reading of Herbert Gorman's *The Place Called Dagon* may have inhibited him from preparing *The Case of Charles Dexter Ward* for publication, given some similarities between those two works; but the similarities between *Ward* and *The Elixir of Life* are still more patent, and may also have contributed to Lovecraft's reluctance to submit *Ward* to a mainstream publisher in spite of several publishers' requests for a novel (as opposed to a short story collection) from his pen. Ransome's novel, to be sure, owes something to Oscar Wilde (Killigrew is approximately a Dorian Gray figure, as Peter Hunt has pointed out),[9] and perhaps still more, in general atmosphere, to Poe. It is unclear how many of the old-time Gothic novels Ransome read; but Lovecraft's novel, written as it was shortly after he had himself completed an extensive reading of Gothic literature for "Supernatural Horror in Literature," can take its place with Ransome's as a tribute to the pervasive influence of Gothic motifs upon subsequent horror literature. *The Elixir of Life*, a fabulously rare work, has not always attracted devotees even among Ransome scholars;[10] but as an effective and occasionally powerful treatment of a venerable supernatural trope, it deserves to find a new generation of readers.

—S. T. JOSHI

---

8. See my afterword to Herbert Gorman's *The Place Called Dagon* (New York: Hippocampus Press, 2003), pp. 186–87.

9. See Peter Hunt, *Arthur Ransome* (Boston: Twayne, 1991), p. 23.

10. Hugh Brogan, Ransome's biographer, makes the remarkable claim that "The only thing of interest . . . is the character of the uncle." See *The Life of Arthur Ransome* (London: Jonathan Cape, 1984), p. 102.

Contents

THE ELIXIR OF LIFE

CHAPTER I
I Quarrel with My Uncle and Meet Killigrew

I suppose when I was young I was a little more particular than I should like any son of mine to be in the matter of lace ruffles, silver buckles, swordstrings, and other of the trifles that seemed to me then the most important items of a man's equipment. Not that I was frivolous. I was not. Indeed I had read rather more deeply than was considered becoming in the more serious literature of our day, and could cap lines from the poets of the classic age with any man who had a taste for that sport. Moreover, my reading had taken a strange path, and led me far from the fashionable Anacreon, to certain strange descendants of Lucretius. There was a Dutch Jew, much persecuted, I believe, whose writings, in passable Latin, had for me a curious interest, and, besides him, there was our own Bishop Berkeley, plain Mr. Berkeley as he was then, whose exquisite dialogues I would recommend, as models of literary form, to all who, unlike myself, are able to make headway after any model whatsoever.

You may think it strange that I should begin the story of the episode that, monstrous as it seemed at the time, yet turned the greater part of my life into a primrose path, leading, I hope, to another end than hell, by the mention, in a breath, of lace ruffles and philosophers. Yet, it was through these things that my adventure began, or perhaps, more exactly, I should say, that lace ruffles and a young man's taste for airing his philosophy made it possible. It was due to these things that I found myself walking alone in the middle of a June night on the great road that leads from London to the north, and I owed the sequel to that strange beginning, partly, to my would-be philosophic conversation, and also, I am persuaded, to the subdued but elegant character of my attire.

I was, in those days, careful to the last degree of my personal appearance, believing that dress is an excellent vehicle of expression, for all who find words too cumbrous or too elusive. I held that the outer show should be the expression of the inner spirit, just as (you will forgive me the metaphor I was accustomed to make play with at the time) the earth changes her dress according to the season, a quaker sobriety in winter giving place in spring to light and joyful tints, which in turn are enriched in the full happy overflow of summer, and finally overwhelmed by the boastful melancholy pomps of autumn. I smile now, as I write down that image, to think how often I used it in those early days, and how often my poor uncle heard it, in excuse of my extravagance, before the adventure began which cast all such trifles from my mind. Still even this theory of mine had its part in the adventure, for it was responsible for the fact that, when I began to walk that great and ancient road, I was dressed in an extremely elegant costume of black velvet, with the finest lace ruffles that my uncle's credit could buy, frilled and primmed by the most incomparable of launderers. My sword was a light weapon, a weapon in hardly more than name, a toy, designed to show that I tolerated the fashion of the day but smiled at it, just as my dress, sober as it was, had an elegance which dallied with the idea that a man may read philosophy, and yet not cease to be a gentleman.

In fact, in many ways, I was a most incomparable young ass, the more ass because so perfectly persuaded of the infallibility of my opinion, and the superiority of my intellect, at least over that of my uncle, with whom, only a few minutes before the adventure began, I was seated in a comfortable closed coach, with an armed servant galloping before us, and another galloping behind. I well understand now how he had borne with me till he could bear no longer, and was determined to be rid of me at the very moment of the expiration of his guardianship. But then I did not realize how near the precipice I had come, or how completely the follies of the previous two years had exhausted my uncle's patience.

He had begun grumbling on the previous day, when we left London. I had replied to his remonstrances over the bill he had received from my tailor with what I imagined then to be reticence and forbearance, but what I now perceive to have been the most intolerable impertinence. He had slept ill at night. In the morning we had not spoken. In the afternoon, he had again broached the subject of my extravagance.

"What do you want the clothes for?" he has asked, in his simple way.

"I believe I dress with sufficient taste to do you credit, sir," I had replied.

"It is no credit to me to have a fool for a nephew."

"Perhaps, sir, you have not. There is a philosopher who maintains that things only are because we think they are, that each man is the inventor of the world he sees, and that the uncle who sees his nephew as a fool . . ."

"You strengthen me in my opinion of you by your words as much as by your appearance."

"But for all you know my words were never spoken. They may be the creations of your hearing. It is even possible that I do not exist."

"If it were not for the sake of my dead brother, I would wish to hell you didn't," said my uncle. With that he turned from me, and watched the pleasant mild landscape of those parts. In the evening, we refreshed ourselves in silence, and, after drinking more than his share of a bottle of port (on account of my age), he fell asleep. He slept, but woke, opportunely for the execution of his resolve, a little before midnight. He looked at his chronometer, satisfied himself of the time, and spoke abruptly:

"Let me see that toy."

"What toy?" I asked, mildly.

"The bauble of a sword for which I have to pay twenty good guineas, a price at which you could buy ten swords good enough to cut off a Scotchman's head with."

"I have not bought it to cut off anybody's head," I replied, and handed him the sword.

"A toy," he growled, "a laughable toy. Do you think if you were alone and attacked, you could defend yourself with such a gewgaw?"

I answered mildly that I was not a soldier, that I thought that in these modern days it was more often necessary to defend oneself with philosophical argument than with a sword, and that in argument I held myself a match for most men, and more of such twaddle.

"You mean, more than a match for me," he replied, "but let that pass. Tell me now, if you were in this country alone, and were attacked by a rogue who knew as little philosophy as your uncle, and had less respect for your father's son, would you threaten him with that ornament?"

I was taken aback, and said nothing, but his next words were a more violent surprise to me.

"You would not. You would beg him to read Mr. Berkeley, and then you would run away as fast as you could."

"That, sir, is unjust."

"I intend it to be. I wish to give you a hearty dislike for me in case you have not got one already. A hearty dislike. You will then be less likely to trouble me again, and more likely to set your face to the world and to find out what it is made of instead of talking stuff, and pretending it does not exist. My guardianship over you comes to an end to-night. I am going to set you in the world, just as you are, to learn your place in it. I am sick of your hair-splitting. We have just reached the top of the hill." (The horses had been walking.) "I beg you to get out. Out with you, sir, in all your foppery, and learn how little it is worth."

He rapped smartly on the windows of the carriage. It stopped. One of the riding servants came to the door, dismounted, and opened it.

I collected my surprise, anger, and such shreds of philosophy as I could find, and stepped down into the road.

"You may close the door, and drive on," said my uncle to his man, and then, to me, "I wish you a good night, and may it be a long time before I see you again."

"Certainly, sir," I replied, "and, for my part, I very sincerely wish you a good night and a better digestion."

With that the stately old carriage went rumbling away down the slope beyond the hill, carrying my uncle in it, no doubt spreading himself, I thought, over the seat I had shared with him, and enjoying his mental image of me stranded in the road. Oddly enough, even then, I could not hate my uncle. I even liked him, told myself I had been something of a fool, and started my adventure with a laugh.

*   *   *

It was midnight when I stood in the road listening to the swiftly dying noise of my uncle's carriage wheels. I was within a few minutes of being twenty-one years of age, and succeeding to the lack of property which, I supposed, was all that had been left me by my father beyond a small collection of books, that had been turned over to me at once, as my uncle did not care for reading. I stood there for some minutes, without moving, in my very elegant black velvet, silver buckled shoes, and cambric ruffles at sleeves and neck. I was five feet and a little more than eleven inches high, looking perhaps slightly less, because of a suspicion of a stoop which I habitually affected, after seeing a certain picture of a Greek philosopher. I was active, strong, and in good health. Indeed I had never been ill in my life. I have often been told since that I was good-looking. I certainly had a straight nose, clear brow, a very white but healthy skin, and an abundance of dark hair. I habitually shaved my chin and upper lip, though my razor had, I think, more of a harvest in promise than in fact.

I stood there in the moonlight, I say, and began my adventure with a laugh. Then, remembering my birthday, and my poverty, I bethought me of ascertaining exactly what I did at that moment possess, and, counting it in the moonlight, made out that I was the master of a gold guinea, two crowns, and some smaller coins. For that, I reflected I could at least obtain a bed, and I remembered that some few miles back on the road we had passed what I had supposed to be an inn. I turned, and began to walk leisurely down the hill. As I walked down the hill my spirits rose up, and before I came to the bottom I was singing, a merry enough little song, pleasant to me, not only for its own sake, but because it was in Latin, and because I had heard it sung, in his cups, in a London tavern, by a student who had gone over the seas after knowledge, and studied in the universities of France and Germany.

> "Gaudeamus igitur,
> Juvenes dum sumus.
>> Post jucundam juventutem,
>> Post molestam senectutem,
> Nos habebit humus."

Thus, by the purest accident, I sang what might have been the motto, the rather satirical motto, of the story I have to tell you. Rejoice while we may, rejoice while we are young, because after our cheerful youth and our old age of grumbling discomfort, an earthy bed lies waiting for us all. For us all, says the song. "The grave will have us," and yet while I was walking that road in the moonlight I was coming step by step nearer the knowledge that it has sometimes been possible to escape the grave, yes, and to escape death, though to tell you so much is already to leap midway into the story I have scarcely begun.

I have often wondered what would have happened to me if I had simply stayed where my uncle left me, and waited for morning to bring what chance it might, or if I had walked on north along the great road. It is, however, idle to speculate. If I had spent a lifetime in wondering I should not have been able to foretell a single one of the extraordinary events that presently swept my uncle, London, and all the childishness of my past life clean out of my mind. It is possible, though doubtful, that even if I had stayed with my uncle, and not been cast out in the road, my life would have been strange. It would at least have seemed strange to me, for there is not on earth one single living man to whom his life with all its circumstances does not in some moment of clearsightedness seem an amazing miracle.

An hour's steady walking brought me to the inn, which must have been only about two and a half miles back on the road, for, though I walked steadily, I did not hurry, and indeed could not unless I had been willing to destroy for ever an exceedingly delicate pair of shoes that I very well knew I should never be able to replace. It was a plain enough country inn, with some sort of sign dangling in the wind. It stood at crossroads, and there was a gallows close by, with the body of some poor wretch, swinging in chains, and making a noise very like that of the inn sign, but of less hospitable portent. Well, I came walking up to the inn, singing "Gaudeamus," and wondering to what extent I should be able to enjoy my youth on the sum of one guinea, two crowns, and a few bits of small change. Outside the door of the inn were three riding horses, two saddled and the third bare, tied to rings set for that purpose in the wall.

I thought to myself that there must be travellers calling at the inn who meant to proceed by night, but, just as I came up to the inn door, singing my song, a man came out, an ostler, and unfastened the horses. He remarked to me that it was a fine night with a bright moon, but an unconscionable hour at which to have to groom horses and stall them, with which, still grumbling, he led the horses into the yard of the inn. There was a light in the windows, and the man had left the door open. I went in, still humming "Gaudeamus" under my breath, and walked into the parlour on the right hand of the door in the window of which room I had seen the light.

There was a small wood fire in the great stone fireplace, always a pleasant thing, and never more pleasant than at night in midsummer. At the end of the table nearest to the fire were seated two men. One had his back to me and to the table, and was lying back in his chair with his legs, crossed one over the other at the ankles, stretched straight out towards the warmth. His head was bowed forward on his breast, and he seemed to be engaged in an almost angry scrutiny of the hearth. I was astonished to hear him humming my tune, "Gaudeamus." He had heard me singing down the road, and, I supposed, had instantly learnt the melody. The other, an older, grey-bearded man, was seated with his back to the wall. He seemed to be a kind of confidential servant, on intimate terms with his master. His face was oldish, unhappy, but not unkind. He stared at me as I came into the room, and into his look there presently came what I can best describe as advice to begone. He looked as if he wanted me to begone, for my own sake. It was a curious look. But, before I had had time to decide whether or not to obey it, his companion turned round, and from his face I could not take my eyes.

I suppose I must myself have been a somewhat surprising figure, standing suddenly in the parlour door of an inn, many miles from any town, and in the middle of the night. My elaborate dress, my buckled shoes, my dainty little sword: none of these things went with foot-travelling, and they must have known that I came by foot, since they had heard my song, and, no doubt, my footsteps on the firm summer road. I should, therefore, not have been at all puzzled if I had seen mere astonishment on the face of the man who now turned from the fire and looked at me with an intentness that I should have resented if I had not found myself, equally intently, staring at him.

His face was clean-shaven. It was an extremely intelligent face, delicate and sensitive to a degree. His eyes were dark and deep-set, his nose fine and straight with a suggestion of wax modelling. The chin though not prominent was firm. I could find no feature that accounted for the strange feeling of distrust that I experienced at first sight of him, unless it were his mouth, which was small, thin-lipped, and yet never quite straight. It seemed always ready to curl. For some reason, I do not to this day know why, it set me thinking of leeches. I judged him, that evening, to be an extremely well preserved man of thirty-eight or forty.

His first surprise at my appearance swept over his face like a summer cloud, and was succeeded instantly by a very different look. It was a look of mental appraisement. There was a good deal of approbation in it, and, more than this, of deliberate weighing of a proposition in which I was somehow concerned. I have seen the same look on the face of a young gallant choosing the colour of a suit of clothes. As I was watching him, before either of us had spoken a word, this look gave way to one of decision, and then this too swept from his face, leaving it merely handsome, cool, polite, even conciliatory.

He rose and bowed towards me.

"My name is John Killigrew," he said, and waited for me to speak.

"Mine is Richard Stanborough," said I, "and I may be permitted to hope that my presence will not disturb the meditation in which I perceive you were engaged."

"It has on the contrary driven it clear away," he replied, "and for that I am your obliged servant."

"In that case, I am glad," I said, and then feeling that at least I must make sure of a bed before I allowed myself to stop in the inn, I asked, "Perhaps, sir, you can tell me if that was the landlord whom I met just now taking your horses, for I suppose them to be yours, into the stable yard. I need to ascertain if he can offer me a bed."

"I think he is both landlord and groom," replied the man who had described himself as John Killigrew, "and I will be frank with you. I asked him to stable my horses as soon as I heard your song as you came along the road. The song is not one that is often heard in England, and I assumed, on hearing it, that here was some poor student coming who would enliven the last hours of what has been, to me, a preposterously dull day. I perceive, sir, that my supposition was an impertinence, but perhaps you will forgive it."

"By no means was it an impertinence," said I. "Indeed your supposition was the very truth. But tell me where you came to know the song."

"I heard it in Germany," said the man, as if it was a distant memory.

"You have studied in the universities of that country?"

"I have."

"Sir, I envy you. I will rejoin you in a moment, when I have spoken with the landlord about my bed."

"There is no need for that," replied Killigrew. "Michael, be so good as to find the landlord and to tell him that Mr. Stanborough requires a bed. Meanwhile, sir, perhaps you will join me in drinking this wine, which is better than might be expected from the cellars of such a tavern in such a part of this country. Michael, we shall need another glass."

I bowed my acknowledgments, and sat down in a chair on the opposite side of the fire, while Michael made his way out, returned with a glass, and went out again to bespeak a bed for me with the landlord. You may imagine that I felt I had stepped directly from my uncle's carriage into the society of a man who would understand me, a man whose attainments, though I did not know them, I already envied with the trustfulness which, although sometimes unfortunate in youth, I cannot think altogether reprehensible. I felt I had stepped from my uncle's world into my own. It was with something like exultation that I immediately broached the subject of philosophy. I blush now to think of the slenderness of the knowledge which then on the morning of my twenty-first birthday allowed me to speak as if I knew already most of what there was to be known. I confess it now. There was an intention in my mind to sound my new associate, to plumb the profundity of those depths which no other living man could guess. I, knowing nothing, dared to set myself to find out what he knew who knew all.

I mentioned my Dutchman to him, and he instantly summarized Spinoza's philosophy for me in a form at once so brief, so illuminating, and so convincing that my presumption was swept from me, and I thenceforward was only too willing to sit at the feet of the man who, I supposed, was the best qualified in the world to be my instructor.

He presently asked me what I thought of Paracelsus, and I had to admit that I knew nothing of him, but thought of him as a sort of Doctor Faustus, half charlatan, half sorcerer, by no means a philosopher. Here he took me up sharply.

"It is true," he said, "that the Cabalistic philosophers do not write in the language of the schools. They are not to be read by every careless runner. But, my friend, if I may be permitted so to address you" (I bowed in acceptance of this title), "let me assure you that there is not one strange phrase, not one obscure image in those tantalizing books which does not shine out with a light from beyond the stars when it is read by one who by dint of labour has learnt to understand it."

"Ah," said I, ingenuously, "would that I could find such an instructor. I am not so blind as not to wish to see, nor so prejudiced as to refuse to search."

"Mr. Stanborough," said he, "I am about to make what you may think a strange proposition. We have known each other but for a very short while, yet I hope you will not consider my offer an impertinence. I do not know your business, nor whither you may be travelling, but we have talked enough for me to know that I should find your company an extreme pleasure, and perhaps I can lessen the tedium of a quiet household by sharing with you what little knowledge I possess of philosophy. Will you proceed with me to-morrow, and honour me by making my home yours for a period that shall be determined by your inclination?"

I was stunned almost by this offer, which seemed to me to be the opening even of the doors of heaven, when I perceived the eyes of the old servant Michael, who was once more seated at the table, again looking at me with that strange expression of warning which I had noticed when first I entered the parlour of the inn. The ready acceptance died on my lips, and, scarcely knowing why, I began making the excuses natural.

"Sir," I said, "I am extremely obliged to you, but you must allow me to point out that I have not with me the clothes that are necessary even for the visit of a night. My whole luggage is the dress in which I am now sitting. My whole fortune a few little bits of metal which jingle in a lonely fashion in my pocket. I can hardly accept a hospitality which I may never be able to repay."

"Mr. Stanborough," said he, "do not answer me at once. I know nothing of your history, nor of your fortunes. You have shown me a little of your mind and character. I am inviting what I know, and not supposing anything that I cannot see. There can be no obligations between one philosopher and another. I am a lonely man. I ask you to help me spend the days in profitable talk and recreation, for my sake, not for yours. See, here is the landlord with our candles. Sleep and give me your answer in the morning."

The landlord stood in the doorway, open-mouthed on observing my costume, but calmed in his apprehensions on seeing the terms on which I stood with Mr. Killigrew, who, at least, had horses in the stable, and, doubtless, saddlebags in his bedroom. He led the way upstairs, and showed us to our rooms.

We wished each other a good night, and separated with bows. I remember, it seemed to me that his bow was a little old-fashioned, and that, as he made it, he tried to alter it into conformity with mine. I dismissed this idea as a piece of ridiculous vanity, and, placing my candle on the chair beside my bed, proceeded to undress. I undressed very slowly, stopping between each article of clothing that I removed to speculate upon this wonderful Killigrew, who, it seemed, was wishful to solve, for a time at any rate, the difficulties into which my uncle's sudden dismissal had plunged me. I went over our conversation, thinking of the things I might have said better, and the things I should have said but had not. Then, more and more often my mind busied itself with that odd look of warning on the face of the old servant. Why did he wish to warn me? Against what? There is nothing very dangerous in a philosopher, I thought, and smiled as I looked at my own dainty little sword, which I had hung on a knob of the chair. The sight of that took my thoughts back to my uncle's carriage, and the moments soon after I left it, when I stood alone in the moonlight, elegantly dressed but practically penniless, on the great north road that lay, grey and straight, under the windows of the inn. I reflected that although chance had given me a few hours of excellent talk, and the society of an equal, it would not do so often, unless I took steps to remedy my position. I told myself that I could not accept Killigrew's offer, until I had made myself something more than the abandoned nephew of an eccentric uncle. I thought I knew friends in London who would help me. I thought of the universities, and suddenly mistrusted my stock of knowledge. One way or other, however, I would better my fortunes, and show my uncle I could do without him. I therefore decided, regretfully, but with a sort of personal pride, to reject, at least for the present, the offer that had been made me. I was sitting on the edge of the bed in my shirt, ready to lie down and sleep on so praiseworthy a resolve, when I heard a very little noise at the door of my room.

I looked at the door and saw it open slightly. Then I saw the head of the old servant Michael. He looked at me, and placed his finger on his lips. I stared at him in silence, as he slipped into the room, and closed it silently behind him.

He approached me on tiptoe. "My master sleeps in the room next to yours," he said, "and so, for my sake, I beg you not to raise your voice. For your sake, I beg, sir, you will listen to me."

"What is it?" I asked, a little offended at being thus forced into conspiracy with some one else's servant in the middle of the night. I was besides conscious that it is impossible to be dignified in nothing but a shirt, even if it is the best shirt that ever was made in London, which I had the vanity to believe that mine was.

"Do not ride with us to-morrow. My master means you well, but his well is another man's ill. There is good in your face besides youth, and he has done harm enough. If you value your peace of mind and the love of God, do not accept my master's invitation."

As you know, I had already decided to refuse that invitation, but such is the strange perversity of the human mind, especially in early youth, that I had no sooner heard the old man's warning, than I reached for my breeches, and began hurriedly replacing them on my legs. I thrust my feet into my shoes.

"For God's sake, sir," said the old servant, "what are you going to do?"

"I am going to tell your master I have decided to accept the offer he has been good enough to make to me."

"You will be sorry for it, but at least I can tell my mistress that I warned you."

With that he slipped from the room as noiselessly as he had come. I followed him, wondering what lady could possibly be interested in hearing that I had been warned. A few steps down the passage there was the glint of light under a doorway. I knocked at that door.

"Be pleased to come in," said the voice of my new acquaintance.

I went in and hesitated on the threshold, aware of my costume. He had not undressed, but was sitting reading, by candlelight, a small book open on a table before him.

"You will, sir," I said, "pardon my visiting you at this hour, and in this attire, when I tell you that I do so to lessen as far as possible the rudeness I am already committing in not at once and gratefully accepting the invitation you have been kind enough to offer me. I shall count it, sir, an honour as well as a pleasure, to ride with you to-morrow."

"My dear sir, I am delighted, and only hope that you will not be disappointed with our very sober hospitality."

I approached the table to shake his hand in token at once of our agreement and the beginning of our friendship. As I did so, my eye, not intentionally curious, fell for a moment on the book that he was studying. I expected it to be a volume of the classics, or some modern philosopher. Its title page was largely printed, and, with the utmost astonishment, I saw that it was a silly little book of contemporary fashions.

We shook hands, and, as I closed the door, I saw him turn the pages of that insane little book, and plunge once more into the most ardent study.

CHAPTER II

I Come to the Old Hall and
Am Warned by a Pedlar

The landlord had not thought to close the meagre curtains of my bedroom, and, long before I fell asleep, the night had turned into a June morning. I did not choose to close them. My mind was moving in such unaccustomed paths, that it was a pleasure to me to see the pale morning sky, and the touch of sunlight on small clouds. I reflected, wisely, I think, that, after all, life and the world were always there, and that from any by-way into which I might be led I could always turn back to them. I perceive now that this is not precisely true; that events do actually change the world to which we turn in escaping from them. For, as Berkeley tells us, it is the eyes that see, and not the things that are seen. I did not, however, apply Berkeley in that manner then, and I am glad I did not. The belief I then held, that life offered me an infinite number of paths, from any one of which I could turn back if I did not like it, is the only belief which does not stifle enterprise in youth.

At eight o'clock, after I had been in bed for six hours, and asleep for four, the sunlight, slowly moving across the room, poured a broad flood on my face and woke me. I sprang out of bed, praised God for the fine day, and dressed as quickly as I could. I wished to shave, but remembered that my razor, with several other small implements of my toilet, were in a bag on the bottom of my uncle's carriage. I idly wondered how soon after our parting he had observed them, and how many miles along the road I should find them if I chose to look. I never doubted for a moment that on observing them, probably after some irascible movement of his feet, he had pitched them bodily through the window. I knew my uncle very fairly well, and that, unless some miracle happened in the night, is a very accurate account of what must have happened. My chin, however, did not really need shaving, and I told myself I would procure a razor in the next town.

I went downstairs, and out into the fresh June air. Two horses, ready saddled, were in the yard, and the landlord of the night before was busy saddling a third. He bid me a civil enough good morning, and remarked that he thought I was to ride the best horse of the three, by which I learnt that he knew I was riding with Killigrew. I made no comment on this news, not caring to share my curiosity with an inn-keeper, but merely looked at the horse, a very pretty roan.

"And I was to tell you, sir, that your breakfast is waiting you in the parlour, and that Mr. Killigrew will be ready to start at any time you think fit."

"And what do I owe you, landlord?" I asked, for I feared the discomfort of settlement in the presence of my new acquaintance.

"The reckoning is paid already," said the man, and, for the first time, a spasm of dislike for Killigrew swept across my mind. I went into the parlour, and found an excellent breakfast set out, cutlets and green peas, I remember, but I had to eat it by myself. Soon after I had done, and was standing before the window, the old man Michael came in, and asked me when I would care to start. I told him I was ready even then, as I had no baggage to pack. A few minutes later I was greeted by Killigrew, who came down muffled in a riding coat, which hid the greater part of his face. He excused himself for not uncovering, by telling me he had caught something of a chill while reading at the open window that morning, before the sun had lifted the night mists. We passed out together into the yard, where Michael was already adjusting the saddlebags to his horse and to Killigrew's. I gave the innkeeper a crown as he lengthened the stirrups to suit me, and, as soon as we were out on the road, complained to Killigrew that he had taken advantage of me in paying my bill while I slept.

"I took the liberty to hold you my guest from the moment you came into the inn, bringing that song with you. You are not going to quarrel with me about that. . . ."

He had me at disadvantage. I could not well say more, and I rode beside him, grumpy and discontented, and yet unable to relieve my temper.

For some miles we rode in silence, and then he suddenly blew my annoyance away by the first words of a discourse on the philosophy of the last century, in which he made great sport of the corrupt Lord Chancellor, Frank Bacon, and his pedestrian habit of experiment. I listened in high good humour, until we met a company of peasants who stared at me with a curiosity that annoyed me, quite wrongly, for my costume was in the last degree unsuitable for horse-exercise, and he must have been a fool who did not stare.

But I will not detain you with a further account of our ride, most of which, excepting the details I have already given you, has passed away from my memory as such things will. Only one thing stands out among all those half-forgotten impressions, and that was one that I did not really notice till the next day. Not once during our ride did I get a clear view of Killigrew's face.

In the evening, at about six o'clock, we came to a small village, where all stared at us with particular curiosity. And we were scarcely clear of that village before we turned from the main road into a smaller one, in very poor repair, partly grown over with grass, which led to a tall gateway, with a griffon on one gatepost, and its fellow lying in the long grass at the foot of the other. In the gateway was standing a very old pedlar, who looked at us so hard that he annoyed Killigrew, who said quietly to the servant, Michael, "Drive that fellow away."

It had, however, just occurred to me that it might be possible to buy a razor from this pedlar, and almost before Killigrew had given his order to Michael, the pedlar was at my side.

Killigrew made a slight gesture of impatience and rode through the gateway. I could do no less than ask the question for which I had beckoned the pedlar, and I asked him, "Have you a razor there in your pack?"

He did not answer this question, but leaning up towards me, and staring into my face, he said:

"Are you the new master?"

"No," I replied.

"Is your name Killigrew?"

I shook my head before realizing that his question was impertinent.

"Then," he said, "in the name of God the Father, God the Son, and God the Holy Ghost, do not go through that gateway."

"You must go now," said Michael. I do not know if he had heard the beggar's words or not. The pedlar turned and walked slowly away, nodding his head, and, as it seemed to me, praying. I thought he was mad, and said so to Killigrew, as I joined him. And I had to go without my razor. He agreed with me and then spoke to the old servant.

"This, I believe, Michael, is our new home, is it not?"

"It is, sir," said old Michael, and then Killigrew turned to me.

"It is as strange," he said, "to me as it is to you. Yet it is the ancient home of the Killigrews. It passed to me from a cousin, who left it twenty years ago. It has been much neglected, but I hear that my poor cousin's taste in books was not unlike mine, so that we shall have the advantage of an excellent library. I have also sent hither a few things of my own, and, I make no doubt, we shall find the house quite ready to receive us. It has indeed been much neglected," he remarked, pointing with his riding switch to the grass on the road, and the rough, unkempt grass of the park through which we were riding. "But nothing could better suit my humour. And these tall trees will stand like sentinels about us to screen our sacred studies from the prying eyes of that foolish world which could make Bacon a Chancellor and delights to think of the ever to be venerated Faustus deep in infernal pits of torment."

It was indeed a strange wild place. A ring of woodland, in which were many trees of great height, seemed to stretch like a wall about the park. Beyond that belt of gigantic trees was the high stone wall with the gateway through which we had passed. Directly before us were more thick woods, and it was not until we were close upon it that I perceived, hidden in these trees, a strange, melancholy-looking old house of stone, covered with dark green ivy, which had grown even to the roof, and waved ragged despairing arms from the grey stone copings.

Some of the upper windows were boarded up, and ivy had grown across the boards. From others, the boards had been but lately taken down, and the torn and broken ivy that had grown on them hung in festoons. The door was studded with iron, like the door of a fortress. The stone steps before it were cracked, and dandelions raised their golden suns from between the cracks. As we rode up, I saw a snake, that had been sunning itself in the last warmth of the day, slip off the step into the long grass under the house wall. The wallflowers growing in that long grass seemed to suggest that the garden had once been cared for, but how long ago?

Killigrew and I dismounted, and old Michael rode slowly off round the corner of the house, leading our horses. We stood on the step, and as I looked back on the gloomy park we had crossed, and reflected that the sunshine which fell on it fell also on the world outside, I was, for the moment, tempted to turn and run. It seemed to me that when that great door should be opened, and when I should have passed into that strange dead house, it would be as if I had died and joined my father in the grey vault where my uncle and I had seen him laid when I was a boy of twelve. Not all my admiration of Killigrew's conversation, not all my pleasure in the new and unexpected, could save me from a cold and choking feeling in the throat, as if my youth were being suddenly taken from me by force. Remember that I was only twenty-one. I looked at Killigrew, hoping to find comfort in some trait of his which I could admire. But he was bending over the keyhole of the door, and his face was utterly muffled in the hood of his riding cloak.

The key grated in the lock, and my companion bowed for me to pass before him. I went in. I could not trust myself to take another glance over my shoulder at the sunshine.

The hall into which we stepped was lofty, and very dimly lit from the ivy-choked windows. But, from a window on the floor above, a narrow beam of sunshine fell on the head of the staircase and lit with a golden, almost magical radiance the figure of a young girl who at that moment began to descend the staircase towards us. She was dressed in white, with a girdle of silver or gold embroidery that caught the light.

Her face was pale, not wholly unlike that of the man with whom I stood, and yet strikingly different. For the mockery that played so readily about his mobile lips was entirely absent from hers. Her hair was that brown which has been touched with red gold. I cannot hope to describe the impression made upon me by that lovely and unexpected vision. I am older now, but even so my pen waits laden with ink above the paper, and I cannot set down a word that does not seem to make Rose Killigrew less lovely than she was. A wood nymph, Troy's Helen, so from time to time I have described her, with what utter failure of expression! There have been Queens of Scotland with something of her head, so lightly set upon that slender, graceful neck. But they were only queens. This was a daughter of the gods, yet with a heart to feel and to console the sorrows of the world.

She came down out of the sunshine, but owed so little to that illumination that, instead of fading as she came near, it seemed to me that she carried the sun with her, and that my eyes were dazzled as they looked at her.

Killigrew said to her, "Rose, allow me to present to you Mr. Richard Stanborough, who is our guest for a while," and to me, "Mistress Rose Killigrew, my sister."

I made the most awkward bow I ever have made in my life, and could find not one single word that I could force my lips to say.

"I hope," she said, "that he will not be disappointed by the poor entertainment we can offer him," and somehow she made those dull, conventional words warm with a real welcome, so that I forgot at once the gloomy fright in which I had stood hesitating on the doorstep. Yet, I had scarcely recovered myself before that fright had been displaced by a new disquietude. This was the mistress of whom old Michael had spoken on the previous evening when he came to my bedroom in the tavern. "At least," he had said, "I can tell my mistress that I warned you." How had she known that I was coming, and why had she wished me to be warned? There was extreme sadness in her face and something which made me glad I had refused the warning. If, indeed, there was some strange danger in coming to that place, I was sure that it did not proceed from her. Perhaps, I thought, she also is threatened by it, and at that thought my heart was suddenly filled with unconquerable joy. I have come, I thought, and perhaps we shall share that danger, side by side. Then I thought, what incredible folly! A brother and sister newly come to a house that had long been uninhabited, and I, romantic youth, was conjuring up horror out of nothing more unusual than the naturally neglected state of house and park. Then again I remembered Michael's warning, and the pedlar, and the physical feeling of gloom with which I had entered the house. I remembered these things with exultation, and I suppose something of that exultation showed in my face as I looked at her, for she smiled, and again I thought I saw both gratitude and pity in her smile.

Immediately afterwards an incident occurred which at the same time brought us near together, and confirmed my original feeling that there was something strange, something unusual in this house.

I glanced at Killigrew and saw that his eyes had been watching the meeting between his sister and myself with an intense and concentrated interest. When he saw me look at him, his eyes seemed suddenly to die in his head, and he to be no more than the polite and hospitable host who is anxious that his guest shall be at home.

He turned and asked his sister, "And is all ready, Rose?"

"I think everything is as you wished."

"The men have gone and the women?"

"There is no one in the house but ourselves and old Michael. I dismissed the others an hour before you came."

I could only see his eyes and forehead, but at this moment I saw those eyes leap again to life, and vertical lines of the most intense agitation crease his brow. I heard a small noise at the back of the hall. One of the doors opened, and a group of village people, men and women, advanced from it, holding their caps and giggling nervously. A large fat man seemed to be their leader, and he, apparently not noticing the startled gesture of Mistress Rose, spoke with peculiarly odious servility, addressing his words to a point in the air midway between Killigrew and myself, as if he did not know which of us was the proper recipient of the speech he wished to make.

"We be come, master, to bid you welcome to . . ."

He got no further.

I saw a look of terror on the face of Rose Killigrew, and I saw Killigrew straighten himself suddenly. She put out her hand and touched his arm. He disregarded her, gripped the handle of his sword, made two or three swift steps towards the group of villagers, uttered a sort of groan of suppressed and violent rage, and, muffling his face still more closely in his hood, ran swiftly up the stairs and disappeared.

The villagers stood abashed.

Rose controlled her terror, and said, quite quietly, "Master Dormer, I think I told you to be gone with your helpers a full hour ago."

"Ay, mistress, but we meant no harm. We do be waiting ever since to greet the master."

"You must go now," she said. There was no anger in her voice.

"Ay, mistress," said the man, and the villagers crowded back and went out through the doorway by which they had come. As it closed behind them, I heard them break into angry discussion and complaint. Then there was a sudden silence, and old Michael appeared at the door.

"Did they see the master?" he asked.

"He has gone upstairs," Rose replied, and Michael hurried up the staircase.

I remembered old home-comings, when I was a boy, and how the villagers always waited in the hall to greet my father, and how there was always a bowl of wine for them, and pleasant speeches on both sides. I could not understand the inhumanity of Killigrew. Still less could I understand his rage, and, as it appeared to me, his flight, before a few harmless country-folk, who had only stayed to do him honour.

Rose and I were alone. I saw that she was trembling. She leaned against the stone balustrading at the foot of the staircase. I was filled with the anger that every young man knows when he stands in the presence of a woman in trouble and knows that he can do nothing to help her. I busied myself with the hilt of my sword.

Suddenly, composed, she turned to me, and said, calmly, as if nothing unusual had occurred: "Mr. Stanborough, you must forgive me. Now that the villagers are indeed gone, we have no servant in the house but Michael. I am chambermaid, and even cook. Let me show you to your room."

"You were expecting me then," I said, again surprised.

"I knew it was possible that Mr. Killigrew would bring a guest."

She led me to one of the doors opening out of the hall, and passed before me, into a small, neatly appointed room, with a high-pillared bed, and furniture of ancient pattern. There was a narrow window opposite the door by which we went in, and low beside that window was a small oak door, that, from its position, seemed an exit into the garden.

"I have done my best to drive away the feeling of death," she said, pointing to some roses in a silver bowl. "There is that feeling in every room of this old house, which has lain empty so long. There is a feeling of death even in the park that surrounds it. But there is one little plot that has been saved from the wilderness. That is the rose-garden. You must see it in the morning. It lies below your window, and this little doorway leads down to it, if you can stoop so low. The old man who has kept fires lit in the house these twenty years has tended the roses, and they alone in the place seem untouched by the finger of death."

"Madam," I said, "there is one other in this place on whom death has not dared to lay his hand. Doubtless for her coming the old man has kept his roses, and they will blossom with the more luxuriance for a mistress as lovely, nay, lovelier than themselves."

It was a silly speech, but, as I have so often to remind you, I was only twenty-one, and, in the presence of Rose Killigrew, no man who was not a fool could speak as neatly as he wished.

She smiled, sadly, I thought, and continued. "He was a strange old man. When he heard that my brother was coming, he took a pack, and said he had been a pedlar before, and could be a pedlar again, and with that he walked out of the house and away."

"We met him at the gate," I said.

"Did my brother see him?"

"He saw him, and seemed displeased," I said. "He told Michael to drive him away."

"I am glad no worse happened. My brother has a peculiar aversion to pedlars. And I was glad that he went away as he did, for I should not have liked to tell him to go, when he had made me so pretty a rose-garden, but you have seen how my brother is with any servants not of his own choosing or Michael's."

"Yes, I saw."

"He might have killed them. In Florence, once . . ." She stopped and went on, "He particularly said that if any pedlars came about the place they were to be driven out. When the old gardener took his pack, I was terribly afraid lest my brother should meet him before he left the park."

Just then old Michael came to the door. "The master is unwell," he said. "He does not require attendance, and asks that you will entertain Mr. Stanborough at supper." He went away.

Mistress Killigrew betrayed no special anxiety about her brother's health, and indeed I felt there was no need, and that his indisposition was no more than an unwillingness to meet us again so soon after his extraordinary behaviour.

"I think I told you, Mr. Stanborough, that now that the villagers have gone, and until the new servants are brought by Michael, I am chambermaid, and, though our supper is almost ready, there are yet some things to be done. I will leave you for a moment."

"Madam," I interrupted, "in the matter of potatoes and such things my sword is at your service." And I think that was the wisest speech I had framed since I had seen her, for she laughed, and at that sweet sound I blessed in my heart my uncle, the innkeeper, Killigrew, every circumstance that had conspired to let me hear that heavenly music.

She laughed, I say, and replied, laughing:

"You are very gallant; but there is no need to sully your sword on such base flesh. The potatoes are already peeled and cooked. They only need to be carried from the kitchen to the table. If you would help me, you may."

She led me to a huge kitchen, with a great fire in it, and dishes on the table ready for whatever was stewing in those iron pots. I hove the pots off the fire for her, and held them while she filled the dishes from them. Then, with great dignity, I carried the dishes at her direction into a room where, by the light of half a score of candles in a huge old silver candlestick, I saw a supper had been laid for us. I well remember that supper. Cold venison pasty was the main dish, and a salad, a salad made by her own hands that knew that art better than any out of France. It was a simple enough meal, but set out with exquisite daintiness. She had planned it, but I had helped, in carrying in those dishes, and, somehow, if it had not been for the empty place, reminding us of Killigrew, we should have been like children who had known each other all their lives and were playing at keeping house. It would be so for a minute, and then, like the faint quick draught that blew about that ancient house and shook the flames of the candles, there would come an inexplicable knowledge that we two were not merely children, but had our parts to play in a more serious drama. And this thought would be succeeded in its turn by sheer pride and joy in the knowledge that, if there were danger in that drama, we two were on the one side. These, of course, were my feelings. I do not know what hers were, on that first night, the most memorable in my life. But, when the meal was over, and we stood up together and said our grace to God, I knew that whatever should come we could not again be strangers to each other.

CHAPTER III

The Rose-Garden at Night and the Fringe of a Secret

It will be readily imagined that when that night I parted from Rose Killigrew, kissing her hand at the foot of the stone staircase, and watching her ascent, I did not feel inclined for sleep. The candles had been lighted in my room, probably by old Michael, and I noticed with pleasure and relief a case of razors and other shaving tackle on my dressing-table, besides several changes of clean linen, and a very handsome suit of mulberry. Mulberry was not a colour that I much affected, but, so far as I could judge, the suit was in a fashion to which I could not take exception, and, in any case, I was glad to have a change at all. I determined to write a letter in the morning to my uncle's housekeeper, and, when Killigrew should be sending to town, to have a small but sufficient wardrobe sent to me. At least, I thought, though my uncle paid for those clothes, yet he is too fat to wear them, and the care and thought that went to their design was expended by myself alone.

Her roses were on the table, and I bent to them and took one from the bowl, and thought of the little hand that had held its stalk, perhaps just as I was now holding it. I kissed the flower, and, as the cold petals touched my lips, I smiled at myself. "Dick Stanborough," said I, "you who care more for philosophers than for women, you are kissing a flower for the sake of one of whose existence you were ignorant yesterday." And then I was petulant with myself, for comparing her even for a moment with other women.

I walked up and down in my room, wholly incapable of following one thought to its end, and freeing myself for the pursuit of another. My thoughts jumbled themselves, and fell one on the top of another, like children's hands in that game of pat-a-cake, when each lays a hand on another, and the hand that is below is pulled out and laid on the top in quick succession. So my thoughts recurred, disturbing, restless, image after image shifting those already in my mind, and presently itself displaced by another. I put my hand to my forehead and found it hot. I pulled the curtain aside, and saw that there was moonlight. The key was in the lock of the little low door, and I opened, bent low, and in a stooping position passed down two shallow steps into the garden.

The moon was not bright and clear as on the previous night, for a white mist hung about the house, and the moon shone through it, as if veiled. My first view of the little rose-garden, which was to be the scene of so much happiness and of so much disquietude, the little garden to which, long afterwards, my thoughts so often turn, was far from clear. I could see that it was long and narrow, and walled by a high trellis, covered with climbing roses. A path ran down each side, and the two paths were joined by numerous crossways, between the rose-beds. I could see the great pale roses in the dim moonlight, and here and there scattered petals on the dark ground, looking at a little distance like a fleet of elfin boats.

I set to walking up and down one of those long paths, trying to collect my thoughts, and to understand exactly what had happened since, twenty-four hours before, I had been turned out of my uncle's coach upon the great North Road. I kept to one path, because, after I had once walked from one end of it to the other, so large a number of gossamers had tickled my face, and, breaking, hung on my nose and eyebrows, that I felt there could be no more, whereas, if I were now to walk on the other long path, I should again have to break through a similar multitude of tiny, intangible, annoying threads.

I looked up to the house. All the windows were dark, except my own. So, for a moment, I thought, and then perceived that some one, with a candle, was slowly going from room to room along the upper storey. Nothing, I thought, could be more natural than that old Michael should be late in going the rounds on this first night in a new habitation. I felt a sort of warmth at the thought of the old man performing that simple office, passing from room to room, that we might sleep secure in the knowledge that in all the house there was no hostile thing, but only the sleepers of the family.

Then, as I turned to continue my walking, it occurred to me, with or without reason, that the hostile thing, the thing that, in spite of myself, I feared, was closely connected with one member of that family, indeed with Killigrew himself, who had brought me hither. Why had the old man begged me not to accept that invitation? Why had Rose Killigrew, for he could have meant no other by "my mistress," wished me to be warned? Why had Killigrew so strange an aversion to pedlars, a harmless if a thieving race? Why had the pedlar at the gate replied to an inquiry for a razor with an adjuration in the three sacred names? And, finally, why had Killigrew been so angered beyond himself merely because a few officious villagers had planned to greet his arrival, as it was very proper that they should? Why was it that on this occasion Mistress Rose Killigrew, whom no evil thing should harm, had been clearly frightened, and that to no common degree?

Then I thought of Killigrew himself, picturing him as I had first seen him, turning from the fire in the inn parlour, to look at me with that curious intentness of expression. I remembered my first strange feeling in his presence, and then the utter abandonment to admiration which had followed in me, when he began to talk. I remembered the exhilaration of those two hours in the inn, when he had talked as I never heard man talk before of the things I had studied, but knew only in my shallow boyish manner. I remembered how it had seemed that God had expressly turned me out on the road, and brought me to the inn, that I might hear those golden words. Finally, baffled by Killigrew, I very naturally turned my thoughts upon myself.

I reviewed my present position, and compared it with that of yesterday. On the one hand, I had been definitely dismissed by my uncle, to whom for many years I had been accustomed to look as guardian. I was utterly without prospects or plans of any kind. And this, mind you, was for me an entire change in the very foundation of my life. I had lived with my uncle for nine years, and before that had always looked upon him as the ultimate fount of pain or pleasure. And now that fat and furious old man had gone rolling away out of my life up to the north country where I had been born, in a carriage that had been in my early infancy the scene of my childish games. It was a coach of ancient design, swung on broad leathers. Its seats were broad, and, for a little boy, high. I had given them names, Ararat and Sinai, the greatest mountains of which I had heard, and, so well was the carriage balanced, that even a small boy, by vigorous movements, could set the whole aswing, and plunge both Ararat and Sinai and himself into the most tremendous swaying of an earthquake. It was, I remembered with a smile, upon Ararat that my uncle and I had been sitting during our last and dramatically concluded dialogue. Upon Ararat now, with his feet upon Sinai, was he, in all probability, sleeping, while the old coach drove on the north road, to rest at last in the coach-house where as a boy I had watched it cleaned and, with difficulty, and the use of hands, climbed up its three hanging steps into its commodious body.

My uncle was the elder son, and his brother, my father, was a spendthrift, though not in any large and showy manner. My uncle owned the greater part of the family property and, like many who have, he knew how to keep. He never allowed his expenses to exceed his income, and he so managed his pleasures that when his expenditure in London threatened to approach his income from the north, he turned very contentedly into a country gentleman, and drove off up the north road, swearing that London was a place for coxcombs and courtiers, but that he, thank God, was an honest country squire and knew how to take his pleasure among folk as honest as himself. My father, on the other hand, could never forget that my grandfather had been the son of a nobleman. He held to the old tradition that sent cadets to Court to make their way, and to Court he went himself, though he was not so fortunate as to obtain any advancement except in the knowledge of how to send one guinea in chase of another. The result of this was that he became almost entirely dependent upon my uncle, who bore with him very good-temperedly, and seldom reminded him of the fact. Indeed, I believe now that many of my uncle's periodical retirements to the north were made to save money not because of any extravagance of his own, but because the family purse was proving too shallow for the upkeep of my father in that state of pleasant sufficiency in which he held that it was fit for a gentleman to appear in the company of His Majesty. I cannot, you see, look back on the figure of my father with any great respect. There is, however, this to be said for him, that no man, woman, or child ever had a cross word for him, that he loved my mother, and that he did not spend her fortune until after she was dead, a forbearance which, on his part, meant much. It suddenly occurred to me to wonder whether by any chance there had been money which by some trick of the law he had been unable to spend, money or property which must come to his son, willy-nilly. It occurred to me that perhaps I was not such a pauper as I had thought myself when I counted my one guinea and my two silver crowns. It occurred to me also that my uncle seldom did things without a purpose, and that it was indeed an odd coincidence that, after bearing with me so long, he should suddenly have flung me forth from his protection within a minute or two of my twenty-first birthday.

A strange protection it had been. My father had died in the twelfth year of my life, and in dying had solemnly handed me over to my uncle with a request that showed that, as he lay on his deathbed, he did to some extent repent of the folly with which he had spent his life in pursuing the vain shadow that is called favour. "Anthony," he said, "I beg you to bring him up as a gentleman, and see that a fair knowledge of the Latin tongue is somehow or other beaten into him. Let him have a knowledge of London, which is a knowledge of the world, but on no account, and under no inducement, suffer him to go to Court, or to set one foot upon the ladder I have spent my life in climbing, of which I am verily persuaded that each step is a hallucination and leaves its climber no higher than he was before. And now, send him away. He is a little young to see death." I remembered that, clearly. My uncle had patted my head and pushed me out of the room, when I was taken in hand by a knot of kitchen wenches who wanted something to blubber over. From them I escaped to the stables, where some hours later I was found, and haled before my uncle, who was sitting by a big fire, mopping his eyes, and taking prodigious pinches of snuff, to which, I think, he wished me to attribute the moistness that, now and then, even showed upon his cheek. He had told me, simply, that my father was dead, and that from that time on I was to look to him for guidance, support, and punishment. My uncle was punctilious in fulfilling to the letter the un-welcome business that my father had requested from him. I was taught Latin by the parson, for a month or two, and then my uncle, much, I believe, against his own inclination, settled in London, that I might be schooled at Westminster. From Westminster I went to Oxford, return-ing, when the universities were not keeping terms, to London. I believe my terms were my uncle's holidays, for he invariably left London the same day that I left it myself, and when I returned thither, I always found that he had but just arrived. I believe he had a half-conscious dis-like of the capital, increased after my father's death. Suddenly, as I walked there in that misty rose-garden, I had a new view of our rela-tionship. I saw my education from my uncle's standpoint, and saw how, as I reached the age of manhood, he had promised himself freedom from me, and, starting for the north on the last day of my twenty-first year, had lost no time in making his life his own again, and in easing his shoulders from their most unwelcome responsibility. I realized that as I had grown older I had not made myself particularly pleasant to my un-cle. I had interested myself in philosophy, which to him was the last abomination. I had cared nothing for field sports, and I can even now see the disappointment on his face when I refused his proffered gift of a leash of badger hounds, to hunt with on our northern fells. I began to see that he was not altogether to blame in wishing to throw me off at the first moment that he could, without violating my father's trust. I was a little ashamed of myself, and thought with real affection of that honest old man, racing like a schoolboy from his books to enjoy the life he had so greatly forgone while protecting a youth whose tastes were in such open hostility to his own.

I had got so far in my meditations, and looking in fancy upon the sleeping face of my uncle, as in the old carriage he hurried northwards to his hills and hounds, had stopped at the end of the garden farthest from the house, when I heard the low, sudden creak of opening a door that is stiff in the hinges. I turned hurriedly, and looked towards the house. There was a light in my window, as before, but I was astonished to see a faint moving glimmer behind a window a little to the right of that, and then a faint light lower in the wall. Some one was moving in that room, it seemed, and entering the garden from another door, like that which led into my room. I stood still. There was the noise of a door being closed with circumspection, and then the light sound of hurrying feet on the other path of the rose-garden, the path that lay parallel to that on which I was standing. Some one, I thought, is now feeling, as I felt, the teasing of the innumerable gossamers, damp with the summer mist. From where I stood, across one of the smaller paths, I could see a few feet of the path on which the hurrying steps were swiftly drawing nearer. I watched those few feet of pathway, merely curious to see who it was who shared with me a taste for the night air. The figure passed at a fast run. It was the figure of John Killigrew, dressed as I had last seen him, but without the cloak. Dimly in the white mist I saw his face. It shocked me horribly. It seemed old, drawn, haggard, like the face of one about to feel the knife of a surgeon. Indeed, I thought of the face of a man I had once seen on his way to be hanged.

I heard him push aside some bushes, and I heard the opening of a light gate and then his running footsteps, fainter and fainter as he fled swiftly into the tall wood that lay beyond the rose-garden. I had been too astonished to call to him, and, I think now, that it is not impossible that I owe my life to that circumstance. I had heard from old Michael that Killigrew was unwell, and in bed. From Killigrew himself I had heard that this was his first visit to the house, and that he knew as little of it as I knew myself. Yet here he was, after midnight, running confidently along a path, finding an exit from a garden in which he had never been before, and making use of a side-doorway out of the house of the very appearance of which he had confessed himself ignorant. Perhaps, I thought, he is indeed ill, and is running in delirium. Yet that could hardly account for the apparently confident knowledge with which he guided his steps. I laughed at myself for the beating of my heart, and went as quickly as I could round the bottom of the rose-garden to the point at which, judging from the sounds, I assumed that he had left it. I saw that a little pathway lay, half hidden under the spreading branches of some small red roses, which, wet with mist, had been hurriedly brushed aside and were still trembling, and that, beyond them, in the trellis, was a wooden wicket which now stood ajar. It was perfectly clear that Killigrew had known both of the pathway and of the wicket gate.

I stepped carefully through the trailing rose-branches, and through the wicket. There was a path beyond the trellis leading into the wood. I walked along it, slowly, for I had not in my mind the least idea of what I intended to do, and warily, because the thought had come to me that Killigrew was perhaps a madman, and might at any moment leap out on me. I loosened my sword in its ornamental scabbard, and thought with some seriousness of my uncle's scorn of its dainty and rather foppish de-sign. My actions were so far involuntary that I had already gone some thirty paces into the wood before it occurred to me that the part of a spy is not a pretty one to play, and that whatever John Killigrew might be doing in his own grounds after midnight, it was certainly not the business of Richard Stanborough, his guest, to observe it. I was on the point of turning back, when my heart was brought into my mouth, and my blood frozen in my veins by a most surprising sound. It came from the wood, only a short way before me. It was a groan that seemed to be forced from a man's lips by the most extreme pain. It ended in an appalling shriek of the most intense human agony. I have never heard such a cry before or since. The shriek ended and was followed by groan after groan, gradually lessening in violence as if the sufferer were losing strength, or as if the pain which had been too much for him to bear were losing its first poignancy.

I could neither move forward nor turn to go back. My mouth was open and my throat felt like parched leather. Before me were only the trees, a faint mist between their trunks, and on the ground dim shadows cast by the moon that shone with lessened brilliance. The groans ended, and the wood was absolutely silent. Then a nightingale broke into song on a tree immediately above me. That heavenly music, lightly pouring from a bird's throat, intensified the horror of the moment. The screech of an owl, or the baying of a dog, both horrible sounds at night, would have been less ghastly than that long, liquid song of careless joy.

It was curious that not for one single moment did I doubt the identity of the man whose groans and shriek of utter agony had poisoned the sweetness of the June night. I knew that the man was John Killigrew.

I was still standing, actually incapable of movement of any kind, when I heard footsteps approaching me from the wood. The sound restored me the use of my limbs, and I stood ready to arrest whoever this might be, who, after murdering Killigrew, was now coming, no doubt, with evil design, towards the house where Rose lay sleeping. I stepped to the extreme edge of the path, and waited with my sword drawn.

As the steps reached the bend in the path immediately before me, I leapt forward, cried "Halt," and expected to find myself face to face with the murderer, or thief, whoever, indeed, had been the author of the pain that had caused that gruesome noise. Almost in my arms, almost on the point of my sword, was the figure of Mistress Rose Killigrew. She was mantled in a light shawl, that covered her hair, but did not hide her face. I saw a flash of scorn pass across it, and then alarm.

"Hush," she whispered, and pointed along the path. "Be quick."

She caught me by the wrist and pulled me swiftly along the path towards the garden. When we reached the wicket, she stopped and listened.

"Spying, Mr. Stanborough?" she said.

"On my honour, madam, no such thing. I came out to compose my thoughts, and, by mere chance, saw Mr. Killigrew, and afterwards heard those frightful groans."

"You saw him?" she said. "When?"

"As he ran through the garden from the house."

"Was his face covered?"

"It was not."

"God grant he does not know."

"Is he badly hurt, madam, and can I not assist?"

"You need not fear on Mr. Killigrew's account," she whispered, "but on your own. I am sorry, I thought you were spying. But . . . Oh, for your own sake, I wish you had not come. Go now, swiftly. Put out that light in your window, and if you hear further sounds be as indifferent to them as you may."

"Let me rather stay with you, madam."

She smiled, and then grew suddenly intent and serious. "Be quick now, Mr. Stanborough. Go. Go. If you would be kind to me, you will be asleep in your room within five minutes from now. Go. Go. I will delay them," and she turned slowly back along the path, while I fled through the rose-garden, closed my little door, blew out my candles, undressed by the dim light that came through the narrow window, and laid me down in the bed.

I thought that I should never sleep, but I was young, I had ridden far that day, and the very excitement of the last half-hour had left me dumb and insensible. I suppose it was about an hour after this that I was conscious of some one bending close over me, watching my face and listening to my breath. I preserved as well as I could the regularity of my lungs' motion, and when I was assured that the watcher had gone, I opened my eyes, and in the early light of the summer dawn saw that my door was being noiselessly closed by some one on the farther side of it. Five minutes after that I was again asleep.

CHAPTER IV
Family Portraits and
Manuscripts of Paracelsus

The mulberry-coloured suit fitted me much better than might have been expected, and, after examining it thoroughly in the tall glass, I was not ashamed to leave my room in it, and seek Mistress Rose Killigrew. On waking I had perceived a hanging bell-rope, and pulled it before reflecting that there was but one servant in the house. My ring had been answered by old Michael with a tray and a light breakfast, which I had thoroughly enjoyed. He had also brought me a bowl of hot shaving-water, and now, with a smooth chin, I stepped confidently out of my room, half believing that the strange events of the night had been no more than an hallucination.

I had somehow expected to find Rose at the head of the staircase, where I had first seen her on our arrival, but, as I left my room, I heard her singing. I guessed that she was in the little pantry, and was moving across the hall to join her, when she came out of the doorway leading from the kitchen. I have never seen a prettier courtesy than she gave me. I bowed, and, as I bent over her hand, she said, "You will say nothing of last night," and then aloud she asked me if I had slept well. "My brother will be anxious to see you. He is, I think, in the library."

She went upstairs, while I followed. At the door of a room on the upper floor, she said, "I have brought you your guest," and motioned me to go into the room. Then she turned and went lightly down the stairs to the hall.

I went in and found myself in a long room, which was both a library and a picture gallery. Shelves of volumes almost covered the walls, leaving space only for a row of family portraits. At the far end of the room, with his back to me, examining one of the portraits with such intentness that he had not, I think, heard his sister's voice, stood my host. I walked towards him, and was close to him before he became aware of my presence. He then turned round, and greeted me. I very nearly betrayed my extreme astonishment. He looked at me for a moment with piercing inquiry, and then resumed his ordinary manner.

"I hope," he said, "that you were not disturbed in your sleep by the restless ghosts of my relatives." He waved his hand lightly towards the portraits on the walls.

"No," I answered him, trying to collect myself, "I slept very well."

Remember that I had last seen him with a face haggard and old, running through the garden like a man running to his death, eager to have it over and be done with it. He had seemed then older than when I had first seen him in the inn. All the previous day during our ride he had kept his face muffled. I had, therefore, only two impressions of his countenance, the first when I had taken him to be a man of thirty-eight or forty, the second, in the night, with that terrible expression, when he might have been any age that is near death. It was for this reason that I found it hard to adjust my thoughts when he turned in the library, and let me see that he could not, at the outside, be more than five and twenty. My whole mental view of my new acquaintance had to be changed in a moment. I had thought of him as a mentor, and given more respect to his age than ever I had given to my uncle's, and now I perceived that he was only a few years older than myself. My confidence in my own judgment was swept suddenly away from me, and I had to reconstruct the whole fabric of acquaintanceship that I had built on the supposition that he was an older man.

"I hope, Mr. Killigrew, that you are recovered from your indisposition."

"I thank you, perfectly so," he replied. "I am, as you have doubtless perceived, a man of singular views, and one of them is concerned with the ridiculous wish of servants to turn even a man's entry into his own house into a kind of theatrical performance. You perceive I am not so far eccentric as not to admit that I owe you some apology for my last night's abrupt desertion of you. You must forgive me."

He waved aside the words which I was about to utter, and turning again and drawing my attention to the picture he had been examining, observed:

"When you came in I was in act of making acquaintance with my good cousin, who preceded me in the occupation of this house, though he left it years ago, and I entered it only yesterday. An interesting face, you think?"

"I was remarking its extraordinary resemblance to your own," said I, glancing now at Killigrew and now at the portrait on the wall. "But for the accident of clothes you might be twin brothers."

"You think the resemblance remarkable?" said Killigrew. "There is not only thirty years between us, but we are even not very closely related. The Killigrew blood seems tenacious of its purpose, and that, judging from this gallery, seems to be the preservation of the family features."

He indicated other portraits on the wall opposite the windows, and we examined them one by one. They were arranged in chronological order, the heads of the house, so Killigrew informed me, and I was indeed amazed at the likeness between them. The last six might actually have been one man in the different costumes of a masquerade. There was a cavalier, a country gentleman of the time of James, an Elizabethan courtier, and so on. The sixth and earliest was a man in the dress of a student of two hundred years ago. In his dark robes and hood, he was just such a man as the John Killigrew who stood by my side looking at his relative across the centuries. There was something in that student's face which would have made it impossible for anybody but Killigrew to examine it with that slightly jeering look. The hood was touched with fur, and out of it the boy's pale face, for he had been painted when quite young, looked with eyes of almost unearthly intelligence.

These eyes were very like Killigrew's own, except that they shone with a translucent purity of purpose, which, much as I admired him, I could not, even in the earliest stages of our relationship, find in Killigrew. This boy, this student, seemed to have set the type for his family for a couple of hundred years. There were only one or two portraits earlier than his, and of them some were probably imaginary. The faces they represented varied very considerably. But after the appearance of that student, the family seemed to have realized that it could do no better, and to have set itself to reproduce him as accurately as possible in generation after generation. There were, of course, minor differences, but, as I remarked to Killigrew, remembering the portraits in my uncle's hall, there is nothing more extraordinary than the way in which family portraits follow contemporary fashions. When it was fashionable to have long necks, you will be sure to find that your ancestor of that date had a neck like a swan's, and when, later, a solid brutishness came into vogue, you will find that at that time you had a relation whose head grew straight out of his shoulders.

Killigrew returned to the portrait he had been examining when I had entered the room.

"A curious man," he said. "He left this house twenty years ago and died, after much travel, in Paris. I believe that strange legends of him still float about this countryside. He had no children, and before he died, sent me his ring and with it the message that he hoped I would better fulfil my duty to the home of our family than he had. By that, I incline to believe that he meant he hoped I would live here, and perhaps have the long grass cut short, and the trees trimmed, and the house a bustle of stupid maids. That I shall not do. Not that I value solitude for its own sake. I think it has been greatly overrated by philosophers, who have often praised its fertilizing action on the mind. I disagree with them. I value, not solitude, in which the mind is wholly at the sport of demons, if you will allow me to use the vocabulary of an older school, but intercourse between two chosen and mutually active spirits. I need companionship to rouse my thoughts from their sluggish habit and to bring them out walking in the open glades of my intelligence, where I may myself perceive that they exist."

"There is not that in your face, sir, which betokens any sloth of mind."

"Perhaps there is not," he replied, glancing now at the portrait of the student, "but, when the mind during years grows to think of one thing only, when it is obsessed by a single desire, or a single regret, the effect is that of sluggishness, however swiftly the mind may hurry round and round the walls of the prison that by the accident of this concentration on a single thought it has built up round itself."

"I do not wholly understand you."

"Stanborough," he said, and he laid his hand affectionately on my shoulder, "you are yet young. The day may come when you will understand too well, when you will know that without companionship the world is an empty, hateful thing, and knowledge a toy to keep a child from crying."

"You are yourself not so old," said I, "as to have reached the limits of experience. Perhaps, when we are old men of fifty or sixty, smoking our pipes over an October fire, we may remember this conversation with a smile."

He laughed, a rather dreadful laugh that I remembered long after, and said, "Yes, I am still young. I had perhaps forgotten that." Then he laughed again and took a ring from his finger and gave it to me to examine.

"That is my cousin's ring," he said, "and when I tell you that every one of those dead Killigrews has worn it, beginning with the student you admire, you will understand that the wearer of it may himself feel old, carrying on his finger the witness of so many lives, even though that witness be only a little bauble of metal."

It was a very plain little old ring, broad in the band, and with a flat indented signet, representing a wheel, and outside the wheel and encircling it a snake with its tail in its mouth.

"It is an ancient symbol of eternity," said Killigrew, and he pointed to the finger of one of the portraits. I looked up and saw a faithful picture of the ring I was examining.

"We have all worn it," said Killigrew, "since the student to whom, so the legend goes, it was given by Paracelsus himself. He was painted, I suppose, before it had been given him, for it does not appear in his portrait. You may see it in all the others."

"Paracelsus himself?" I said.

"Yes, the greatest and wisest man since . . . but there is no one with whom he can be fittingly compared. I share my ancestor's admiration for him, and, in the shelves at the end of this room, is a small collection of his manuscripts, which I sent hither a few days before setting out myself."

"Manuscripts of Paracelsus!" I exclaimed, feeling that by the mere handling of such things I was many steps nearer the thoughts of a great man than ever I had been at Oxford.

"No less," said Killigrew, smiling, and led the way down the room to a broad-shelved bookcase, in which lay a black, iron-clamped box. Killigrew took a key from a small bunch that hung on the wall, and made me remark it.

"If you care to read these manuscripts at leisure," he said, "you will always find the key here, and I shall be delighted to think that I am not alone in my study of them."

I cannot describe to you the absurd vanity and gratification with which I heard him make this offer. I instantly saw pictures of myself reading the manuscripts of Paracelsus by the light of candles. Candles were essential to my imagination, and I scarcely wished to look at the manuscripts by daylight. I pictured myself reading of strange things, of the Elixir of Life, of the Philosopher's Stone, of all the mad romantic quests a thirst for which had not been quenched in me by the delicious, sober dialogues of Bishop Berkeley, or the fine spiritual enthusiasm of Spinoza. In my picture, of course, I saw myself exquisitely dressed. I had no desire to ape the traditional student, and so, after Killigrew had opened the box, and shown me the manuscripts that lay there, and, to my great relief, had closed it again, without suggesting that I should look at them more closely in the sacrilegious daylight, my mind, boy-like, continued straight along that bypath, and I reminded Killigrew of the scantiness of my wardrobe.

"You picked me from the highway, sir, and I come to you clothed as a beggar."

"Are you referring to the very handsome suit of black in which you walked into the inn on the North Road?" said he.

"I am," said I, "and I had intended to ask you if it will be possible to send to town from here, without unduly causing trouble to my host."

It will be the easiest thing in the world," said he. "To-morrow, new servants of old Michael's choosing will arrive and he will be riding to London, to fulfil some small commissions of my own. If you will entrust him with letters, I can guarantee their safe delivery. And," he added, "may I congratulate myself on the supposition that your wish to send to London implies a willingness to remain here for some little time?"

I blushed, perceiving that I had in fact announced my intention. At the same time, I knew that he wished me to stay, and I think that, what with the sight of the manuscripts in the black box, and Mistress Rose Killigrew, I would have almost forced myself upon his hospitality, even if he had been unwilling, or if I had not myself been eager for more of his company, which was indeed the case.

"No, no," said he, "you have no need to blush, since I begged you to remain here as long as you should wish. I was quite honestly congratulating myself on the fact that you are willing to accept an invitation which was really the prayer of a somewhat lonely man."

I was amazed that any one could speak of loneliness with so lovely a creature as Rose Killigrew moving graciously about the house, and at the same time I was surprised at the strange elderly tone of his speech. After all, I thought, he is at most only five years older than I, however much older he may be in the matter of learning and genius.

"I beg," he said, "that you will do here exactly what you wish. There are these manuscripts to amuse you. If, anywhere, they seem obscure, I shall be happy, not to explain them, for that, perhaps, I could not do, but at least to set my reading of them beside your own, that we may by comparison approach a little nearer to the truth. For exercise," he continued, "if you do not care for the paces of the nag you rode yesterday, you are always at liberty to take my own. And, when the society of a philosopher becomes tiresome, and you also weary of yourself, my sister, I am sure, will be happy to entertain you."

I thanked him, and looking from the window, saw Mistress Rose, plucking roses in the garden below, and secretly resented his supposal that his own company or solitude could be preferred to being with so beautiful a creature. Then I remembered how we had met last night, and how I had seen him, running with a worn, deathlike face, and the horrible groan and cry. All these things seemed quite incredible in the presence of the man, after our quiet, polite conversation. But, for all that, I felt that my curiosity was painted on my face, which, for some moments, I kept turned from him.

He observed my action, and came nearer, so that he too could look down upon the rose-garden.

"Ah," he said, "I see my sister is already at her favourite business. Let us forget that there are such things as philosophies and books, and go down to join her among the roses."

Nothing could have better pleased me, and presently, leaving the house by the great doorway, we walked round it, and through another doorway in the trellis, into the little garden.

"Mr. Stanborough is so far pleased with our new house that he is to-morrow sending to London for more clothes in which to honour us. I assured him that this would be good news to you."

"I am very pleased," she said, "but I had already learnt that Mr. Stanborough has an adaptable nature."

"How is that?" asked Killigrew with a sudden look of suspicion, which I could not understand.

"He had not been an hour in the house before he offered to peel potatoes with his sword," she replied. There was exaggerated relief on Killigrew's face, and he laughed.

"There was fortunately no need," she said, and laughed herself, but I could see that there had been fear in her mind, now passed. Of what was she afraid? And of what was Killigrew suspicious? If all these hidden feelings were apprehension that he had been seen last night, if she were afraid lest he should know he had been seen, what was it that lay between them? What was it that had happened away there in the wood, within earshot of where we were standing?

We walked slowly down the path, Killigrew leading, followed by his sister. I walked last, and noticed yet another puzzling incident. He bent down to taste the perfume of a flower, and she, seeing that I was about to do the same, cut it with her scissors so that it fell on the path, and trod upon it, as if it were a thing of evil. Then, before I had recovered from my surprise, before, indeed, I had quite realized what she had done, she plucked another flower, and offered it me herself with a smile at once serious and sweet. Killigrew saw nothing of this.

He came, at the head of our little procession, to the place where there was the overgrown path and the doorway in the trellis, through which I had seen him run last night, through which I had myself passed before meeting his sister.

"Whither does that path lead?" he asked, with the most exact air of one who, for the first time, is looking at a new possession. I looked with astonishment at his sister, but she answered at once: "It goes into the wood."

"I must explore it," he said, "but do not let me take you from your flowers. Mr. Stanborough will stay with you. There is no need that he should make his ruffles a sacrifice to my idle curiosity. And these brambles have thorns."

He made his way carefully through the roses, and disappeared beyond the trellis.

For a moment, I stood, staring at the green, rose-hung trellis, through which he had gone. I remember my mind fastened itself on one particular rose, and I stared at it so hard that I returned to consciousness of my surroundings with an unpleasant suspicion that I had been squinting. Rose Killigrew had already moved a little way up the other path. I followed her.

"Mr. Stanborough," she said, "I fear you are a very honest gentleman."

I felt that there was some meaning not altogether flattering to my vanity in her words. Wherefore, not trusting myself to answer a remark of the purport of which I was doubtful, I contented myself with a bow.

"I am glad of it," she said, "for honesty is a rare plant, but, for your own sake, I must beg you not to cultivate it too openly in this garden. If, for example, my brother, instead of walking on into the wood, as I hope he did, had taken it into his mind to watch through the trellis, and to see how you took his departure, do you imagine that he would have found it difficult to perceive that you knew a little more of him than he had chosen to show you?"

"Mistress Killigrew," I replied, "I admit that I do not know how to swim in mystery. I throw my arms, and my convulsive gestures betray my lack of practice. I beg you to tell me one thing."

"Do not ask," she said.

"Only one thing," I pressed.

"Ask it, but I will not promise you an answer,"

"Tell me what is the secret of last night, and why you asked old Michael to warn your brother's guest not to accept his invitation."

"Those are two questions and I cannot answer either of them yet, though I will tell you that it would have been better for you not to come, but now that you are here . . ."

"Now that I am here," I said, "you can at least tell me if the secret concerns yourself, and if it is something that you fear on your account as well as upon mine."

"I fear for both of us."

"In that case, madam, I have yet another reason for being glad that I have come."

She leaned down over a rose-bush and half whispered, "And I too, I think I am glad that you have come. But you are very young, and must learn to cloak your honesty."

"Madam," I replied, "yesterday was my twenty-first birthday."

"So old," she smiled, "and I am twenty, but hundred of years older than you, for all my life I have been living with my brother, and you have known him but a day."

"And a night," I said.

"Yes, a night." Then, as we were close together, she touched my sword, that sword at which my uncle laughed. "You would really have killed me with this?" she said.

"If you had been other than Mistress Rose Killigrew, I should have done my best," I replied awkwardly.

She looked at the sword curiously. "It is a toy," she said, "among the weapons of men, just as you are a child smiling into the face of this world's evil. Nay," she said, "do not be angry with me. I have been alone so long that I have grown to think aloud, and you need not quarrel with me for a thought, and that thought not unkind."

CHAPTER V
Life in the Old Hall and a Budget of Letters

It is extraordinary to me now, years afterwards, when my mind has settled in its ways, to remember with what speed the life in that old house seemed to become my life. Before I had been there a week it seemed that I had lived there for ever. The secret background to the simple days we spent seemed to be natural to existence. I saw that Rose Killigrew lived her life without letting the knowledge of whatever danger there was darken the passing moments of her simple pleasures. We laughed and were merry, when it would, I suppose, have seemed more natural to an observer from without if we had moved solemnly about with grim faces and never a song on our lips. That may have been because we were in love, but of love in due course. At the beginning of our friendship we were unaware of it ourselves, though it was not for that the less delightful.

In the evening of the day the morning events of which have been described in my last chapter, I settled myself to the table in my room, to write two letters. This was always a serious business with me, and is still. You would perhaps set a higher value on these reminiscences if you could know the difficulty with which each sentence has been dragged into existence and flung before you, like an unwilling schoolboy. There have been times indeed when I have sat for nigh two hours looking at the feather end of my quill, not for want of matter, but for lack of the hard industrial courage that would make me set pen to paper and keep it moving there. These confessions are, however, sadly out of place. They have been prompted by the sight of the two letters that I wrote that evening, both preserved among my uncle's papers. I suppose Mistress Barber, his housekeeper, dutiful woman, handed her letter over to him when she went to Bigland, and that he kept it ever after, as he kept many other useless scraps of writing, bills from coach-menders, recipes for mixing snuffs, and so forth. Anyhow those two letters are before me now, and through their erasions, and the irregularity of the ink (I so often had to dip afresh, so often let the liquid dry on my pen), I can see, as if it were yesterday, how I sat in that room, as a boy of twenty-one, and wrote by the light of three candles, with Mistress Killigrew's bowl of sweet-scented flowers before me on the table.

I copy the letters here. The first was addressed to my uncle's housekeeper, Mistress Barber, who had been my nurse.

"MY DEAR OLD BABKINS,

"It may be a very long time before I see you again, as on the journey my uncle and I had a small dispute and he continued the journey alone, so that I am staying with my friends and no change of clothes to put to my back. Will you give to the bearer of this letter my best lilac, my blue brocade, my plum, my riding equipment, and ten of the shirts with sleeves having those frills which you did yourself to my design. Also I have but one pair of shoes and have no riding boots. Please be careful to send as many pairs of coloured hosen as truly match the coats or breeches. Dear Babkins, you will remember better than I what is required. And please send the other letter that the bearer of this will give you to my uncle at Bigland by the first messenger. Dear Babkins, I send you my love.

"(Master) DICK"

The word in brackets was inserted at Mistress Barber's request by the steward who read the letter to her, she being illiterate.

The second letter was addressed to my uncle, Mr. Anthony Stanborough, Esquire, at Bigland, in the county of Yorkshire, not far above Rievaulx. This letter was more carefully written.

"SIR,

"Lest you should be in any way anxious as to my fortunes after my somewhat sudden parting from you on the road (and, sir, I find it difficult to imagine you in any anxiety), I have pleasure in informing you that I fell among friends. I have taken the liberty to send to Mistress Barber to ask for certain clothes which are of too youthful design to be of any service to you. I take the further liberty of reminding you that when you expressed your desire to be rid of me you had not given me any information as my standing in the world. Indeed, for all I know, I may be a beggar, in which case I thank you heartily for maintaining me so long. If, on the other hand, I am not a beggar, and if your dislike of me is as deep as it appears now to be, I should feel happier if before handing over to me any property of which I may be possessed, you will repay yourself out of it for the very considerable expenses to which you have been put on my account.

"Sir, I kiss your hand in duty,

"RICHARD STANBOROUGH

"Killigrew Hall, near the village of Bent in Huntingdon."

To these letters I received in due course replies characteristic of the writers. I will give you my uncle's first.

"To Richard Stanborough, at Killigrew Hall, near the village of Bent in Huntingdon:

"JACKANAPES,

"I have read your insolent epistle. If you were younger I would make the journey south with the especial purpose of chastising you. But you are of age, and a duel between us would be scarcely seemly. You are not a beggar, though nearly so. Your father left you an income of some two hundred a year, and an uncle very much too good for you. A considerable sum is standing to your credit, and you can draw upon it by visiting my attorney, Gillard, in the Temple, a lousy, unwholesome fellow, but honest, which is unusual. I have no intention of apologizing to you, but I am an old man, and therefore say that only unbearable exasperation of your own causing made me tell you I would not see you again. When you wish to see your uncle again, you may come to Bigland, but not for long, and, for God's sake, no ruffles.

"ANTHONY STANBOROUGH

"P.S. I threw your knickknacks out of the window as we were crossing the Nidd.

"P.P.S. The chub are feeding well, and on dull days I have done well with trout. It is a sad pity you do not take to angling."

The second reply, from Mistress Barber, was less humiliating to my vanity.

"MY OWN DEAR BOY AND RESPECTED MASTER,

"I am sending the cloes you asked for and with them a cake, baked this day. We all drank a long life to you on your birthday, my dear boy, and however things are between you and master, be sure that they will turn out right. Many is the time I've spoken for you when you were a bit of a boy, and please God, the master will feel the wrong side of my tongue the first time he comes to London, or sends for me to go home into Yorkshire. The cake is rich, and should not be eat at one sitting.

"Your old nurse and faithful servant,

"JANE BARBER, her mark X

"Written by the hand of the House Steward, who sends his respectful compliments to Master Dick upon his coming to the years of maturity."

The cake arrived with the clothes, and for all Mistress Barber's care it had left its imprint on a brace of collars and ruined them for ever. However, this small matter was amply atoned for in my eyes by the pleasure it and Mrs. Barber's letter gave to Rose. A great, solid Yorkshire cake it was, and made my stomach ache like a child's. But somehow, a cake, and such a cake in that old empty house, and that strange secret life, was like a firm handgrip out of the world of human kind.

You may perhaps be asking why, if my life in the old hall was so strange, so full of secret fears, I did not walk out of the park and away to the open road, where I could have turned my steps to London or to the north. You may wonder, indeed, why I did not instantly fly, after the experience of that first night in the rose-garden, when the song of the nightingale, that purest of nature's melodies, served but to brim over the cup of an unnatural horror. At the time I asked myself these questions, and could not give myself an answer. It is a strange thing that the mind may be as it were resolutely blind to contemporary facts, which, from a little distance, stand out so clear as to make all else seem of small significance. Now, when I look back on that strange time, I perceive that every one of those moments of strangeness, of fear, was deprived of its influence on me by being somehow connected with Mistress Rose Killigrew. I perceive now that for me those dark, unwholesome places were lit up by the white radiance of her who shared them with me, and that the ecstasy of that sharing made me even welcome all that, by intensifying the strangeness of our surroundings, intensified the feeling of comradeship which had so miraculously sprung between us at my very first coming to the place. It was as if a mortal walking with an angel should feel himself on earth distant from his companion, but, in hell, nearer by the very fact of the visible opposition to his alliance. Such a mortal would be glad to walk in hell, for the sake of that feeling of companionship, and I was glad to have left ordinary life for this place of mystery, because it brought me near Rose, and I had not the vanity to suppose that in other circumstances she would care for my society.

I see now clearly that Rose was the principal reason of my willing stay in that strange place. I could not have left her. But, at the time, I gave myself other reasons, and I would not for a moment deny that there was much truth in the arguments which I nightly invented to save myself from the admission that I stayed for Rose's sake. The principal one of these reasons was the very man who seemed to be the origin, the fount, of all that was unexplainable in the daily events of our life. So far, I have perhaps only succeeded in letting you feel the strangeness, the singularity of Killigrew. You think of him as of something sinister and dark. All this he was, but if you would truly see the man, you must think of him as, in his better moods, of the most delightful, charming talker that the world could produce. I had heard good talk at Oxford, and listened to and taken part in a score of the philosophic disputations, the principal result of which is an unweening conceit in Oxford students, and a readiness to argue, and to contradict the opinions of others, which make them wellnigh insufferable until experience of the world has worn away their confidence in the nurture of their university. I have mortified my vanity by setting down as accurately as I could remember it the ridiculous talk to which I treated my good uncle. You will have learnt from that that I was no unusual specimen of the cubs of Oxford. Cublike, I began my acquaintance with Killigrew by a conceited attempt to find out what he knew–that is to say, by an assumption that I knew more than he. But, within a few moments of the beginning of our conversation, my conceit had been swept from me. I had realized that here was a man who knew not only more than I, but more than any of the learned pedagogues who had taught me nothing except a useless self-confidence. I had exhibited my petty knowledge, and he had picked it up, played with it in a few golden sentences, and tossing it back to me an hundredfold enriched, had soared on into realms which, even in fancy, I had never touched. My conceit fell prostrate before him, and in a few minutes he undid all the harm that had been done me by the university. With him I could not preserve the tone of equality that had been natural to me in conversation with my professors. I became in an instant his very humble disciple, and at his first mention, for example, of Paracelsus I was ready to assume that that alchemist alone possessed the secrets of the universe. Yet, fresh from Bishop Berkeley and Spinoza, if any other man had mentioned the Swiss alchemist, I would have been ready to laugh him to scorn.

Killigrew gave me a profound mistrust of my own knowledge, and nothing is more stimulating to a young man, unless, indeed, he be of those whom nothing can stimulate, or else incorrigibly vain. He suddenly introduced me to a new world of thought, and I flung my modern philosophy aside like so much rubbish. He had talked to me on that first night of the cabalistic thinkers, and already on the next day the blood rushed to my cheeks when he showed me a box of manuscripts by the man whom, twenty-four hours earlier, I would, without knowing a word of his teaching, have cheerfully described as a charlatan. I begged for further enlightenment, and Killigrew was ever ready to instruct me, and never was there a more entrancing teacher. At the universities my instructors had treated me as an inferior and I had felt their equal. Killigrew treated me as an equal, and I grovelled before his mind, while delighting in the spiritual excitement of treading unknown paths with a companion at my side who seemed not to observe that I was feeling the novelty of my surroundings.

All our reading, all our conversation, had a single direction, although at the time it seemed to me infinitely various. Paracelsus, Lully,

Cornelius Agrippa, these were the philosophers we studied, and I learnt for the first time of the strange spiritual background of the world in which we live. The answers of the modern thinkers seemed empty beside these glowing pictures of a spiritual universe, and, with my mind itself aflame, I read of the spirits of water and the spirits of fire, the personal essences of being. I read of Salamandræ, and, when I asked Killigrew if such things indeed existed, he took me into the laboratory where from time to time we illustrated our researches by experiment, and from that place I went forth, perhaps under an hallucination, but certainly with the conviction that I had, for an instant, actually seen one of those strange essences floating in the green flames of our chemical furnace. We talked of the creation of life, and I read the curious tale vouched for by one of the secretaries of Paracelsus, of the occasion when that marvellous man did in fact produce homunculi, creatures like man, but small in stature. I found nothing fantastic in the account, how one of these was a king and one a queen and a third a tailor, and how they were preserved alive in bottles covered with parchment, and how in the middle of one night there was a noise that woke the alchemist, and he ran into the laboratory to find that the king's bottle had fallen to the ground and broken, and how after long search for the king, a little scratching noise had directed his attention to the upper shelf, where the escaped homunculus was scratching at the parchment that covered the bottle of the queen. I found nothing fantastic in all this, and nothing incredible, and I was presently to be myself a witness of such things as make it impossible for me to-day to disbelieve in similar events, although I well know them to be traps of the unclean spirit set for the snaring of our poor human souls.

From such beginnings, Killigrew gradually led my mind towards a single subject, and that the quest which had engaged the minds of all the alchemists from first to last, and, in the end, absorbed me also, the quest for the Elixir of Life. How many lives have been spent in that search, for a potion, a powder, that should conquer death and leave man free from the lurking shadow that dogs every footstep of his swiftly-passing days. This came to be the most persistent topic of our conversation. As we rode in the wild, unkempt grounds of the old house, or sat in the small room that made our laboratory, or read in the library under the portraits of the Killigrews, this came to be the common subject of our speculation; and some time before the events that made the subject for ever loathsome and horrible to me, I was myself secretly fired with an ambition to follow the paths of those old alchemists, and if possible to go farther than they. I say that this was a secret ambition, but I suspected then that Killigrew knew of it, as he knew of everything, and I know now that by every means in his power he fanned that flame until it came near consuming me in the white heat of its unbearable intensity. Perhaps it would have done so altogether if my mind had not had another occupant of a very different nature, and if alchemists and philosophers with all their dreams had not now and again been bundled bag and baggage out of my head by the entrance therein of the simple purity of Mistress Rose Killigrew, to whom, indeed, on the Last Day I must acknowledge that I owe my salvation, my rescue from the very gate of hell. If ever a girl was an instrument of God, that girl was she whose presence in the house made so strange a contrast to our talk of magic and witchcraft and all that kind of knowledge which the devil puts into the hands of men.

Our way of life was quiet and regular in the extreme. When Michael had come from London with my clothes and Mistress Barber's cake, he had brought with him two servants, a man and his wife, who relieved Rose of such active participation in domestic affairs as the dishing of potatoes. None the less, she was always busy, and every room we used (there were many that were never opened) bore traces of her charming presence, in flowers and in spotless cleanliness. It was as if she had set herself to surround our secret life of speculation with the sweetest kind of reality, as if, indeed, she were working against Killigrew in a struggle for my soul between the powers of good and evil.

In this struggle, of which I was but half aware, old Michael took a part. He seldom spoke to me, and then only of the simplest matters, of such things as come within the province of a servant. But he was often present during our conversations, and once or twice when with boyish enthusiasm I had launched into a triumphant pæan over some discovery in those old manuscripts, or when, with glowing eyes, I discoursed to Killigrew on the wonder of the Elixir of Life, and how its possessor might make the world anew with the wisdom he would gather through the centuries, I used to catch the eye of the old man looking at me with an expression of such ineffable sadness that more than once I broke off short in the middle of a sentence. Then Killigrew would glance up, and old Michael, visibly shrinking into himself with a kind of terror, would move away and leave us to ourselves.

Our meals were taken for the most part in the great hall. Sometimes we all dined together, sometimes Rose and I alone, and sometimes when Killigrew and I were busy with experiment or discussion Michael was instructed to bring our food to us in the library. There were occasions when Killigrew would throw aside his solemnity, and laugh and joke with us, though there was never much heartiness in his laughter, and I liked him better when he watched our growing happiness with what seemed then to be a grave benevolence.

The days followed each other with regularity, marked for me one from another by the progress of my friendship with Rose on the one hand and my advancement in my new studies on the other. Rose and I would meet in the little garden, and she would ask me questions of the world I had left, and I would tell her of Mistress Barber, of my uncle, of the house in the north, of Oxford, of London, until at last she seemed to know my old life as well as I knew it myself. She would often ask for tales of this or that, and, by these questions, she kept alive my affection for all the simplicity I was in such imminent danger of losing. I learnt, too, a little of her life, and how they had lived abroad, in Florence and in Paris, always alone, always separated as if by high walls from the ordinary life of the world.

Sometimes I rode with Killigrew, sometimes by myself, rarely with Rose. With Killigrew or by myself my rides took the character of meditations. I think I was oldest of all when I rode by myself. Then I would drop the reins, and let the horse make his own way at his own pace through the trees or over the broad stretches of long grass, while I sat musing on his back, my mind full of bright visions and plans for the spiritual conquest of the world, or rather for conquest of the spiritual resources of the world. I would find the Philosopher's Stone, I would find the Elixir of Life, and, in the end, turn the world into an earthly paradise peopled by immortal beings. When Rose was with me not one of these things entered my mind. I was again a boy of twenty-one, and we galloped side by side like children, and sang and laughed as the wind disarranged our hats, or blew light pennons of her hair about her eyes.

Yet she was not always thus. At the first opportunity after our encounter at night in the wood, I had asked her to explain many of those things which I did not understand and which were disquieting in themselves. Later, I asked her again.

"Mr. Stanborough, she said, "you are asking me for a secret the whole of which I do not know myself. If I were to tell you what I know, you are too well accustomed to honesty to be able to stand for two minutes in my brother's presence without his instantly being aware of your knowledge."

"Do you know why he brought me here?"

"I do, and if I were to tell you now, I should, I think, be serving his purpose, for, Mr. Stanborough, I know you better than he, being so nearly of your own age."

"But he cannot be half a dozen years older than we."

"No," she said, shortly, and turned away.

I persisted in my inquiries.

"Shall I be glad or sorry when I know what he wishes from me?"

"I fear you will be glad, and I pray that Heaven may so enlighten you that you will be sorry. Nothing that I could say would do anything but increase your readiness to fall in with his views. But . . . but, think, if he should . . . if he make you any proposal, think, I pray you, upon the sound you heard on the night of your arrival here, and ask yourself if he can be as fortunate as he appears."

More than that she would not say, and when I was still begging her to enlighten me, I saw her looking with a startled expression over my shoulder. I turned and saw that Killigrew was approaching us. I do not think he heard our conversation, but her manifest fear lest he had made me more careful in future not to ask her such questions as might involve her in his displeasure.

There were thus two currents flowing side by side in the general stream of my life at the old hall. There was my interest in philosophy, my enthusiasm as a pupil, my unbounded admiration for Killigrew, which made any suspicion of his intentions seem almost blasphemous, and my increasing affection for Rose. Then, besides all this, there was the strange feeling of untrust which mingled with my admiration of Killigrew, the secrecy that sometimes clouded the sweet purity of my intercourse with Rose, the knowledge that there were many things in our life there which I could not understand, and, lastly, a perfectly inexplicable dread of the old house in which we lived. Sometimes, returning to it after a long ride through the park, I had to turn my eyes away from it as it stood there, with its untrimmed ivy, its boarded windows, and the grass-grown drive that led to it. Sometimes I felt that the reason of my discomfort lay in the park itself, and that there was a breath of poisonous horror in the very wind that swept over the long rank grass about my horse's knees.

CHAPTER VI
Love in the Rose-Garden and
Love Before a Looking-Glass

Perhaps you will remember that, on the night of our first meeting in the tavern on the North Road, it had seemed to me that Killigrew, in saying good night to me, altered his bow until it was in closer conformity with my own. That slight circumstance was brought vividly to my mind by two similar incidents which occurred, shortly before that series of swiftly succeeding, startling events which lit up as if by lightning flashes the darkness in which I had been dwelling, and the gloom of the doorway which I was on the point of entering. The first of these small incidents was connected with no more spiritual a matter than the taking of snuff. Like most of the youths of my time, I indulged in this habit, and carried the dandyism which I applied to my dress into the details of my equipment as a lover of tobacco. I possessed accordingly, bought by my uncle's money, and, like my sword, an object of his aversion, an extremely pretty little tobacco box, French work, enamelled, and very small. It annoyed my uncle, because, as he said, one could buy a bigger snuff-box for a twentieth of the money, and, if one were going to take snuff, why, then, the bigger the box, within reason, the better. I was very proud of this box, and took occasion to offer a pinch of snuff to Killigrew, with the particular short bow, then fashionable for a gentleman performing this trifling service for another. Killigrew accepted my offer, but I was surprised to see that he took snuff in an altogether older manner. In fact, he took his pinch and applied it to his nostril precisely as if he had been my uncle himself. Very well, there was nothing in this. Any man has a right to be old-fashioned if he wishes. But, a week or so later, we were talking in the library, when Killigrew produced a snuff-box as small and as pretty as mine, and offered me a pinch, and took one, not in this ancient fashion, but as elegantly as I was in the habit of enjoying my tobacco myself. He took snuff like any young man of my time, and no longer like the old men of a previous generation. A small thing to notice, you may say, but you must remember that it was precisely such small things that, until Rose came into my life, were alone allowed to share the interest I gave to my philosophy. I was puzzled with this, and resented Killigrew's action, on his own account, and only indirectly on mine. I felt unaccountably displeased that a man from whom I was learning the very service of the world should so far lessen himself as to learn from me the very insignificant art of taking snuff in a gentlemanly fashion.

But I dare say I should have thought no more of it, if it had not been for another incident of the same sort which occurred on that day. I had tired of reading, and, looking from the window, had seen Rose in the garden. I went down into the sunshine and joined her. It was a fine day in August. A cuckoo, remarkable that year for its extreme lateness, was calling not far away. There were many butterflies fluttering among the roses, and then with swift little wings climbing up and up till they topped the rose-covered trellis, and flew away into the blue sky, or, at the end of the garden, into the wood. I have once already tried in vain to describe to you the beauty of Rose as I first saw her, radiant in the patch of glowing sunshine at the head of the staircase in that gloomy house. She seemed lovelier still when, leaving my books, I came out to her in the garden. She wore a soft grey gown, and in the girdle of it were some roses, and more of them in a basket she was carrying.

"The roses in your room are almost dead, Mr. Stanborough," she said, "and I think it will rain before night, wherefore I am gathering now, for rain-soaked roses will not live at all."

She was so beautiful as she stood there that I had not a word to say. I looked up at the sky, and saw that there was, indeed, the promise of rain, in a certain darkness on the horizon, as well as in the oppressive heat, but I could not find words even to give her the result of my meteorological observations.

She laughed, and at that words did indeed come to my lips, but not at all the words I wished for. I had not wished to say anything of the kind. I did not think I had the right to say such words until my future was very much clearer than I could see it then. But the words were out of my mouth before I had time to be aware that I was breaking a seriously-made resolve.

"Rose, Rose," I said, "I beg you leave your flowers for a little while, for I have something to say to you, and you must be patient with me and let me say it out."

Her laugh faded suddenly.

"That was not what you had meant to say, Mr. Stanborough." She always has known me better than I have known myself.

"Mistress Killigrew," I said, blushing, "it is said now, and I cannot take it back if I would. I beg you hear me out." And with that grown bold, I offered her my arm, and she laid her hand upon it, and we walked together to the end of the garden where there was a little stone seat with a screen of roses, red and white.

As we walked together down that path, her hand resting on my arm, I felt a wall of silence rising between us, and when we reached the little arbour it had become an impassable barrier. I looked at her, and she was so near, and yet that wall seemed to set her so far away that I felt as if the walls of my throat were closing together to prison my heart that was leaping like a wild thing trying to escape.

At last I said, "Oh, Rose, you know right well what I wish to say to you."

She answered nothing, but twisted a rosebud that was hanging out of her basket. I could not bear to see that she was moved, yet, to my infinite pain, I knew that her heart beat fast, as the roses at her breast rose and fell.

And then I was suddenly, dreadfully ashamed. I knew that I had no right to sit side by side with her on the stone seat. I felt the blood rush to my face with nothing but shame at my presumption. I knew that I should be happier if she were on a high throne and I a supplicant on the lowest step of the dais, and I knelt beside her and whispered:

"Oh, Rose, if you will not have me there is nothing in the world for me."

With almost unconscious fingers I was touching the rose on her knee, but then, and it seemed to me the bravest act of my life, I took one of her hands and then the other, and put them together and held them in both mine.

To my surprise I knew that she was near crying, but she asked with eyes that smiled, as it were, through a mist, "And what would Mistress Barber say?"

She would say, 'Thank God for another bairn.' . . ."

"A bairn is a little child. . . . I have never been a child. . . . Do not ask me. . . . You must not ask me, or not now. You do not know what you are asking. I can never leave my brother. You do not know what is behind this life. I could only run away with you, and I cannot run away. I wish I could."

"Rose!" . . .

"My dear," she said, "I have one thing to say to you, and that is that I am a wicked, worthless woman to have said what I have. I can marry no one, you least of all, because I love you."

She bent forward and kissed me.

"Go, go," she said, "I should not have done that."

"But Rose," I stammered.

"If you love me, go just now," she said. "This evening . . ."

I kissed her bent head and went away towards the house, staggering like a man drunk, and with blind eyes, scarcely seeing the path. The cuckoo called close to me, and I began counting my steps until he should call again. Such strange tricks does the mind play when the heart is stirred. I had taken twelve steps when the cuckoo called again.

I have written all this down, which should be secret between Rose and me, because of what next occurred, which showed that from John Killigrew it had not been secret.

I went into the house, not directly by my little door into my own room, but round and in at the great door. I think I must have been walking on tip-toe, not purposely, but naturally, for I felt almost as if I were in a church, and my mind was full of the picture of Rose in the garden, and the sound of her voice when she had called me "my dear." It therefore happened that Killigrew, who was in the room next to mine, did not hear me. The great door was open because of the heat, and so was the door into that room. You may imagine my sensations when, as I stood in the hall, I heard these words:

"Oh Rose, you know right well what I wish to say to you. So that is how they do it. And then they kneel."

I looked through the door of the room with the distinct feeling that I had taken leave of my senses. Facing the side wall, against which stood a very large mirror, was Killigrew. At that moment he knelt before a chair so placed that he could see himself in the glass as he did so. He was imitating my attitude exactly. He was a little dissatisfied with his performance, and once or twice altered his position, and, worse, the expression on his face. Then, toying with his fingers with an imaginary flower, he whispered:

"Oh, Rose, if you will not have me there is nothing in the world for me."

He repeated this once or twice, while I stood stupefied, and then he said to himself: "Modern love, modern love . . . . Yes, they certainly do it now in a different way."

I was filled with a tornado of opposing desires. Black anger and burning shame were mixed with astonishment so complete that it made me incapable of any action whatsoever.

I have since more than once thanked God that I did not stain my hands with blood on that occasion. The restraint which prevented me from running into the room and wringing the man's neck was not put on me by myself. If any other man but Killigrew had done such a thing I know only too well that I should have killed him, and you may judge of the extraordinary influence of Killigrew's personality by the fact that when I became capable of action my only thought was to get into my room and, if possible, let him remain in ignorance of the fact that he had been observed.

I slipped into my room and closed the door behind me. Instantly I heard the noise of a chair replaced in the next room, and then the closing of that door. I was drawing on my riding boots which had been sent me by Mistress Barber, when I heard Killigrew reopen his door and come to mine, which he opened. He stood in the doorway, and I knew that he wished to ascertain if I had seen or heard anything of his extraordinary performance.

"Ah, Stanborough," he said, "so you are going riding. Do you ride alone?"

"I ride alone," said I, busying myself with my boots.

"And my sister?" he asked with his eyes on my face.

"Is in the garden."

"I have something to say to her," he said. "I wish you a pleasant ride, but keep your eye upon the heavens, for there will be rain before evening." With that he withdrew.

The moment he was gone, I was again filled with furious anger against him, an anger which something stronger than myself prevented me from expressing. It was not that I was afraid of him. It was that I was afraid for him. In spite of my wrath, I thought more for his dignity than for my own. My shame was for him. It was as if I had seen a god stealing apples.

A few minutes later, with the help of old Michael, I had saddled the brown mare, and was galloping furiously through the long grass, careless of my direction, anxious only to obliterate my immediate discomfort that I might think once more of those strange, sweet words in the rose-garden, which had been spoilt for me by the knowledge that another than I had overheard them.

I crossed the broad, open grounds of rank grass, where thistles and campions, lifting their heads almost to the level of the mare's chest, showed for how long the place had been neglected. Then, riding along the edge of the wood, I came to an overgrown pathway, and turned in there under the tall trees. For some minutes I had enough to do in keeping my hat on, in saving my face from the whipping of the branches that swung over the path. By the time the path opened into a narrow glade, soft underfoot, good ground for the mare, I had so far lost my mood of mingled shame and anger as to be able to return to that which had immediately preceded it. I slowed the mare, and presently dropped the reins on her neck, and, while she walked slowly onward, thought of the change that afternoon had brought in my position in the hall as far as concerned Mistress Killigrew.

I had learnt much since morning, and in the first place the strange new fact that I loved her, which fact had, as it were, disclosed itself to me by my first words in the garden, words that I had not planned, words that even the day before I could not have supposed myself capable of uttering. It seemed a curious thing that the mere involuntary uttering of a few words should have revealed to me the possession of the most important thing in my life. I knew now that I had loved Rose Killigrew ever since my first sight of her on the staircase—that is to say, it seemed to me that I had loved her all my life, for, boy-like, I already counted my life as beginning at midnight on the North Road, when I took leave of my uncle. I knew, too, that I should love her until my death, and that knowledge was true knowledge, for I am already on the downward slope of life, and never for one moment has that fair image been displaced, or that sweet friendship, which I hold the better part of love, been broken. I am setting things down as honestly as I may, and you may perhaps the better understand my feeling and my youth if I tell you that the mare nearly unseated me when she plunged forward, startled by a loud and cheerful cry which I let forth, bringing my hand down with a great slap upon my knee.

Had she not said that she loved me? True, she had said that on *that* account she could not . . . but what had she said she could not do? She had said she could marry no one, me least of all, because she loved me. Because she loved me. The words fairly sang themselves in my head, and made the rest seem nonsense. She loved me. Then all was possible, I thought, for I loved her, and I was yet young enough to believe that against two lovers nothing on earth can stand, unless it were the very powers of hell. I was in this defiant, joyous temper when, coming to the end of the glade, and to the edge of the trees, I saw across an open space the grass-grown road that led from the house, and, a little way along it, grey and desolate, the great gateway and a little of the high wall that encircled the Killigrew lands.

I put the mare to a light canter, and rode to the gate, and through between the griffon on the gatepost and that other that lay forlorn upon the ground. Perhaps I wished to reassure myself that there was a world outside that wall, a world of simple human folk to which I could take Rose, a world in which, I smile to say it, there would be but a small place for my philosophy.

I pulled my horse up short when I saw that sitting on the fallen griffon was a man, and that man the pedlar I had spoken with on my first coming to this place, when on my twenty-first birthday, in my fine black suit, I had ridden out of my old life and into my new on the horse that Killigrew had lent me, after that night in the inn at the crossways on the great road running north and south through England, some forty miles away.

On that occasion I had not given much thought to the pedlar, except to regret having spoken to him when Killigrew was clearly impatient of his presence. But I had often remembered his strange words, when he had bade me in the three holy names not to go through that gateway into the place where, as it had turned out, I had found the greatest happiness of my life. I looked at him now more narrowly, and saw that he was even older than I had thought. I judged him to be nearly eighty years of age. He had blue eyes, so blue as to compel observation of their colour, and there are many blue eyes that a man may see every day and not know but they are grey or brown. His long, straw-coloured hair, splashed with white, hung to his shoulders. He was sitting on the fallen griffon, leaning forward with his chin resting on the head of his stick. His pack lay beside him on the ground. He looked up at me with quick interest, and then crossed himself in the Popish manner.

"Young man," he said, "you are riding out of the gate of hell. Come near to me that I may see the marks of the flames upon your face."

"Pedlar," said I, "were you not here some months ago, when I rode in at this same gate with Mr. Killigrew and his man?"

"I was," said the pedlar, "and I warned you then. Do you not now feel in your heart that you are damned for ever and for ever to the torments of hell?"

"On the contrary," said I, "but two minutes ago I was thanking heaven in my fashion for the greatest happiness God has given me on earth."

"Come near to me," said the pedlar.

I was tempted to ride on, but remembering suddenly that this was perhaps that very old man who had kept the rose-garden, and so given great pleasure to us both, I dismounted and stood before the pedlar.

The old man stared into my eyes, and I stared back, determined not to be put out of countenance by him, an old hawker. At the same time, as I looked into his eyes, and he into mine, I knew that, pedlar or no pedlar, he was an extraordinary man, and I thought of the fanatics of whom my father had told me, who, during the early years of the Restoration, walked even in the streets of London denouncing the licence of the times and calling down curses and the hatred of the mob on every gentleman that passed with well-dressed hair or clothes other than the ashen-coloured rags in which those vagabonds were content to await the day of judgment.

"Your soul is as yet unspotted," he said at last, "but how long will it remain so in that place of evil?"

"Tell me," I asked, "what it is that makes you speak in such terms of this old house?"

"Is she also safe?" he asked, "or are you saving your soul alone?"

"If you are speaking of Mistress Rose Killigrew," I replied, "I would advise you to keep a hold on your tongue, for I will suffer no impertinence even in thought towards that lady." Then, remembering the rose-garden, and feeling that I was taking a ridiculous and haughty tone to an old man who could at the worst be but a harmless lunatic, I added, "But perhaps I mistake the spirit of your words."

"There is light in darkness," said the old man. "Tell me now frankly, what I suspect from your quick words. Do you love her? Boy, do you love her?"

Something stronger than myself prevented me from resenting this question, and, unconsciously catching the pedlar's tone, I answered, solemnly, "So help me God, I do."

"Take her from that house of devils while you may."

"I have asked her to marry me," I said, "though, master pedlar, I hardly know why I should tell you so."

"For fifty years the clouds have been gathering about that house. For fifty years I have seen the sky darken and narrow, closing in upon it, and for long before that I believe the devilment has been in the house and in the owners of the house. Soon the thunder will rumble in the clouds, and the lightning leap forth and the house be licked up in the flames of retribution and the devil cast out for ever."

"I beg you to tell me plainly what you mean."

"Tie up your horse to the hinge of the gatepost, and come near and listen to me."

I obeyed him, I knew not why, and threw myself on the grass beside him, in the shadow of the gateway.

"Do you know that within the memory of man the Killigrews who have lived in that house have had no children? Do you know that the grandfathers of the oldest men living in the village told their grandchildren the same tale. It is always so. There comes a Killigrew to the house, and lives there for a little while, and goes away. Years pass, and there comes a Killigrew, another, and he lives in the house, and then he too goes away. I am an old man, and I have seen this happen twice. And the man or devil who rode in with you is the third of that race that I have seen, and all were young men, and all alike, like twins, but in the eyes of each one lay more evil than in the eyes of him who went before. The third, that one who rode with you, rode with his face muffled, but I have seen him since, and he is young, like the others, but there is that hidden in his eyes from which the worst of human sinners would turn away."

"He is a strange and learned man," I answered, "but I have seen nothing but sorrow in his face, sorrow and fear, but not wickedness."

"Of what is he afraid," said the old man, "but of the wrath of God?

And it is not he who fears, but the devil who has entered into that family, or the house, and possesses each one of those men who come to take their place in the house that has never known their fathers. The place is in the hands of devils. It is a place of death. There is not a family in the village but has its tale of one who went into that great desolate park and never returned. It may be thirty years ago, it may be a hundred, it may be more, but every cottage has its reason for fearing that great house. It may be a little child found strangled in the wood. It may be a man called in there to fell trees, and found the next day bled to death, his throat cut by his own axe. This stone beast on which I am sitting has been a tool of death."

"What do you mean?"

"A little girl strayed from the village, and when they found her she was lying here, crushed by the stone beast that had fallen on her from the gatepost."

I suppose I shuddered and moved, for he went on.

"Ay, young man, you may well shrink, but if you knew all that is written against this house in that great book that on the Judgment Day will be read in a voice like the sound of many clear trumpets, you would not shudder only. No, with your eyes blind with terror, and your hands to your ears shutting out that awful accusation, you would fly, looking neither to right nor to left."

At this I made sure that I had to do with one of those mad fanatics, but his next words again aroused my curiosity.

"I am an old man now, a very old man, and not far from my death, but before I die I know that I shall see the end of this house and of all that is therein, and the wrath of the Lord falling upon it even in hailstones like red-hot coals. It is for that end that I wait, that I have waited these twenty years. Ay, there is not a man in all the countryside that does not know that the end is near, and that I . . ."

"Tell me what it is that you have against the house."

"The greatest injury that was ever done to man was done to me in that house, and I will tell you of it, and you shall judge.

"Twenty-five years ago there was a Killigrew in that house, and with him a young maid, just such another as Mistress Rose, and beautiful. I had a brother, older than myself. In our youth we had been here, and, when I was about sixty years old (I was not a pedlar then, and if I were to tell you my name you would know it at once) my brother prevailed upon me to come here again. We came here, and, old men though we were, we loved that lady. I love her memory still. It is a strange thing, old man's love, and a rare thing. It took my brother and me and made us mad. We loved each other, but during that time we more than once fought each other with our weak fists, and once we fought with swords. And she would walk in the rose-garden there, an angel, while our love for her turned us two old men into fiends. And all the time that Killigrew looked on and smiled, and watched us narrowly. And there came a day when I could bear it no longer, and I laid myself before that lady and begged her mercy. And she laughed at me, and then, at the sight of my great pain, she hid her laughter. She hid it, and I knew that she hid it, and the pain of it haunts me to this day. And then I broke out against my brother, and, madman, accused her of loving him, and told her he was ten years older than myself. And at that she could not hide her laughter, and said that we were two kind old men, but that she could never care for either of us in that way. Well, I did not say good-bye to my brother, nor to Killigrew, but walked away out of this gateway, and wandered on the high roads. At last, after five years, I came back here again, and, with my pack on my back, walked up to the house, and there met Killigrew, who fell to laughing. I cursed him, and, as I was cursing, I heard her voice and my brother's in the rose-garden close by. I left Killigrew and went to the garden, and there was that lady walking, with a young man at her side. The young man turned and looked at me, and I knew that not only did he speak in my brother's voice, but that the eyes that looked at me out of his smooth face were the eyes that had been my brother's.

"I asked for my brother, and then I heard Killigrew, who had come into the garden, laughing behind me. I spoke to that young man as my brother, and he turned as white as bleached linen, and answered not a word. Killigrew said that my brother had gone away soon after I had gone myself. I said he lied, and that he had taken my brother's soul and set it in a young man's body. I raved, I accused him of sorcery, of witchcraft, and he laughed. Then that lady laid her hands on the shoulders of that young man, and looked earnestly in his eyes. And whether or not she saw there what I saw I cannot say, but she suddenly put her hands to her own throat and fell on the ground. They tried to prevent me, but it was I who lifted her. She was dead. Just then I heard the crying of a little baby. That was her child, a daughter. The same night they drove away, Killigrew, the young man, and the little baby. . . . They left me with the body of her whom I had loved. God revealed to me then that Killigrew was not a man but a devil, and that he had bought my brother's soul. I cursed him as he drove away. He shot at me twice with his pistols as I stood there cursing him. He missed me, though I stood directly before him in the lighted doorway. The bullets are even now in the wood of the doorposts.

"I buried that lady, where she had fallen, in the rose-garden. For twenty years I stayed there alone, wrestling with the spirit of evil, and tending the roses that make a garden of the place where she lies dead. Then, after twenty years, she came again. Mistress Rose Killigrew came, and brought in people from the village, to prepare the house for her brother, and when I saw her first I thought the years were wiped away, and that here again before me was that lady whom I had loved. She thanked me for my care of the roses, and I could not tell her why I had tended them. Then she spoke of her brother, and that he had said that he would bring a guest with him, a young man to share their solitude. I knew that Killigrew had come back again, and I left my roses and came away and waited by the gate. When I saw you, I thought you might be the new master, and that I had been mistaken. When I knew that you were not, I thought of my brother, and warned you not to go into that place where death walks in a rose-garden and the souls of men are bought and given to the devil. Then the servant told me to go, and I looked at him, and I know that he was my brother himself."

"Really," said I, "that is a little more than I can believe. For on your own showing, your brother would now be very nearly a hundred years old."

"You are welcome to think me mad, young man, but that house is the abode of devils, who will presently be cast out, and, if you love that maid, take her away at once, before the day of vengeance. For I know that the day comes swiftly, and I am the instrument of God."

He rose from the stone griffon, and stood, raising his hands above his head, as if preaching.

"Woe, woe to that house where death is secret and life is an abomination. Woe, woe to the buyers and sellers of souls. Woe to that spirit whose thirst for evil is not to be quenched, who sports with the bodies of men, who feeds on death, who mocks God Himself with hideous resurrection."

His words were ringing horribly in my ears when with trembling hands I unfastened the mare, and galloped away from him, along the grass-grown path towards the house he was cursing, the house that for me was nothing but the gloomy casket, in which, like a star in darkness, shone the presence of my beloved.

CHAPTER VII

A Disappearance:
The Clog with the Chipped Heel

Before I reached the house, rain was already falling, not a violent storm, but the big slow drops that shine, almost white, against the dark sky. I rode into the stable-yard, and called loudly for Michael, because I wished to get indoors before the rain had ruined my clothes, or at least taken the crimp and curl out of my lace-cuffs. Michael did not answer. I stooped low on the back of the mare, and rode in through the stable-door, to be in shelter from the rain. I called again, and set the rusty clapper swinging in the old cracked bell that hung by the door. Still Michael did not come; so I made the best of a bad business and unsaddled the mare, and gave her food and a little water, as soon as she had cooled from our brisk ride homewards. It was beginning to be dusk in the stable then, and I made my way swiftly across the yard, for the rain was still falling, though there was a line of clearer sky below the purple curtain of the clouds.

Wishing to save my clothes, I went straight into the house by the door that led to the kitchens. I found there only the man and his wife whom Michael had brought from London soon after my first coming. I asked for Michael. They did not know where he was. The woman rolled the flour from her sleeves (she was baking) and said that Master Michael was a queer steward not to be at hand when the gentlemen wanted him, a silly servile speech. Servants are not like that in the north country, and I have never been able to accustom myself to the servility of the south. Mistress Barber, in like circumstances, would have wished Master Michael to the devil, roundly called me a fool for getting myself wetted, and then set to with a whisk of her skirts to warm me a hot drink against the rheumatism, and to see that new dry clothes were upon my back before I had had time. to cool. That is the north-country way, and I was impatient at the empty words of the woman who stood now in the kitchen looking at me, and trying to please me by fanning the ill humour which I did not feel. The man helped me off with my riding boots, which were dirty from crossing the yard, and told me that he had not seen Michael since he had gone out to saddle the mare for me.

I supposed that the old servant was busy somewhere in the house, or that he was in the garden, plucking weeds for Mistress Rose. It occurred to me to ask Killigrew when I met him in the hall. I needed to say something, and this inquiry was the first speech that came into my head.

"No," said Killigrew, "I have not seen him. In fact, I have wanted him. I supposed he was in the stable."

"He is not there, and the servants have not seen him."

"Perhaps he is with Rose."

At that moment Rose came down the staircase, from one of the rooms on the upper floor.

"Have neither of you seen old Michael?" she said. "He was to have helped me in the garden."

"An extraordinary thing," said Killigrew, "but it seems to me that old Michael has disappeared. Here is Mr. Stanborough has been looking for him, and you and I. . . ."

And so it happened that I did not that evening hear from Rose what she had almost promised to tell me. She had been very fond of the old man, and could think of nothing but his disappearance. We thought of all the possible places where he could be, or where he could have met with an accident. We searched the house thoroughly, went down into cellars, and, with a ladder, into the lofts. At least, Rose stood at the foot of the ladder, and I went up into the lofts, which for many years had been a very metropolis of jackdaws. Killigrew, to my surprise, took as active a part in the search as either of us. I had not thought that Killigrew could be other than indifferent. Until late at night we searched, and at last Killigrew and I went out with a lantern and made sure that the old man had not fallen in some kind of fit and lain in some dark corner. I did not get the chance for three words with Rose on the subject of our morning's conversation.

In spite of the protests of the two servants, we left the great door on the latch, unbolted, so that Michael should not find himself locked out, if by chance he had been detained, perhaps in the village; though I, for my part, thought that unlikely, as I had spent the afternoon at the gate with the pedlar and seen no one ride out.

In the morning I rose late, not by intention, but because I slept longer than usual, and was not awaked by the coming of old Michael. And indeed, when I woke, I lay abed, considering what might have happened to that old man. My conversation with the pedlar had made me more apprehensive on his account than I should have been. I lay abed, thinking of the old servant, and, as I lay there, one image of him came so clearly into my mind, that it was as if I saw him. I remembered a day when, by chance, one of my shoes had slipped under the armoire. Old Michael had looked for it, and, at last, perceiving its whereabouts, had knelt on the ground, and reaching under the armoire had brought it out. It had been a slow business, his kneeling and searching, and I saw him in my mind's eye, with extraordinary clarity, his bent back, his thin legs, and the upturned soles of his clogs. I do not know what south-country folk would have called them. They were leather shoes with wooden soles, and out of the heel of the left clog a small piece had been chipped. I had noticed this clearly, as I watched the old man's back and speculated at the right name for such shoes. And now, as I remembered the scene, that detail sprang vividly into my mind.

It occurred to me at once that here was a means of finding at least whither old Michael had gone. I rose, dressed, breakfasted with Killi-grew, and, anxious perhaps to have the credit of discovery in Rose's eyes, if indeed my quest should prove successful, I said nothing of my plans. After breakfast Killigrew rode off, as he said, to make inquiries in the village, though I have now very considerable doubts as to whether he went so far. If he did, he did not go for any other purpose than that of exercise.

I saw Rose for a moment in Killigrew's presence. She was pale, and I thought she had been weeping, and selfishly wondered if, supposing it was I who had disappeared. . . . She asked if we yet knew anything of Michael. Killigrew told her the purpose of his ride. I listened, but, full of hope, said nothing of what I meant to do. She left us to deal with the business of the housekeeping, a business which she treated with a sweet, diligent seriousness, like a child playing at house. She is older now, but, in this particular at least, she has not grown up, and even now when I see her arranging the manifold details of our life which fall within her province, I see her still as a serious child at play.

As soon as I was alone, I set about the execution of my plan. I went first to the stable-yard, and there in the soft mud by the door of the stable sought for the print of Michael's clogs (I shall call them so, though they were not such clogs as Mistress Barber would have called by the name). I presently found several clear imprints, and, as I had hoped, the cracked piece from the heel of the left foot was easily noticeable. Now the rain of yesterday had softened the ground, but there had been a drought for some weeks before that, and so no old footprints in the yard. I found in the soft mud clearly-marked prints leading from the stable, but they disappeared as soon as they left that part of the yard, close about the stable-door, which is always soft. I therefore concluded, as I had expected, that Michael had left the stable soon after I had rid-den away—at any rate, before the storm.

I had learnt that, which was little; but I also learnt that he had been wearing that easily recognizable pair of clogs, and it seemed to me to be pretty clear that I had but to cast round the house in widening circles, and unless he had gone too far before the moistening of the ground, I should pick up the trace of that chipped heel. It is curious, but I set about that business with a light heart. I did not for a moment suppose that I should come upon Michael's corpse, or indeed evidence of any shocking kind. There are powers in the mind quite beyond those simple processes which the best of our philosophy has only catalogued and described. We know far more, it seems to me, than we can ever explain away by stating how it was we came to know it. I knew, as I set about that search, as surely as that the sun shone, and that yesterday's curtain of cloud had given way to a mere flock of flying white lamblets in the heavens, that Michael was alive and well. The only question that exercised my curiosity was, Where? Rose, I think, was less at ease than I, but then, she knew more of the secrets of that house. If I had known as much of Killigrew then as I was to learn in the ensuing forty-eight hours, I should, quite wrongly, have set about my search with more anxiety.

I had a fairly easy task, for there were not many outlets from the house. I walked out from the stable-yard, noticing in the grounds only the hoof-marks of the brown mare, and, newly printed, the hoof-marks of the black horse on which Killigrew had ridden away. I walked round the house and through the side door into the trellised rose-garden. I walked to the foot of the rose-garden along the path that led from my own little door, and then, to the left, to the other path parallel with the first, that led from the small garden door out of the room next to mine. Here, so early, I came upon footmarks. There were several, and I bent to examine them. Most clearly marked were footmarks leading towards the house, heavily indented at the toes, the footmarks of a man running, not the footmarks of old Michael. The feet were small, neat, well-shod. I put them down at once as those of Killigrew. The same feet had also left prints going in the other direction, away from the house, and, side by side with them, I perceived other footprints, which, it seemed to me, were those of which I was in search.

I shifted the little branches of the rose-trees that hung across the path at the level of the knees, and went through the little wicket-gate in the trellis, out of the rose-garden into the wood. Here I eagerly examined the path again. The trees had protected it from the rain, so that the footprints were not so clear as in the garden, but here they were, unmistakably, the neat footprints of Killigrew, and the marks of the clog with the chipped heel. I followed them along the path, with as much excitement as I used to feel when I traced a philosophical idea through the ages, once a favourite amusement of mine. Here and there when the branches were thick over the path the footprints disappeared altogether, and then, suddenly, there they would be again, faint, so faint that I could scarcely trust them, until a little farther on where the path was moist I found other examples of an encouraging clearness.

Ever since that first strange night, when for one moment Rose had thought that I was spying, I had avoided this little path into the wood. I had never gone farther along it than the point at which, after being petrified by that horrible shriek of pain, and by the song of the nightingale above me in the tree, I had leapt out on Rose with my drawn weapon in my hand, and she had hurried me back to the house, and remained herself to face whatever mystery there was. I had felt in honour bound not to pursue that inquiry, and therefore, well as I knew the rest of the Killigrew estate, this little woodland path I had most scrupulously left unexplored. Now, I felt, it was a different matter. I was not concerned with anything more mysterious than old Michael, and his disappearance justified me in following his footsteps even if they led into a part of the wood that I had decided, though never promised, not to examine.

So I followed the footprints without misgiving, until they led me through a close thicket to a small stone hut. I have written the place down a hut. That is not an accurate description of the impression it made on me, although the word came naturally to my pen on account of the small size of the building. It was a small stone building, overgrown with ivy. Even those parts of it that were not covered with ivy were green with the brighter green of moss on damp stone. It had but one window, and that a narrow, vertical slit above the level of my head, glazed, but hidden from any one who did not search for it by the close overgrowth of ivy-leaves. There was a wooden door to the place. It was closed. I pushed at it, but it did not give at all, so that I supposed it was not merely latched but locked. The roof was of moss-covered stone tiles. There was a small stone chimney. I should think the building was about seventy or a hundred years old. It reminded me of certain drawings of Sir John Harrington's which will be remembered with a smile by those who know them.

Now at the door of this strange little building the marks of the clog with the chipped heel came to an end. There were two or three imprints close to the door, as if there had been a moment's wait, perhaps for the unlocking. But the other footprints not only seemed to indicate that Killigrew or whoever it was that made them had gone in there, but also that he had come out, and walked on farther along the path. I took it to be the head of a well, or some such place. I tried, as I have said, to shake the door and failed. I then resolved to follow the other footprints, and perhaps see what had become of the man who had carried away the key, if indeed a suspicion which now began to form against my judgment were true, and Michael had been shut up in that place. Still the place was so small that I could hardly suppose any one shut up in it un-willingly and there had been no sort of hesitation about the steps of the clog with the chipped heel. For some minutes I examined the hut from all sides, thinking that perhaps there might be some hidden exit at the back. I wondered whether it was in that hut that the drama or accident of my first night here had taken place. Was it within that tiny green prison that Killigrew had been so tortured as to freeze the night with that solitary, dreadful cry? In any case, I reflected, the hut could not run away, and I did not want to get help from the house to break it open, and in doing so perhaps alarm Rose unnecessarily, before I had ex-hausted my private inquiry.

The path curved and wound through the wood, so that, though I had not altogether lost my bearings, I was yet surprised when it brought me suddenly to a full stop in some bushes beside a low stone wall. I pushed my way through the bushes, and broken and bent boughs showed that some one else had been in the habit of doing this same thing. I found that from the farther side of them I could look down on the stable-yard of the house, with a practical certainty of being unseen.

"Ah," I thought, "so it was here that Killigrew was standing when I crossed the yard to the kitchen."

The supposition was the flimsiest hypothesis, but I believe it was ac-tually correct, for, working from it, I decided that he must have taken a quicker path back than that by which I had come; and searching round with a view to verifying this deduction I found clear footprints going off at a tangent from the path. I followed these footprints. They were not so easy as those on the path, though there was even here a track that had evidently been used before. At the end of about ten minutes of my pains-taking progression, I arrived, with a back that ached from stooping, at the path again, opposite the little stone hut. I found two prints where the man had jumped from the grass on to the path, and then I turned directly to the door to compare these with those I had originally observed.

A theory had now formed itself in my rather unwilling head. Assum-ing that Killigrew was responsible for the neat footprints, as I believe he was, and Michael responsible for those of the chipped heel, which I al-ready knew, then I told myself a story something like this. I own that the wild words of the pedlar had more than a little to do with firing my imagination to this extravagance, which I should not have thought of without that stimulus, my brain being now, as always, not of an inventive character. I said to myself that Killigrew had beguiled the old man to come with him to the hut, that in the hut he had done away with him by some wicked means, and that he had then gone to that post of observa-tion by the stable-yard in order to appear with the correct modicum of astonishment and distress, he also looking for his victim.

A stupid little story it was, but that was what struggled awkwardly about in my mind, while with bent back I peered at the ground before the door, and moved slowly like a gravel-pecking hen to look at the footsteps I had already examined.

I stood upright with such suddenness that it seemed to me from the pain that I had almost broken my back. For whereas when I had been here before the prints of the clog with the chipped heel came to the door of the hut, and there ended, I now saw, before my nose, a new set of these prints, leaving the hut and going towards the house on the path to the rose-garden. Michael had been in the hut ten minutes before and had now left it.

I tried the door. It was fast as before.

I turned back to the path, and now, with new-awakened interest, I followed these fresh tracks towards the house. There was no mistaking them, and they led me the whole way to the wicket-gate in the trellis and into the rose-garden. There they turned to the left, as if to take the path that led up to the little door out of my room. I had got to the corner of the path before I heard a strange sound, the noise of a grown man sobbing. It seemed to me that I knew the voice, and yet I could hardly believe it possible that a man of Michael's age and dignity could weep aloud in a garden at midday.

Close round the corner were Rose, with wet cheeks, and a youngish man, a man of five and thirty, talking to her. I did not wish her to think I had listened to them, and I made a little noise with my feet on the path, and proceeded towards them, carefully observing the tracks that I was following.

I was close to them, when Killigrew appeared walking down the path. The man instantly walked to meet him, and passed him without speaking. Rose wiped her eyes and bid me a good morning which I scarcely noticed, for, in the moment when the man had turned and moved off, I had noticed the prints that his feet made in the ground. I had been afraid that they would obliterate those on which I was intent. Now the prints made by that man's feet were precisely those. At every other step he took he left the mark of the clog with the chipped heel.

CHAPTER VIII

The Strange Servant and My First Love-Letter

Killigrew came up to us, just as, recovering from my astonishment, I was returning Rose's greeting. He looked at her face in a way which I secretly resented, for it seemed to me that he was trying to read there what she by an effort was concealing from him.

"You are not up so early to-day," said Killigrew, "but we all slept late after last night's unnecessary anxiety."

"Has Michael returned then?" I asked, "and who was that man?"

"No," he replied, looking intently at Rose, "Michael has not come back. It seems, however, that he had business of his own beyond the village, and he has sent us this man, a cousin of his, to fulfil his duties towards us. The man should have been here yesterday in the afternoon, if he had understood his message, and then we should have known no disquiet."

I did not believe a word he said. I doubt if he intended me to believe him. I think he was merely putting off a truthful answer to my question until the time when it would better suit his purpose. He went on:

"My dear Stanborough, I do not know what is in your mind, but I promise you that to-night we will have a talk that shall clear up for you many puzzles with which I perceive that you have been troubling yourself."

With that I had to be content, for Killigrew was one of those men whom it is impossible to question if and when they do not wish to be put to the inconvenience of refusing an answer.

Nor during the whole of the rest of that day did he give me an opportunity of speaking with Rose alone. Either he was with us, or I was with him and Rose was elsewhere. It was as if he had determined to prevent us from explaining to each other anything that needed explanation, and, God knows, there was enough. I was in a fever to speak with Rose, to beg her to tell me what she had meant to tell me the evening before. I wished to tell her of the pedlar, and to learn why she had been weeping, and what strange grief she could share in common with that man, a full inch taller than Michael, in different clothes, but wearing Michael's shoes, with whom I had seen her in the garden, I remember that day as a long-drawn-out impatience, politeness barely sustained in the perpetual presence of Killigrew, who with unutterable calm walked with us, sat with us, or drew me aside to speak of indifferent things.

We walked together in the park not far from the house, under the shading trees, which were taking on their gaudy autumn colouring, and now and then, when there came light puffs of wind, showering little clouds of gold and umber leaves about our heads. We talked of politics, a subject wholly foreign to the lips of Killigrew, and then as always distasteful to me. We spoke of the Scotch rebellion of the year before, and of what would have been if it had succeeded, and given us one king instead of another.

He saw my impatience of that subject, and spoke of Paracelsus and the manuscripts I had read during the last few weeks. On any other day I would have discussed them with him with delight. Even then I admired the swift subtlety of his mind as he seemed to twist in and out through the mystical reasoning which had almost baffled me, lighting his path as he went, like a glowworm moving through the dusk of those strange thoughts. Yet, all the time, though I listened and admired, I was waiting for the end, and wondering when and how I could persuade Rose to set my mind at rest, and let me help her to break whatever cords those were that kept her from being mine, though on her own confession she felt for me some little of the love I felt for her.

During that long and, as it seemed, interminable afternoon and evening, when Killigrew was like a shadow before me and behind me, wherever I moved, there occurred two incidents, one of which confirmed the happiness at which I seemed to be grasping through a mist of doubt, and the other doubled my perplexity, though it might well have altered the remainder of my story.

I scruple to write down the first, but if, when you read this, you are in love and doubt, you will understand how much it meant to me—this little thing, this tiny incident, so small, so slight, as almost to seem without importance. If, on the other hand, you have not that privilege, it is possible that you will smile, and think to yourself that you at least are above such triviality.

For it was nothing more, though to me nothing less, than the pressure of a hand. There were no words between us. Killigrew made that impossible, and yet it happened that the touch of fingers did more perhaps than any words could do to give me confidence and happiness, and even the trust that so short a while afterwards was to determine the happy issue of my adventure.

We were walking all three together, Rose between us, when my hand touched hers. Killigrew was talking, but I do not remember what he said, although I believe I answered him. For as we stopped for a moment at the end of an avenue, her hand was in mine. I think I took it. I felt her little hand tremble in mine. It was as if there was a parliament of her little fingers, making up their minds, and then her hand nestled into mine so frankly, so trustfully, that I knew, as if she told me outright, that something had happened which removed the barriers between us. I knew not what it was. I scarcely cared. But I knew that she would never again say "you least of all," and for the rest of that strange day I walked in exultation, careless of the future, careless of all save the memory of those little fingers in mine and the message they had given me.

The second incident was of a very different character. More than once during the afternoon I had thought I had perceived the strange servant, he of the chipped heel, whom Killigrew pretended had been sent by Michael, either watching us or following us, as if waiting for an opportunity.

In the evening, I went into my room to prepare myself for supper. I was scarcely in the room when I heard a gentle tapping at the small garden door. I opened it, and a man who, for a moment before he spoke, I thought was Michael, pressed a book into my hand.

"Keep this secret for the sake of all of us from the eyes of him who is master here," he said, "but, I beg you, read it as swiftly as you may."

He instantly disappeared into the gloom of the garden. I closed the door, and had just time to see that it was a little book of closely-written parchment leaves bound in pale vellum that had turned grey and yellow with age and damp. Then I heard steps in the hall, and Killigrew, apparently determined not to leave me even for a moment alone, came into my room. I slipped the little book into the breast of my shirt, as I busied myself, alike for Killigrew's observation and my own need, with the arrangement of my linen.

Killigrew sat idly on the edge of my table, and congratulated me on my taste in kerchiefs, of which I had emptied a number out of a drawer. Half bantering, half serious he talked on, as he alone could, teasing me for my foppishness, and flattering me by making me feel that at the bottom he was envious, and at the same time making even this indolent playful talk the ornament, the accompaniment of his ingenious philosophical ideas. I have every reason for hating the memory of Killigrew, but I can never think otherwise than that he was the finest talker I am ever likely to hear.

But as Killigrew talked I kept my face so turned that he could not see it, for, the more I thought of my late visitor, the more certain was I that he was the man I had seen with Rose in the garden, the man whose grief had brought tears to her eyes, the man of whose presence Killigrew had given so lame an explanation. I began to entertain a strange suspicion. If the thing had not been incredible, I admitted to myself, I should have supposed that this man and Michael were one and the same. I laughed at myself for the idea, but it returned with increased insistency. How could a strange servant sent by old Michael dare to parade his woes before a mistress he had never seen? How could his sorrows affect her? And, what sorrows could he have, of so deep a nature as to make him weep aloud, an action abhorrent even to the commonest hind?

We supped late that night, later than usual, and with unusual ceremony. When we came out of my room the table was already laid in the main hall, and the new servant, or Michael, as I shall call him, for my heart even then told me that it was he, though my mind rebelled against this supposition, was waiting behind Killigrew's chair. Rose came down the staircase, and as I offered her my arm to lead her to her place, she gave me a little paper note, just at that moment when Killigrew could not see what passed between us, as I stood with my back to him at the foot of the stairs. It was a little note folded twice over, like a little paper butterfly, and I had already concealed it when we crossed the hall and sat down.

Killigrew continued the bantering, semi-philosophic conversation he had begun in my room. He talked to a silent audience. Rose was grave, and I thought she had been weeping again, and, when I was not thinking of her, I was preoccupied with the strange man who stood at Killigrew's elbow, the man whom I had seen that morning in the garden.

He was dressed in plain brown clothes, such clothes as were fashionable twenty years ago for the livery of a house steward or confidential servant. He was, I thought, a little taller, perhaps an inch taller, than Michael. He was clean-shaven, whereas Michael had been lent a greater dignity by his flowing grey beard. But he had Michael's forehead, and I should have said Michael's eyes, if it had not been that the settled gloom of Michael's eyes was here replaced by a look of mortal anguish, of dreadful, violent remorse. His was a fine face, though not a face promising any very particular intellectual qualities. There was a weakness perceptible in the chin and what I can best describe as a lack of premeditation. You would have said on looking at him that here was a man who had sinned without counting the cost and had suddenly awakened to the knowledge that his sin was mortal. The dreadful thing about that tortured face was that it was the face of a good man.

And now, as we sat and supped, he went silently from one to the other, with bread and wine, fulfilling small menial duties whose very triviality seemed to intensify the depth and *abandon* of his grief. And Rose sat there at the table, beautiful but sad, she also with a deeper melancholy than I had ever seen in her, and, more than that, with an anxiety which she was quite unable to conceal.

It was a strange meal, there in that hall; with the high panelled walls, and the candlelight flickering on the blue surface of the armour of dead Killigrews of long ago, and on the lilac curtains that shaded the narrow windows, this one of painted glass, that boarded up, long broken, and never restored. A strange, uncomfortable meal, for there were three in that room disturbed each in his fashion, and one so calm as to heighten by his calmness the agitation of the others.

Only now and then, when Killigrew glanced at the servant, I thought I saw his calm disturbed by a moment of scornful impatience, and thought of Satan angry and jeering at the remorse of those other devils he had tempted to their fall.

We had scarcely come to the end of the meal, when Killigrew spoke to the man for the first time.

"Go," he said, "and prepare the library as I told you, for Mr. Stanborough and I shall be sitting there to-night."

The man bowed without saying a word, and went out into the kitchens, and presently returned carrying some wine-bottles, which he took with him up the staircase.

Killigrew became even more insufferably calm and, as it were, joyful after the man had gone. He poured out wine for us, and lifting his glass asked us to join him in a toast.

"To youth," he cried, but there was something so sinister in his tone, even while he smiled, and held his glass high in a mock enthusiasm, that, though I answered him, "To youth," and drained my glass, the wine seemed to dry in my throat, and I felt as if I had been drinking in honour not of youth, but of death.

Soon after that he prepared to leave the table.

"My dear Rose," he said, "I beg that to-night you will excuse Mr. Stanborough and myself if we leave you alone. We have a matter of considerable importance to discuss, and as it may well be that 'the humid night' will have 'rushed down the sky' before we have finished our discussion, we will bid you good night. I beg you will go early to your rest, for it seems to me that you are fatigued."

There was an abominable tone of irony in this last remark, but it was so disguised that it was impossible to resent it openly.

Rose bowed. I saw that she could not trust herself to speak. There were tears in her eyes. I was more than ever disturbed.

"And now," he said, turning towards me, "you perceive I have counted upon your indulgence to give me the pleasure of your company in the library. I have much to say to you."

We rose, and he bent over Rose's hand with a gravity that I found hateful, and waited for me at the foot of the staircase.

Rose gave me her hand to kiss, and looked straight into my eyes, with a strange look, as if she thought it possible that we should never meet again, a look which seemed to draw my soul out of my body and to be loath to let it go.

I bid her good night, and though she did not speak I knew that her lips moved, and that she wished to say good night to me. She turned suddenly away, perhaps because Killigrew was watching her. She walked to the great hearth, and stood there looking down on the embers that burned there, with her arm resting on the panelling above it. I think she was weeping.

She turned for a moment, and smiled at me with dim eyes.

"God be with you," she said.

"Thank you," said Killigrew, and led the way upstairs.

She turned again to the fire, and I followed Killigrew, searching meanwhile for that little note that she had given me. Perhaps in that, I thought, I should find some help in whatever difficulty or danger lay before me.

CHAPTER IX

I Am Invited to Eternity and Refuse the Invitation

I walked upstairs with Killigrew, in a state of considerable perplexity. I could not, for the life of me, think where I had placed the butterfly note that had been given me by Rose. I felt here and there about my person, and more than once as I went up the staircase looked behind me to see if by any chance I had dropped it. It had disappeared, as completely as if it had been a snowflake. That was, in itself, a sufficient reason for my agitation, but there were other reasons equally compelling. I made sure that Killigrew was going at last to explain some at least of the mystery that hung about the house. There was a gravity about his invitation to the library which precluded any supposition that he merely wanted company. For a moment the thought crossed my mind that he had observed with displeasure my intimacy with Rose, and was about to upbraid me for my use of his hospitality, and perhaps to tell me that that hospitality would not be further extended. My mind ran this way and that among these doubts and suppositions, now remembering the hundred curious incidents of my stay of which I had in vain sought an explanation, the words of the pedlar, the miracle, if it was a miracle, of the old servant, Michael, and now asking myself with the most poignant doubt whether, in case of my dismissal by Killigrew, I could persuade Rose to come away with me, and my uncle to let Mistress Barber care for her until I could put matters in train for our marriage. If, indeed, she would marry me. For she had not said so. I think that there were in my mind as I went up that staircase at least as many notes of interrogation as the steps I climbed.

Killigrew carried a candle, and, at the head of the staircase, turned and held it so that he could see my troubled face. It seemed to me that he was not displeased by what he saw there.

In the long library, Michael had already lit a number of candles. A small fire was burning in the hearth. There were two chairs set near the fire, and on a little table between them were glasses and bottles of wine, a tobacco jar, and three or four of those long slender tobacco pipes that give a peaceful savour to discussion. When I saw them, I felt reassured that whatever it was Killigrew had to say, it was nothing hostile to myself. Nowadays when I smoke such pipes, I invariably remember with a shudder how near I came that night to the loss of my immortal soul. But then everything in the room seemed to promise no more than a peaceable and pleasant conversation. Everything? No. There was one thing that disquieted me, but only for a moment, and that was the strange anxiety visible on the face of the servant. He looked at me with solicitude and at Killigrew with distrust and even hate. I thought he was about to ask me a question. He did not speak, but he put into his look so much warning, so much anxiety, that I stared at him open-mouthed. Killigrew noticed me, and looked from my face to the object of my regard, but the servant had already turned away, and his master saw nothing but his brown back, as he bent over the logs in the fireplace, and set others to dry in front of them, that we might feed the fire when it sank low. I thought there was a shadow of anger on Killigrew's face, but it was gone in a moment, and his voice was that of one perfectly at ease.

"That will do now," he said. "You can go to bed."

The servant, Michael, or as I thought then, that young man with Michael's eyes, looked at me, but finding himself observed by Killigrew, merely bowed, wished us a good night, and retired.

Killigrew poured wine into our glasses, and taking the lid from the tobacco jar, began with leisurely care to fill one of the long pipes, inviting me to do the same. I did so with unsteady fingers. I felt that Killigrew was watching me narrowly, and I determined, if possible, not to betray by any question my eagerness to know the subject of his intended conversation. We filled our pipes. Thin wooden splinters lay at the edge of the hearth, and with these we lit our tobacco from the fire. We moistened our lips with wine. For some minutes not a word was said by either of us. Killigrew, I think against his will, was compelled to be the first to speak.

"My dear Stanborough," he began, "I will tell you at once that the two months during which you have honoured us with your company have been two months of preparation, of probation, perhaps, for what I have to say to you to-night. I could not say it to any one in whom I was unable to place a very particular confidence. During two months you have, I may say, given continual proof of the rightness of a decision made at our first meeting. You have convinced me that I was not wrong in supposing that you might fitly share in a good fortune denied to all the rest of mankind."

"I do not understand you."

"I did not expect you to understand me, though I dare say that without my telling you you will know of what subject I wish to speak to you."

"Truly," said I, "I have not the faintest idea."

"But consider, my dear Stanborough. Look back on your stay here, and ask yourself if it has not occurred to you that certain incidents in our life, perhaps in my life, perhaps in the life of one of our companions, require, let us say, some more than ordinary explanation."

A host of questions I had been asking myself rushed together into my mind. I hesitated, wondering how much he had observed, and then decided to commit myself as little as possible, but, where I could, to answer him with sincerity.

"You are right," I said.

"For example?"

It was clear enough that he wished to learn from my lips what I had noticed. I dared not speak of the pedlar's warnings, nor would I betray myself, remembering Rose's caution, by saying anything of that cry in the garden, during my first night at the Old Hall. I could not with politeness allude to the oddities, if they were no worse, that I had noticed in his own behaviour. But there was the question of Michael's disappearance, and, as I more than half believed, his reappearance. This incident had, it was true, been covered by a few words from Killigrew, but I had not even at the time thought he meant me to believe them. So I answered boldly:

"I found it hard to believe you, sir, when you told me that the servant who has lately waited upon us was sent here by Michael, a mere substitute found in the village. He is very different in appearance, but I have reason to think that he is old Michael himself, or, if that is not so, that there is something in old Michael's disappearance of very unusual significance."

Killigrew puffed out a cloud of blue smoke which veiled his face. From the cloud came the words, "I wonder if you would be so good as to tell me those reasons."

I told him frankly the whole story of the clog with the chipped heel, though, of course, I did not make any mention of the strange agitation I had observed in the rejuvenated Michael, nor of the book that had been given me, as I supposed, by him, nor of his tearful conversation with Rose.

Killigrew was silent for a moment. Then he said:

"You make small bones about accusing me of being a liar, but, I admit it, I was ready to deceive you for a few hours, as I did not wish to precipitate our discussion. And your observation, on the accuracy of which I congratulate you, saves me much tedious explanation. Of course, you are right in supposing that Michael is Michael still. He, and the change in him, form a perfect induction to the subject I want you to consider. What, exactly, did you notice in Michael?"

"It seemed to me a few days before his disappearance that he was perceptibly older, unnaturally older, than when first I had seen him, and, when he reappeared, he seemed to have recovered his youth. He had removed his beard, but the loss of a beard could hardly account for so remarkable a youthfulness as I now see in him. I feel, with conviction, that the man is Michael, yet, when I look at him, I should be willing to suppose that Michael had a son, and that this were he."

"Precisely," said Killigrew, "a return to youth. You could not have described the phenomenon in exacter terms. I almost feel that I need say no more. Your penetrating mind . . ."

"Has certainly not solved that riddle. I am puzzled by it, Killigrew. The thing might almost be a miracle."

"And if I were to tell you that the phenomenon might be repeated and is no miracle at all?"

Killigrew blew an alley-way through the cloud of smoke before him, so that he could see my face.

"I should," I replied, "be as far from understanding as ever."

You are modest, my dear Stanborough. I credit you with greater perspicacity than you are willing to avow. Do you really find no explanation, or is it that you do not wish to admit that you have found one?"

"I promise you I have no explanation at all."

"Not in your reading, during the last three months? Is there nothing in Paracelsus, nothing in Lully, nothing in Agrippa, nothing in the Historia Alchemicorum to throw light upon this puzzle? Does it not occur to you, Stanborough, that what man has sought, man may find, and that the lives of so many wise men can hardly have been thrown away upon a wholly fruitless quest?"

Suddenly, I perceived his meaning.

"No, Killigrew," I laughed, "you will not persuade me that Michael's rejuvenation has been worked by the Elixir of Life. If that were so, what need for secrecy? If the Elixir had been discovered, why, the whole world would have rung with the fame of the discoverer."

"And the discoverer tied to a post in the middle of a pretty bonfire, and burnt as a wizard, with the comfort of hearing half a score of parsons reading texts and promising him that the heat he felt now would be nothing to the heat he would begin to feel as soon as he were dead. No. The histories are written, with honour, of those who failed. Theirs is the glory of the quest. But he who finds, must keep his treasure secret as the grave if he does not wish inopportunely to find a grave himself. Why, has it not occurred to you that, apart from the matter of sorcery, which is but an excuse, men would never knowingly tolerate the presence of an immortal among them? Men die at peace with their fellows only because they are persuaded that sooner or later those they leave behind will die also. If they knew that there was one man on earth who would not die, they could not themselves with resignation lie down on their death-beds until they had destroyed this unforgivable insult to their mortality. Indeed, when a god comes on earth, we have seen that man's instinct is to kill him with as many circumstances of disgrace as possible. He who is in possession of this secret shares it only at the peril of his life. I am putting my life in your hands at this moment. . . ."

He paused a moment, and then continued:

"Yes. That is the attitude of the world. A murderous jealousy. I do not think it will be yours. Consider the long avenue of thought, stretching through the ages, back into the past, and on into the future. Remember the shortness of human life. Not only to the immortals themselves, but to mankind, the greatest benefit that has come to the world is this, that a few chosen men of intellect may prolong their existence, and gather into their knowledge more than the experience that can be gained by a race along that road for the short normal period of years before death plucks them from it, and drops them, broken and useless, their work in vain, upon the dung-heap of mortality."

"But, Killigrew, this is tremendous, great. . . . 'Has come,' you say? Why was I not with you when you discovered it? When did you discover it? Tell me. And why did you let old Michael taste it, not yourself? . . ."

"It has been in my possession already two hundred years," said Killigrew. "I will not tell you how it came there. It is enough that in the metamorphosis of Michael you have seen the proof that I possess it. You have seen Michael once regain his youth, and, though I hid my face during our ride hither, you saw me in the inn, and I imagine you were not altogether unobservant of the change in my appearance."

"Yes. Yes."

"I drank from the Elixir on the night we came here, and I shall presently drink from it again. . . ."

"Again?"

"Yes," said Killigrew. "I will tell you precisely what the Elixir is. It is not, as men suppose, a drug that once for all restores a man to youth, and keeps him young. On the contrary, it merely takes him back at each drinking, approximately, to the age at which he first drank. He then grows up, again from day to day, like any other man."

"Then the first drinking has no effect."

"No apparent effect. It is only at the second drinking that the effect can be observed. At the second, and at each subsequent drinking, the owner of the Elixir returns to the age at which he first tasted that strange, but by no means miraculous, fluid."

"Then you? Those portraits? . . . Two hundred years? . . . ." I stammered, as the idea slowly presented itself to my brain. At first it had been as if I were merely listening to extraordinary words.

Killigrew stood up, took a candle, and walked to where that row of portraits hung on the wall above us. I followed him. He laid his hand on my shoulder.

"Yes, Stanborough," he said. "I assure you that the remarkable likeness you noticed in those portraits is not the result of chance, nor an example of the persistency with which a family reproduces its characteristic features."

He lifted his candle to one portrait after another.

"The portraits are all alike, though they illustrate the history of two hundred years of painting. They are all alike, because they are all portraits of one man, and, my dear Stanborough, that man is speaking to you now. I was that earnest student. I was that grave, armoured cousin of his, that cavalier. . . . You remember the song of 'Gaudeamus'?

> 'Vita nostra brevis est,
>   Brevi finietur,
>   Venit mors velociter,
>   Rapit nos atrociter,
>   Nemini parcetur.'

"That is the general belief of mankind. They see death coming swiftly, abominably snatching first one and then another, and sparing not a man. They look at each other's heads, and see skulls thinly clothed, presently to be stripped and cleaned by loathsome means. For them death is the longer part of man's existence on earth, and life merely the antechamber to the courts of that all-powerful Emperor. But, Stanborough, they are wrong. In my own person I have defied that tyrant, and shall defy him for ever. . . ."

I looked at him, as he stood there, holding the candle up to the portraits, and, as it were, addressing his remarks to those old editions of himself. I was amazed that I could ever have supposed that they could be portraits of different people. But, while I looked at them, a thought came into my head concerning them, and I looked at them again, and shuddered. The portraits were all portraits of one man, but, throughout the series, that man changed, for the worse. The pure enthusiasm of the student was never repeated in the later portraits. It seemed to me that evil had crept into their eyes. And the face of Killigrew smiling up at them, mocking, boasting, seemed the worst of all, and filled me with distrust, which, however, was presently swept away by his conversation.

"Killigrew," I said, "you could have trusted me at first. Why did you not tell me? Why did you set up such a hedge of deceit as I see you raised between us?"

"For the simplest of reasons. That I did not know you. I have pointed out to you that the possession of this thing is not likely to be honoured by the world, unless you count a public, painful death an honourable reward for discovering the secret of life. I had to be sure that I could trust you, before putting my safety in your power."

"But why do you tell me now?"

His answer took my breath away.

"Because I propose to share it with you."

"Your secret?"

"The Elixir."

My pipe broke in my fingers. Bits of it dropped on the oak floor and broke again. I stared at Killigrew. I scarcely know how I found my way to my chair. Killigrew set the candle on the table and sat down. He did not stop talking.

"Immortality is a very lonely thing in this world where all move through their lives with no other end before them than the grave. For me, friendship with men is like friendship with butterflies who live for a day, and die. I have long needed a companion who should live with me, and, in a life of philosophical speculation, share with me my unique experience. I needed such a companion, but I had come to think I should not find one, when chance brought us together, and you walked into the inn with 'Gaudeamus' on your lips. If I had been superstitious I should have taken that as an omen in itself. But no augury was needed. I suspected at once that here was the companion for whom I had hoped. Do not take this as too extravagant. You were young, a philosopher, and yet a gentleman of my own rank, with a taste in dress that showed you had not been narrowed by philosophy into one of those snuffy pedants from whom the world is hidden by a wall of books. You perceive that you did, indeed, promise me much, when you came singing into the inn on the Eve of Midsummer, when I, sitting glum before the fire, had just been telling myself that solitude was the price I had to pay for my eternity. I begged you to visit me. You consented. By that very consent, you proved yourself the possessor of an adventurous mind, not to be balked by the false wall of a convention. You came here. We read and talked together. I found in you a mind equal to my own, its complement, more rash than mine, and for that reason well adapted to lift mine with it on speculations which, alone, I should not have attempted. . . ."

I do not blush to set down here his ridiculous flattery of me: or rather, I blush less, for, by the warmth of my cheeks, I observe that even now, after all these years, I am blushing, because I know that before you reach the end of my story you will have seen the other side of Killigrew's false, glittering coinage. If I had but read the book that was even then in the pocket of my coat, I should have known these shining compliments for the snares they were. I will, however, spare you from hearing all. He continued in this strain for some time, and, I am ashamed to say, did indeed succeed in blinding my better judgment.

"Together," he said, "we shall be able to explore all the enticing byways of knowledge, free from the fear that attends the mortal inquirer, who knows he must die before he has got fairly started on his way, even before his road has left the town, and given him a prospect of the mountains."

He well knew how to influence the generous, ambitious heart of youth.

"Living from age to age," he went on, "comparing, with the full understanding that can only be given by personal experience, the results obtained by one generation with those obtained by another, we may bring infinite benefits to mankind; and, at the least, we ourselves will move on earth with knowledge only less than that of God."

My own impatience made me interrupt him.

"Where is the Elixir?" I asked. "Let me see the thing for which so many thousands have given their lives in vain."

He took a small key from a ribbon that hung about his neck, inside his shirt.

"I shall show you the Elixir, when it is yours as well as mine and Michael's. It is not here. He and I alone use this key, which shall presently be placed in your hands also."

"But what of Michael?" I asked. "Does he, too, possess the Elixir? Why is he not your ally? Why is he not your companion? Do you need a third?" I spoke, merely to be reassured, for, with boyish presumption, I felt that Michael was unworthy of the post to which I had been invited.

"Michael," said Killigrew, "could never be other than he is. I let him drink of the Elixir some years ago, because I wished him to know if supposing I found a suitable companion, I should indeed be able to share my power with him. The experiment succeeded perfectly, but Michael could be only my slave, not my companion. And it is convenient not to have to change one's servant, with one's manners, every time the earth renews its population."

The fashion-book came into my mind, which I had seen Killigrew studying so diligently in his bed-chamber at the inn. I remembered also the fantastic parody of myself, which, with an anger I now felt was not justified, I had seen him perform. I did not intend to mention these things, but they prompted my next question.

"One's manners?"

"Yes, the owner of the Elixir, I have found, loses none of his experience each time he regains his youth. And, with his experience, he retains his habits, ay, and his manners, so that it behoves him to study how young men behave, lest among them he should appear old-fashioned and, at his next rejuvenation, positively eccentric."

The night wore on. The dry logs placed in readiness by the fire were thrown one by one among the ashes and consumed. The candles burned near the sockets of the candlesticks and were renewed, though the flames of them wavered in a mist, for the smoke of tobacco and the fumes of wine had thickened the air in the room. I began to be conscious of the great dark spaces about us which the candles did not illuminate. And still Killigrew talked on, now seriously, now with a touch of sarcasm, and now with one of those rhetorical flights which on this subject displeased me, though I strove to hide from him the fact that I did not admire those gilded sentences in which he took manifest pleasure. It occurred to me that this very trick of occasional rhetoric was one of the things that Killigrew had brought from one of those earlier generations, with which, as with my own, he had been contemporary.

I sat there, trying to make my mind realize that Killigrew meant me to share his fate with him, to be separate from the race of men. Killigrew's long separation from mankind had perhaps blunted his understanding of them. He should have offered me the Elixir at once, let me drink it there and then. I should not have resisted him, and I shudder now when I contemplate the fate that might so easily have been mine. But he talked on, and while he talked, my mind, half stunned as it was, yet thought of many things. I know now that Rose was praying for me that night. Her image was continually before me, as indeed it always is, when I do not see her close at hand or walking under the hollyhocks in the garden, through the window of this room where I write. She had been in my mind, as it were, in actual conflict with the thought of the Elixir. Her presence was about me all that night, but I suppose it was because I had come almost to think of her as part of myself, that it was a shock so violent as to take the blood from my face when I thought that perhaps to drink the Elixir would be to separate myself from her for ever. I believe there has never been a lover who has not wished to die before the death of his beloved.

For a long time I dared not put this question to Killigrew. At last, however, I forced some courage to my tongue.

"And Mistress Rose?" I asked. "Has she drunk of your Elixir?"

"No," he said, "her twenty years are twenty years, no more."

I was profoundly relieved, but a moment later was again plunged into doubt. How could I drink the Elixir, if she had not? Killigrew, however, continued.

"I wish to speak of that. I do not ask you to condemn yourself to spend eternity with me. You are young. I have not been blind to the relation between my ward and yourself. You could not have made a more fortunate choice, for she, alone in the world, can share your immortality. You and she shall drink on the same day. I offer you Rose and the Elixir together. You shall marry her, spend your youth together, and return again and again to the age at which your love began. Not in the history of the world has there been so fortunate a love. . . ."

I started up.

"Sir, let me see Rose at once. . . . Let me speak with her of this. . . . I have not the right . . ."

"My dear friend," he said, "it is now early morning, and Rose is asleep. Moreover, it will be better . . . your word will have more weight. . . . You shall carry the phial to her, having yourself already drunk. I know her. . . . When she hears that. . . ."

I could not answer him. What right had I to speak for Rose? "And yet," I thought with exultation, "an immortal youth, an immortal love!"—and it was this, rather than the thought of philosophic speculation, that fired my spirit. If Killigrew had offered me the potion then, I should have drunk. There, I have made confession. It was no strength of mine that saved me from the pit he had dug for my feet.

*   *   *

For some time now, the candles had shone paler and paler against the rising dawn. The fire was low. The candles were like moths surprised in daylight. Killigrew bent, picked up a large pair of leather bellows, and began to blow life into the dying embers of the fire.

With the approach of dawn, I had pulled my chair nearer to the fire, and was now leaning over it. To that circumstance I suppose I owe my salvation. For, when Killigrew blew with his bellows, a cloud of fine wood-ash spurted up and into my face. My eyes smarted, and I sneezed. I plucked out my kerchief, and, with the kerchief, there shot out and dropped on the floor that very butterfly note which Rose had given me on the previous evening, the note which I had sought in vain on my way up the staircase. Killigrew saw it, but I was swift to pick it up. I felt that in this moment one word from Rose would be a great refreshment. This is what I read:

"*I beg you, if you love me, to refuse any proposal that may be made to you by Mr. Killigrew, for my sake.—R."*

That was all, but it brought back the whole of my distrust of Killigrew. I knew now the reason of the anxiety I had seen in Rose's eyes. I would have refused Heaven itself if she had asked me to do so in such terms. I remembered what she had said to me before, and asked myself if Killigrew could be as fortunate as he wished me to suppose. Till that moment I had been like one asleep. Now, with these words from Rose before my eyes, all that Killigrew had said, his flattery, his promise, went for nothing. I remembered the pedlar, old Michael's warning, and a thousand other circumstances which told me that I had reason to fear this man who had offered me more than had been offered by God Himself, when first I came into the world. A line of Vergil came into my head and wound itself among my thoughts:

"Quicquid id est, timeo Danaos, et dona ferentes."

Why, of course, I perceived, it was precisely against this that I had been warned. I saw that Killigrew was hiding much from me. He had told me either too much or too little. This gift, this Elixir, whatever it was, I feared its giver. I feared him most of all at this moment.

Killigrew blew out the candles, and the thin threads of smoke rising from the quenched wicks in the light of the morning seemed to represent the destruction of the magic of the night. I was free.

He saw the change in my face and the note in my fingers. Unwisely, I think, for his own purpose, he asked me what that was.

"Nothing," I replied, and held it in the flames that his blowing had waked from the embers, until it was burnt almost to my finger-tips. Then I dropped it, waiting to see that it was consumed, before rising from my chair and walking to one of the windows.

I felt as if I had been stifling for a long time. I opened the lattice, and breathed the cool air of the morning which poured in to disturb the stale smoke of our vigil. I looked down into the rose-garden, and saw the sunlight already gilding a corner of the trellis. These things had an extraordinary effect upon me. It was as if the sun were sweeping before it the night and the evil of the night. And, as I stood here, at the window, taking deep breaths of the sweet air, I felt I was clearing my lungs of poison.

More than that. I perceived, suddenly, the unreality of my boyish pretensions to be a philosopher. I knew that I was simpler than I had wished to believe. I thought of my uncle, and of Mistress Barber, that good, homely old woman, and of Rose. I told myself that I wanted Rose, as I wanted the sunlight, unsmudged by magic. I wanted to free Rose from this house and all its secret ways, not to drag her further into the power of Killigrew, and myself become bound to him by a terrible obligation. I had a vision of the hills at morning in the north, and Rose and me lying in the heather; and then I heard a low nervous laugh behind me, an uncomfortable, ominous little laugh, and I knew that the realization of that vision depended on the next few moments and on what I might say to Killigrew.

I turned and saw Killigrew watching me.

And then, I write this down without shame, I was frightened. I knew then not a hundredth part of what I was afterwards to learn of the nature of his Elixir. The whole monstrous evil of the thing he had kept carefully hidden from me. I scarcely suspected it. And yet, as I stood there, I was afraid. I felt, rather than knew, that Killigrew was stronger than I. I felt his two hundred years of life crushing my bare twenty-one, and forcing them in the way in which he wished that they should go. It was as if I were pulling against a huge, invisible giant, and yet there was nothing before me but that slight man, whose thin lips were smiling while his eyes seemed to be looking for something in the air between us. It was not my own wishes I was afraid of. I had been offered immortality, but I wanted something better. I wished to keep my soul and Rose. No. The last few minutes had shown me what my wishes were, and how little, how simple a man I was. I was afraid of something else. I knew that Killigrew expected me to agree to his proposal. He had, as he said, "put his life into my hands." He had told me his secret . . . how little he had told me I had yet to learn. And, as I looked at his face, his thin lips, smiling always, and his impenetrable eyes, I felt the words that he expected coming, in spite of myself, into my mouth.

"Well, Stanborough," he said, "you have not given me your answer. The Elixir waits. Let us now go and drink. . . ."

Then suddenly my fear overmastered me. If I had not shouted I felt my words would have said just what I did not wish to say. I stepped towards him as if I were going to strike him.

"No, no," I shouted. "Never. You shall not make me. I will have nothing to do with it. May God help me to keep my life and Rose's life from you. God help me. God help me."

That, or something like that, is what I shouted at him.

I was blind. For a moment I scarcely saw him. Then a feeling of joy came into my heart. After all, I had said it. I had won. I knew now that nothing Killigrew could say or do would make me take back those words. Then I saw Killigrew again.

His hands were close at his sides, his fingers working like claws. Surprise, rage, and suspicion were struggling in his face. I thought he would spring upon me. In that moment I should have been glad of the physical conflict.

"God damn you for an hysteric fool!" he said.

"You have not told me all. I will not share what I do not understand."

His reply confirmed the suspicion to which I had thus rashly given expression.

"Has Michael dared . . .?" he asked, suddenly, with a look of the most infernal malignity, and then brought himself up short before finishing his sentence.

"No, he has not," I replied. "If you need to be angry with any one, I should myself suffer. I have told you. With the help of God I shall keep my hands clean from touching your Elixir. I do not trust you or it."

Killigrew's face changed again. The ugly lines of hate and anger were smoothed out of it as if by magic.

"Come, come," he said, "we are using strong words to each other without necessity. For my part I apologize freely. I misunderstood my *guest*" (he laid emphasis on this word, and I was, boy-like, instantly ashamed) "and I hope he will forgive me. You will, I need not ask you, you will keep my secret, though you do not wish to share it. Of all this matter we will say no more. You refuse to share eternity with me. Let me show you that I can partake of the pleasures of mortality. Let us drive away by horseback exercise the humours of discussion. The ground is firm, the sun is up, and a pleasant wind is blowing from the hills. Let us go out, and rejoice, 'juvenes dum sumus,' for you, my dear Stanborough, will not be juvenis for ever, since you condemn me to solitude in my eternal youth."

The evil had cleared from his face so swiftly that I began to doubt if it had ever been there. With his return to calm he had regained much of his influence over me. I was ashamed of my suspicions. I was so glad at this peaceful ending of our discussion, (for, after all, Killigrew was the guardian of the girl I wished to marry,) the tension of my feelings had been so suddenly relieved, that, fool that I was, I supposed the question settled indeed, and did not see that Killigrew had never been more dangerous. So easily was I conquered by his manner and my own anxiety, that I forgot that in refusing to share his Elixir I had made myself his mortal enemy. Like a child, I was delighted at Killigrew's forbearance, told myself that I had wronged him, blamed myself for the violence of my words, and did not suspect that from that moment on I was in imminent peril of my life.

CHAPTER X

I Ride with Killigrew and
Meet the Pedlar Again

Ten minutes later we were lightly cantering side by side across the neglected park. It was about six in the morning of a beautiful day, a light
mist rising from the ground, which had frozen during the night, but was
now soft and easy for the feet of the horses. The trees were changing
their colours, before throwing their summer garments aside to face the
snow in nakedness. There was a freshness in the air which, as I took in
long and grateful breaths, I felt was an antidote, indeed the only fitting
antidote, to all that strange talk. It was as if I had stayed too long in a
laboratory, where an alchemist was boiling liquids that gave off a heavy,
pungent steam. I felt my lungs were full of a poisonous air, and that
every breath I drew as we rode under the blue autumn sky brought me
towards the full enjoyment of a life I had come dangerously near losing
altogether.

No man refuses a proffered gift, however small, without feeling afterwards a strong desire to be confirmed in his refusal by some proof
that he was right in making it. I have come to the conclusion that the
thing which men most fear in life is regret. Killigrew had offered me a
gift which he alone could give, a gift which hundreds of learned men
have spent their lives in seeking in every corner of the world. I had refused it. I knew that my refusal was final, that the offer would not be
made again. I craved with the whole force of my nature for strength to
resist the half-smothered feelings of regret which forced themselves to
light. I snatched greedily at every confirmation of my resolve. I told myself that, had I accepted, I should now be riding with a burdened heart,
separate from mankind, and timorous of my fate. I told myself that I
should have disobeyed the command of one I loved above all else and
destroyed my hope of removing her to a place where the shadows were
less mysterious, and where life ran its course in the open. Yet the regret
was there, though I was glad beyond measure to ride in the cool morning air, and to know that my life would be like that of my fathers, and
that in the end I should grow old and die, and be buried in a stone vault
with the family blazon over my grave. If only Rose were to share these
things with me, I thought, then indeed I had nothing to regret.

Killigrew seemed to have fallen in with my mood. His brow was
clear, and he talked only of the day and the things we saw as we rode,

small, simple things, the very thought of which was rest and refreshment to my spirit. He pointed out a squirrel, and asked me if certain small bright-coloured birds, called tom-tits, were common in my part of the country. In fact, we rode like plain country gentlemen, whose philosophy is bounded by a knowledge of the weather and the points of a horse or a dog.

He seemed to have set himself to chase away the cloud that our long discussion had brought upon my spirit, and indeed he was so successful in this that much of my old admiration for him returned, and forgetting the many reasons for my mistrust of him, I began to think that he was really a delightful companion. I planned, when I should have persuaded Rose to marry me, to make Killigrew often of our company. Such is the power of youth and of love that I readily accepted his immortality, for belief in which I had indeed been prepared by many incidents, and, now that he was in smiling mood, thought of him merely as Rose's guardian. If, now and again, I looked at him with the thought that long after I was dead he would still be young, and riding on autumn days through the long grass, that thought was swiftly banished by the remembrance that I had a happiness greater than his, in that he was Rose's guardian, while I . . . I did not finish my thought, but in my mind sang those words which, even now, send a tremor through my blood . . . "you least of all, because I love you."

Hitherto, when I had ridden with Killigrew, we had made a circuit of the park, or taken devious paths through the belt of woods, now walking our horses, and now, when we came into the open glades, galloping over the soft turf, where the close presence of the great trees kept the grass short. We had never gone beyond the wall that encircled the estate and, as it were, separated it from the world, and made it a strange kingdom of solitude fit for a philosopher. On this occasion I was surprised when Killigrew proposed to ride to the gate, and out into the open country beyond. I took it as an additional proof of his kind intentions towards me, that he was breaking his custom only on my account, to drive away the effect of our last conversation by the sight of our honest eighteenth-century England.

"Killigrew," I said, as we rode towards the gate, "I am thinking that you will be glad to be rid of one who has treated with seeming ingratitude a very generous offer. I have already prolonged my enjoyment of your hospitality. I must not presume upon it for too long."

"My dear sir," he replied, "I am not blind to the fact that there are other reasons for your stay here besides that of my pleasure in your society. I should be sorry indeed if by leaving us now you punish my sister for my high esteem of yourself."

I cannot tell you with what relief I heard these words. For, if he had shown me that he too thought that my absence would be welcome, I should have been in a sad quandary, not yet having persuaded Rose to marry me, and so having no right to speak of that project with her brother. With her brother, I reflected, following Killigrew's example, when he had spoken of her as his sister.

He guessed my thoughts, and answered them.

"No," he said, "Mistress Rose is not two hundred years old, and she has not the misfortune to be my sister. She has, however, spent her whole life in my care, and has become accustomed to think of herself as such. You may be at ease on that point," he added, with a smile which, grateful as I was for his information, I did not altogether like.

It may seem curious to you that I did not press my questions further, having learnt so much. If she was not his sister, was she his daughter? If not, who was she? Perhaps, if I had not loved her, I should have asked these questions and compelled an answer. But the plain truth of that matter is this. For me Rose was Rose. So long as nothing happened to make her something else, I was content. I loved Rose, and that was enough for me.

We rode out of the gateway, and I looked with half a shudder at the stone griffon in the grass, remembering the pedlar's story. But the pedlar was not there. We followed the road by which we had travelled that day, not so very long before, although it seemed that a lifetime had passed between that day and this. We came to the village, a long straggling street, small thatched huts, a spread of grass bitten short by donkeys and thin ragged ponies, which lifted their heads and stared at us with the melancholy habitual to such beasts. One of the donkeys put back its ears and opened its mouth, and let out that dreadful noise which is its only substitute for speech. That horrid, grisly trump was the announcement of our presence to a group of small boys who were playing on the grass. They looked up, and, on seeing us, fled into the village, which lay beyond the common.

We slowly followed them. As we rode down the long street, we could see the children hiding in the doorways.

A few old men lifted up their hands and cursed as we rode by.

Old women made the sign of the cross, and presented their hands at us, with the middle fingers closed, and the first and little fingers extended, which I knew to be a precaution against the evil eye. But for the most part the people in the village hid themselves as we approached. The village might have been a village of the dead, the only living inhabitants of which were crones and old men who took us for invading devils.

It was a strange experience for me, who remembered how when I rode with my uncle or my father, as a little boy, into the small town near Bigland in the north, the men would all doff their caps, and the women run out from their cottages and bob courtesies, and the children wait in the road, smoothing their pinafores, and offering posies. My uncle always stopped and took the flowers, gruff though he was sometimes, and each posy he lodged somewhere about his person, in the buttonholes of his coats, in his pockets, in the ribband of his hat, so that after one of these excursions he would return home decorated like a wandering simpleton at a village fair.

"Of what are they afraid?" I asked Killigrew.

"It is a long story, and a foolish," he replied. "They have all had their heads turned by a crazy lunatic pedlar, who has made them think I am the devil himself."

"The pedlar who was at the gate when we rode hither?" I asked.

"The same," said Killigrew. "He has his brain turned by spite or by some imaginary misfortune, and he has, so I am told, turned the brains of the villagers. It is the old story of the tailless fox. Mad himself, he would have all others mad, and it seems that in the village he has succeeded. No matter."

As we were nearing the end of the street, I looked back, and saw a group of villagers and children who had come out into the road now that we had passed, and were staring at us as we rode away. As soon as they saw that they were observed, they set to crossing themselves, and again separated swiftly into their cottages. I remembered what the pedlar had said to me, and I felt a coward and afraid when I saw that I shared the abomination which was evidently felt for Killigrew by the uneducated audience of that strange man. I was to have yet another proof of the horror in which the villagers held the inhabitants of the great house.

Just outside the village we met an old, old woman, bent under a load of sticks, slowly making her way towards us along the road. I think she was deaf, for she did not seem to hear the hooves of our horses until we were close to her. Killigrew drew up, and, I fancy, in an attempt to dissipate the gloom which our reception in the village had thrown upon my spirits, wished to enter into conversation with her.

He made some simple remark, such as "It is good weather for the season." I forget exactly what he said. The old woman took no notice, but hobbled on towards him, her eyes on the ground, clearly unaware of his presence. She walked almost into his horse's chest. She was horribly startled, and looked up suddenly, loosing her load of sticks, which rattled to the ground. Then, peering upwards, she saw Killigrew, and apparently recognized him. She lifted her hands as if to shut out the sight of him, and broke into a gibberish of words taken from the Holy Bible. "The transgressor . . . weeping and gnashing of teeth . . . a millstone hanged about his neck." She screeched these words and many more, with all the signs of intense fear. I had heard how Killigrew had addressed her, with the utmost gentleness, but now his face became suddenly dark, and he lifted his riding whip. Suddenly, he lowered it again, and turning his horse out of her way, rode past the old woman, and broke into a swift trot.

"What ailed the old crone?" I said, lightly, though the incident had made a most unpleasant impression upon me.

"Years ago, in the great storm that blew down many of the trees, and one of the griffons from the gateway, she lost her daughter, a little child, through the accident of her sheltering close under the gate-post. I suppose the pedlar has taught her to attribute the storm to me instead of to God."

I made no reply, and we rode on in silence. I was glad when we came to a point where we could see a fine stretch of broad rolling country. A better stretch of country for the chase of the fox I never saw in my life.

"That is not a thought particularly suitable to a philosopher," said Killigrew.

The picture of Paracelsus, seated in his study, came into my mind, and I blushed at my secession from the strict ways of the learned. But I answered, not altogether frankly, "I do not understand you."

"You were thinking that this would be a pleasant stretch of country over which to gallop a horse."

"I admit it. That was what was in my mind. But how did you know? Have you the power of knowing the thoughts of others, as well as the Elixir of Life?"

"No," said Killigrew, "I must be content with the Elixir of Life, but that, in giving me unusually prolonged experience, gives me the semblance of unusual powers. But this was no miracle, but a very simple matter, such a deduction as even your wretched Verulam would have found easy."

"How?"

"You looked at the landscape first as a whole. Then your eyes took a direct line across country. I saw them note certain obstacles. At one of these obstacles you involuntarily moved your whip, and tightened your knees, so that your horse started. I knew from that that even in imagination you were on horseback. It seemed that you had mentally jumped a fence, and, by the exhilarated expression of your eyes, I made sure that you had thought that the experience would be a pleasant one."

"Truly no miracle at all," said I. "I am ashamed to be so legible."

"You have no need," he replied. "But, seriously, what say you to turning your imagination into a reality? Those fields are indeed inviting. I foresee some pleasant leaps. Our horses are, I think, fairly evenly matched. What say you to a race?"

Nothing could have better suited my humour. I instantly agreed.

"Come now," said Killigrew, pointing with his whip. "Do you see that low mound, with a tree upon it, an ash, I fancy. It stands just so high that we shall not lose sight of it. Let that be our winning-post."

He had pointed to a tree that stood on a low hill, on the skyline, I suppose five miles away.

"Let the race be serious," he said. "There shall be a stake."

"Agreed," said I, "if it is within the limits of my purse."

"No," said Killigrew, "I think of a stake that will make you ride your best. If you win, I promise you that you shall find no opposition on my part to your marriage with my ward."

"If I lose," said I, "I must warn you that if I have her own permission I shall make as light as may be of any opposition you may feel inclined to offer."

"Honestly spoken," said he. "If you lose, you may do as you please, though I will not promise not to thwart you. If you win, you will know at least that one difficulty will not be raised. Now, sir," he continued, "are you sure you will not change horses?"

I did indeed think that he had slightly the better horse, a big black. But I was riding the brown mare, and we had become well accustomed to each other. I set this fact against the advantages of the other, and said I would keep to my mount.

"Very well," said Killigrew, "away with us," and he leapt his horse over the low bank at the roadside, and was off at a speed that left me despairing, till I remembered that whereas Killigrew only rode occasionally, my brown mare was in the most excellent condition, and that this, in the course of five or six hard miles, would certainly have some influence in the result.

I did not wait to think these things, however, before patting the mare, and leaping the bank, and making away after Killigrew. I felt the mare gather herself together, and get her pace, though I touched her once with the whip to show her that this was not a mere canter in one of the glades of the wood in Killigrew's park, but an altogether more serious business.

At the first start Killigrew on the big black got a lead of twenty or thirty yards. For a couple of miles he preserved it, and the mare showed no inclination or power to make it up. She took her jumps like a pheasant skimming a hedge, but always landed a foot or two inside the hoof-marks of the black.

The pace was not one of which any man, however hard a rider, need have been ashamed. I lost my hat in the first minute, and the wind in my hair turned the exhilaration of the race into a sort of ecstasy. Now and again I saw the little hill with the ash-tree against the sky, nearer each time, but for the most part my eyes were on Killigrew, my whole mind watching the space between us, and calculating how small was the chance I had of getting rid of that interval before we reached the end. At the beginning of, I suppose, the third mile, I perceived that at last I was actually gaining. I rose in my stirrups and shouted with triumph and joy. I saw Killigrew look at me over his shoulder, and bring his whip down on the haunches of the black, which sprang forward in answer. I did not touch the mare, but patted her neck, and shouted to her endearing epithets, all manner of idiocies. My voice broke like a boy's. I nearly cried, with nothing but excitement. Something of my eagerness caught the mare, for I saw that in spite of Killigrew's efforts, we were now markedly gaining ground.

At the crossing of a stream, the black jumped a little short, and had to climb the bank. It was the matter of a second, but my mare cleared the stream and bank, and I knew that the black was tiring.

There was a slight rise beyond the stream, and the black did not recover its stride before reaching the top. From the crest of the rise I saw the ash-tree now not a mile away. The black was faltering. I drew level with Killigrew, screaming like a madman, and then, as I passed him, settled down into silence, thinking only to preserve my lead and avoid accidents until the end.

When I looked back, some two hundred yards from the foot of the little hill on which our winning-post stood, outlined against the sky, I saw that Killigrew had fallen fifty or sixty yards behind. He flourished his hat in a salute, and I imagined the mocking look that I felt sure had come into his eyes.

But I had no time to think of Killigrew. Close before me was a long hedge, not high in itself, but made higher by the fact that the bushes of which it was composed had been allowed to shoot, so that above the hedge was a thin wall of greenery, not enough to impede or trip a horse, but quite enough to test his confidence in the judgment of its rider. I chose the point in it which promised the easiest crossing, and, encouraging the mare, struck her lightly for the second time in the race, and made for it. The mare answered my touch, and showed that she had yet speed and to spare. We were coming up to the hedge. She had shown in her gait that there would be no balking, that she meant to clear it. We were close upon it, when a man leapt suddenly from the low ditch in front of the hedge, shouting and waving his arms, directly in our path.

There was no time given me to think or to save myself. The mare swerved violently to the right, and, going at top speed, tripped, and fell within a foot or two of the man. I had fortunately been hurled from my seat as she swerved, and fell heavily close under the hedge.

I was stunned, but only for a moment. I opened my eyes and saw bending over me the old pedlar with whom I had talked at the gate. It was he who rising suddenly from the ditch had made the mare swerve and caused my fall. Killigrew, sitting on his panting horse, was watching me with his mocking smile.

The pedlar inquired if I was hurt.

"No thanks to you that I am not," I replied, staggering to my feet. "Is the mare hurt? Do you know you lost me such a race as I shall never ride again in my life?"

"Young man," said the pedlar, solemnly, "if I had not lost you this race you would never have ridden again, because you would have been dead. Be so good as to look beyond the hedge."

He parted the stems, so that I could look through. There was a drop of thirty feet at least, within a yard of the other side. If I had jumped that hedge, both the mare and I would have lain dead at the bottom a moment after. It seemed it was a quarry or had been used as such.

I was ashamed of my hasty rebuke, but before I had time to make an apology to him, I heard the pedlar address Killigrew, in the following strange words:

"John Killigrew, have you forgotten that fifty years ago, in this same place, a young man met his death, riding for a wager against another of your name?"

"Was it here?" said Killigrew carelessly.

"You, John Killigrew, may have forgotten, but God does not forget, and 'Vengeance is Mine, saith the Lord.'"

With that the pedlar broke into such prophecy as I had heard from him at the gate, so that I was inclined to be impatient, and to put him down for a madman, only that, half stunned as I was, I remembered that the John Killigrew of fifty years ago was the same John Killigrew who, sitting idly on his horse, was looking quizzically and with complete indifference now at the pedlar, now at me. I knew that there was a deduction to be drawn from these data, but my head spun, and it was all I could do to keep the world steady before my eyes. I could not draw that deduction to save my life, and stood staring stupidly. The thought of the mare first roused me to consequent action, and I walked unsteadily to where she stood, having picked herself up, cropping at the hedge which had veiled the pit where we might so easily have ended our days together.

By a miracle she was unhurt. She was bruised, no doubt, and very muddy, but she was no worse hurt than myself. She thrust her soft muzzle into my bosom when I petted her and whispered to her. I tried to mount her and failed, narrowly escaping another fall to the ground.

"You seem to have had a lucky escape," said Killigrew.

"I do indeed," said I, again trying to mount.

With great difficulty I got into the saddle. We set off slowly homewards, and presently found a small cart-track, which led into a road. The pedlar walked with us.

Killigrew told him angrily to go about his business.

"This is my business," he replied. "You must go through the village, and if they see in the village what has happened to this young man in your company, it may go ill with you, for they do not love you in the village, John Killigrew. The time is not yet. The millstones of God have yet a little grist to grind, and for that reason I walk with you."

Killigrew said not a word. And we proceeded in silence, for which I was grateful; my head ached as sorely as if it had been pounded in a mortar.

It was nearly two hours before we reached the stone gateway, when the pedlar stopped.

"Young man," he said to me, "may the Lord guard you in that house, and as for you, John Killigrew, be assured that the end is not far off. I have no more to say to you than that."

As we rode through the gateway, I heard the pedlar set to praying in a loud voice, and I heard Killigrew curse under his breath. I looked at his face, and saw that it was distorted with anger, and that it was old, far older than I had remembered seeing it before. I tried to think of that, but I could not think of anything except the pain in my head, and, absurdly, of the mud with which my clothes were freely plastered. Of that alone I obtained a clear idea.

CHAPTER XI

Murder No Murder

As we neared the house, Killigrew became suddenly attentive, inquired particularly as to where my bruises were most painful, and asked for a precise description of the pains in my head. Such was the man's charm of manner when he chose to be charming, that in spite of the fact that I had the strongest reason for suspecting him of a cunning attempt upon my life, I found myself actually grateful to him, and when at last we entered the door our relations were those of doctor and patient. He accompanied me to my room, helped me to remove my clothes, insisted that I should rest, rubbed, himself, my worst bruises with an ointment that increased my confidence in his good intentions by giving me instant relief. It did not occur to me until afterwards that all this was done to prevent me from seeing Rose, and, indeed, so simple was I, that I entered eagerly into Killigrew's plan for saving her anxiety by keeping my accident a secret from her until the worst effects of it should have passed away.

"You will be fully recovered before night," said Killigrew. "A little stiffness, perhaps, but at least with a clear head."

My head was anything but clear, and very painful, so painful, indeed, that when Killigrew brought me a draught and promised me that it would put an end to that torment, I drank it rapidly, without reflecting for a moment that if he wished to get rid of me by poison I was giving him an excellent opportunity. I wonder that he did not take it, unless it was that his resolve had been shaken by the words of the pedlar and that the event had not yet occurred which threw all his foresight to the winds, and made him utterly careless of all except a single desire. But that is to anticipate.

My pains left me soon after I had swallowed Killigrew's medicine, and a few minutes later Rose, who had, I think, been in the garden, came to the door of my room.

I heard her voice outside, inquiring what was the matter, and whether I was hurt. Michael had told her, no doubt, of the state of the brown mare.

Killigrew went to the door and replied, in his easy, mocking voice: "No. Our young philosopher is quite unhurt. He has had a fall, but a few hours sleep will cure the worst of his injuries."

"Is that true, Mr. Stanborough?" she asked.

"Yes, yes, quite true," I answered feebly, and there and then, as I believe, fell asleep. At any rate, I heard no more. Killigrew had so far made use of his opportunity as to give me a sufficiently powerful sleeping draught.

It was then, I suppose, about two o'clock in, the afternoon. About fifteen hours later I awoke, with the presentiment that something of grave import was at that moment occurring not far from me. The mind of man works in ways that are too subtle for the perception of his common or brute sense, and, so it seems to me, often pursues a chain of reasoning that is entirely hidden from his conscious observation. It was as if, in my sleep, I had a clearer idea than when I was awake of the things that were happening about me. Awake I thought mostly of Rose Killigrew, or of myself. Asleep my mind, as it were, enfranchised from selfish preoccupations explored alleys and narrow wynds of speculation that were hidden from it in the day.

If you do not know this sensation of waking on the eve of some immediate, urgent business, you know not what, as if a trumpet had called you to the full possession of your faculties and warned you that you needed to make instant use of them, I cannot hope to describe it to you. I can only say that when I woke, still conscious of a slight pain in my head and of the stiffness in my limbs, I found myself already half out of bed, and groping for the tinder. Before I had realized what I was doing, or why I was doing it, I had the candle lit, and was drawing on my breeches, with deliberate speed, my eye already seeking other articles of my apparel, that not a second might be lost. I was half dressed before I asked myself why I was dressing at all.

My answer was given me upon the instant by the sound of a violent altercation outside my door.

I blew out my candle.

The voices were those of Killigrew and Michael.

It must have been already near dawn, for I found that I could have done without the candle, if I had waited a moment until my eyes were accustomed to the faint light that came through the latticed panes of my window.

I caught the mention of my own name. One voice was as cool and quiet as freezing water. It was Killigrew's. The other, which, for a moment, I thought was the pedlar's, had in it an indescribable quality of agitation. It was denunciatory, but it was the voice of one bitterly conscious that he had himself sinned. It was the voice of a man afraid in spite of himself, but determined to say on, mastering his fear as the danger into which he was forcing his way became gradually inevitable. There was the strangest possible contrast between those two voices.

The violence of the altercation was all on one side, and that side, of course, the weaker of the two.

I sat, a stocking in my hand, and felt that any man would churn his thoughts beyond control against the wall of Killigrew's indifference.

I heard the door of the room next to mine open, and they passed in. I remembered that from that room also there was a door into the garden, and, presently, when I could hear no more, moved silently across the floor, and opened my own door, the little garden door, an inch or maybe less. I heard the steps of the disputants on the long path of the rose-garden.

This time, at least, I had enough at stake to guard me even in my own mind, which is scrupulous on such points, against any suspicion of spying. Enough had passed. I knew enough of Killigrew to be sure that I was justified in keeping the closest watch upon him. My mind was clear now. I remembered the words of the pedlar, and the circumstances of my accident, and, feeling pretty certain that he had already made one attempt on my life, I hurriedly finished my dressing, and, closing the little door carefully behind me, slipped out into the cool damp air of dawn. I heard the voices of the disputants, faintly now in the direction of the wood at the end of the rose-garden. I hurried down the path, and found the wicket at the bottom open. I passed through, supposing that they had been going towards the hut, from which, on that first night of my stay in that place, now so long ago, had come those agonizing sounds, the hut in which, I now believe, had occurred Michael's metamorphosis. I followed, but was presently arrested by the sight of broken brambles and footmarks in the deep wet grass, showing that they had left the path.

Presently I saw them. Killigrew was walking in front of the new servant whom I had now become accustomed to regard as Michael. His was the manner of one avoiding discussion, and Michael's that of the man who is determined to have his say out, feeling that he may not say it again. Perhaps, if I had been more alert in mind, I should then have perceived what now, when I look back upon that scene in memory, I clearly see, that Killigrew was deliberately drawing his companion away from the path and from the house. He moved on with quick, short, impatient steps, and Michael followed him, determined not to be shaken off.

Suddenly Killigrew stopped, in a little open space under some beeches.

"Listen," he said, and looked sharply round.

I was by this time close to them, and it was the merest chance that enabled me to secrete myself behind some thickly-growing hazels.

For a moment there was silence, and then Michael's voice broke out again, insistent, almost hysterical.

Killigrew interrupted him at once:

"Moderate your excitement," he exclaimed, sternly. "Even at this distance you may wake Rose and that fantastic boy."

"And, if Rose should hear us?"

"She would learn," said Killigrew, "that our relations are not what she supposed."

"And what if she already knows? What if she knows already that you have done her irreparable harm, that you killed her mother? . . ."

"And your share in that?"

"That you have been the cause of my ruin and of all that is miserable in her life? What if she already knows who was her father?"

"You told her?"

"I told her. Her at least you will no longer be able to deceive, nor that young man."

Killigrew looked at him with such calmness that the man was stung again to violence. His voice was raised, his whole body shook, as he continued:

"John Killigrew, you tempted me to my ruin. I fell, deep, though not so deep as you had wished, and I shall expiate my sin in hell. But one sin I have not committed. I have not, by silence, allowed you to snare that young man as you snared me, and to do to Rose what you did to the woman I was mad enough to love and bad enough to desire at any cost to herself or to me. You ruined me, John Killigrew. You shall not ruin him also."

"So it is to you that I owe that nincompoop's rejection of immortality?"

"It is to me that you owe your inability to lead that young man into eternal damnation."

Killigrew drew his sword, slowly, as if with an absent mind, ran his finger along it, bent it once or twice against his thumb, and then with careful exactitude pricked a beech leaf that lay before him on the ground. He lifted the leaf on the point of the rapier.

"It is very like a human heart," he said, looking at it with an expression of mild interest.

Michael flared out at him again:

"How many have you sacrificed to your monstrous greed for life? How many have you murdered that the Elixir might be red with power? . . . with power that I have shared. . . . My God, that I have shared. I have fed, like you, on the deaths of your victims. Unclean. Unclean. I also. O God, forgive me my sins, though I cannot forgive. Let me suffer in hell, but let no other be led into the evil that this man offers as a prize. May Rose be spared the full knowledge of my iniquity and his. Poor child . . . poor child. . . ." His voice rose and fell irregularly, and he wrung his hands, as if they were bound with imaginary fetters that somehow hampered him from speaking.

"You forget," said Killigrew, "what you owe to what you are pleased to call your sin, even while you try to shift it to my shoulders."

"I do not forget. I owe to it, and to you who made it possible, the certainty of eternal torment. I owe to it that I tricked the fairest of women into becoming the bride of my old age. I owe to it that I became your slave, dependent on you for all, compelled to witness your sins, and, worse, to benefit by them. I owe to it that I not only tricked that woman, but, when she died on learning the truth, I fed and let you feed on the very life that I had loved. Devil, I am your servant no longer. I am a sinner, but I repent. I am not your servant. I ask nothing from you. I care not what you may do to me. I have saved Rose from such suffering as I inflicted on another, and . . . no, I am telling you too much. You stand there, cold, and I say more than I wish to say. Devil, devil, I am not your servant, and do what you will, you are the servant of Satan, who dares not enter the presence of my Master."

"Are you sure that your Master, as you call Him, needs such a servant as you?" taunted Killigrew.

Michael covered his face with his hands. Suddenly he snatched his hands away. His face blazed with anger, and he yelled aloud: "Devil's words . . . devil's words."

There were tears in his voice.

"No," he shouted, "I will not listen to you. I will not listen to you. Be silent. Devil, devil, devil. . . ."

Killigrew's next words had the effect of calming the storm that was shaking Michael. They were deliberate and clear.

"Ass," he said, "you have neither the courage of sin nor the courage of virtue."

Michael was silent for a moment. Then he asked slowly:

"And had you, before your heart was turned to stone by the steady flow of iniquity in your veins? No, you too felt remorse, once, and conquered it. Thank God, miserable sinner that I am, that I do not seek to conquer mine."

"Ah," said Killigrew. "You know that I felt remorse. Have you ever seen me show any?"

"In your own words I have seen it written that you wished to die. You made even that resolve one of your victims. You drowned it in the deaths of others. You killed even that little scrap of virtue, and became wholly evil, wholly damned, a blot, a stain on the very sunlight."

"I have learned what I wished," said Killigrew. "You have read what was not intended for your eyes. I had forgotten that you knew Latin before you sold yourself to be my servant. Did you tell Stanborough what you read there?"

Michael seemed suddenly struck dumb.

I could not tell what was coming next. I supposed that they were speaking of the book which I had not yet examined. But, even so, there was much in their talk which I could not understand. I felt a wish to show myself, and demand an explanation. But I was incapable even of the smallest action.

Killigrew did not look at Michael, but seemed to wait for his reply. He seemed to meditate. Then he asked, suddenly:

"You showed that book to Rose?"

To that question, Michael did not reply.

"Kill me," he said, waiting, upright in the moonlight not two yards from where Killigrew stood, pricking the ground with the point of his sword. "Kill me, and may my death be the means of your undoing."

Killigrew looked at him, and laughed.

"Bah!" he said, "you forget that but for my elixir you would long ago have died."

With that, idly as it appeared, and without undue haste, he raised the point of his sword to the level of his hip, and lunged upwards, so that his sword transfixed the unarmed man who stood before him, entering in the region of the heart and coming out between the shoulder-blades.

There was no noise of any kind. Michael collapsed at the knees, and fell forward, Killigrew withdrawing his sword with a jerk that twisted the body to one side as it fell.

Killigrew then stooped, picked up the body with apparent ease, and threw it into the bushes. It seemed to fall to pieces in the air. Then he wiped his sword with a wisp of grass, and walked leisurely away.

At that moment, the power of action returned to me. I sprang forward, the whole horror of the scene I had witnessed concentrated in the desire to avenge the unfortunate man I had seen murdered. I sprang forward, I say, and, as my senses leapt to action, a sudden shock of unbearable pain in my head brought me to the ground like a shot hare.

I suppose my fall of the previous day had been more serious in its effects than I had known. I have imagined since that some slight concussion of the brain was suddenly intensified by the rush of blood to my head, as, burning with passion and indignation, I sprang from the spot where I had been held motionless by horror and before that by weakness during the scene that had ended in that calm and effortless assassination. I feel sure that I owe to that accident the fact that I am alive to-day.

If I had indeed fallen upon Killigrew, with my toy sword, to match my indignation against his passionless skill, there could have been not the slightest doubt as to the result. He would have played with me, taunted me a little to satisfy his anger at the thwarting of his plans for the capture of my soul, and, when he had tired of that, would have spitted me with as little compunction as he had shown in murdering the defenceless Michael.

And, if he had killed me, Rose would have been alone and at his mercy, and the happier part of both our lives would never have been lived. I have written this down as accident, and I leave the words as they stand to show how by the attribution of the mercies of Providence to the sport of chance a man may easily fall into ingratitude.

I do not know how long I lay there, in the damp grass under the tree where I had fallen, but, when I came to myself, the sun was up and the ground was broken into little pools of golden light. I had fallen on my face, and as I struggled to my knees I observed with some surprise that I had my sword in my hand. For a moment I remembered nothing of what had happened, and then, suddenly, the whole scene came back into my mind, and I saw the horrid jerk of the falling body as Killigrew plucked his sword away.

I stood up, and walked out into the small open space where Killigrew and Michael had stood. There was nothing on the ground, no blood, to bear witness to the thing that had there been done. Presently, looking at the ground, I saw a tuft of plucked grass, which I took to be the tuft on which Killigrew had wiped his guilty sword. I bent to examine it, forcibly checking my revulsion. There was no blood on it. I began to doubt my own memory, and to think that I had dreamt. Then the picture came into my mind of Killigrew picking up the body of his victim and throwing it from him into the bushes. I forced my way through the brambles, and came at once on the proof that I had not dreamt. Yet, it was not that which I had expected.

There were the plain brown coat and breeches of the dead servant. On the ground not far from them were his shoes, wooden-soled, the heel of one of them chipped, as I had already had occasion to notice. There were the black silk stockings. But . . . I can hardly bring myself to describe it . . . the clothes were almost empty. Not quite. There was something there, but it was not the body of a newly-murdered man. A little way apart there lay an old skull. The jawbones were not with the skull. I found them in the long grass. In the neat brown coat, that had, as it were, fallen in on itself, there was a bundle of dry brown bones. The stockings were not empty, but enclosed, loosely, knee-cap and shin. I picked one up by the foot, and these bones fell out from it, followed by a shower of the little bones that once had been a human foot. All these bones were brown. There was no flesh on them at all, and when, with a movement dictated rather by horror than by curiosity, I jerked at the coat, it came away from the breeches and spilled a grotesque collection of vertebræ and thigh-bones on the ground.

CHAPTER XII
The Loss of the Elixir

I cannot hope to make you share the frightened horror of that moment. Remember that I had seen and talked with this man, and that there, before me, on the ground, was evidence that he had been dead for a considerable time. What with the conversation I had heard I found no difficulty in understanding that phenomenon, but it was no less horrible because I understood it. Michael had shared with Killigrew the Elixir that I had refused. He had been kept alive by it beyond the natural term of his existence, and now that Killigrew had murdered him, his body had undergone in a moment the long process of dissolution that in the grave is an affair of years. That much was clear to me, but it did not still the dreadful shaking of my legs.

It was some minutes before I could sufficiently control myself to move, and get back as swiftly as I might to the path, where, if I should meet Killigrew, my presence would not raise in him a suspicion that I had been a witness of his crime. A rabbit ran nervously across the path before me, and soon afterwards it was followed by a weasel, a little slim brown animal, with a black tip to its tail, its teeth showing white, intent on its pursuit, and scarcely heeding me, although I was not two yards from it when it shot by. So, I thought, did Killigrew hurry towards the end he had appointed for himself. He had tried to kill me, and would doubtless presently make a second attempt. He had killed Michael. And Rose? Was she to be sacrificed also so that not one should be left alive who knew his secret? That thought brought me sharply to myself. I hurried towards the house.

Rose was in the garden, gathering fresh flowers. She turned at the sound of my steps.

"Dick," she said, "you are up. You are not badly hurt? I did not know quite what I feared last night, but Mr. Killigrew gave me no chance. Tell me. . . . No. Come near to me, and pick these weeds from the ground. He is watching us. He must not see your face. There is something in it that frightens me. Dick, Dick, tell me that you read my message in time. You did not agree. You did not yield to him. Tell me, tell me what it is that is in your face, and makes me so afraid."

I stooped and began picking weeds from round the roots of the little rose-bushes. And she, while she talked, went on bravely cutting flowers, and making them into a posy. Where Killigrew was, I do not know, but he can have seen only the most innocent of pictures.

"Dear Rose," I said, my face bent to the ground, "I read your message, just in time. I obeyed you. I have refused the strange thing that Killigrew offered me."

"Oh, thank God for that," she said. "I have learnt much that I did not know only two days ago. Killigrew is not my brother. Michael told me. . . ."

"Rose," I said, in a voice scarcely above a whisper, "I have something to tell you that will shock you. Can Killigrew see your face?"

She answered me by dropping her posy of flowers on the path. She bent to gather them up and I helped her.

"Rose," I said, "Michael is dead."

She opened her lips, but said nothing.

"Killigrew killed him," I said, "this morning. They quarrelled."

"He was my father," she whispered.

"Oh, Rose, I should not have told you . . ."

"It is better so. He wished to die. He had drunk of Killigrew's Elixir, and some strange sin, he did not tell me what, had made his life a burden. You saw him that night. You heard him, here in the garden. He was glad to die. . . . He told me enough to make me glad for his sake. It was he who warned me that night, and bade me give you that message . . ."

"Rose," I went on, "I am afraid for you. Killigrew has killed Michael, and as for me . . ."

"Tell me," she whispered.

I told her as shortly as I could the story of the race and my fall, and the words that the pedlar had used to Killigrew.

"Yes," she said, "he meant to kill you. . . . For you see, you know his secret now, and he has no power over you because you refused to share it with him. Dick, listen. Have you repented of what you did not mean to say and said."

"Rose." No other words would come to my lips.

"I have really never had a father," she said, "but when that poor man, who was Michael, told me that I was his daughter, he told me that if I would please him I would . . ."

She stopped, as if she could not speak. Then she went on quickly to the end of the sentence.

". . . Do what you seemed to wish. No, Dick, he may be still watching us. You must keep your face from the house. And, my dear," she said, "I do not yet know how it will be, for there is now something else that I must do."

There was the noise of a door opening from the house, and steps approaching. Rose whispered swiftly:

"Be on your guard, for your own sake, but, as for me, if for some time you do not see me, do not be disquieted, and, above all, do not ask for me."

Killigrew's voice fell like cold water on my burning ears.

"If you can stoop over a flower-bed," he said, "and not cry out with pain, we may be sure there are no bones broken. Good morning to you, my friend, and did you sleep well? But I need not ask that, for it is clear that sleep has come to your aid as well as my poor doctoring, or you would never be out of bed, and walking."

I heard my own voice wishing him good morning, as if in a dream.

"Are you not stiff?" he asked.

I told him I felt a slight stiffness in the legs, but scarcely more than a man feels when he rides after becoming unaccustomed to the saddle.

"Youth, youth," he said, smiling; "no wonder that you feel that you have no need of my Elixir."

It was hard to believe that it was the same man whom only a few hours earlier at most I had seen murder a defenceless fellow-creature with as little compunction as if he were killing a wasp. There he stood talking lightly and easily to me, as if perfectly indifferent to the probability that I suspected him of an attempt on my life, and to Rose as if she were indeed his sister and not the daughter of his victim. He did not seem to care what we knew, or whether we knew it. He bent over the flowers, with his back to me, as if he were clothed in a suit of mail. I believe he knew that I could not lift a hand against him. It was as if he were an evil spirit, not a man, and so invulnerable. I knew myself that I could not fight him. If we had stood up to fight, I think I should have waited for him to kill me. He was separate from men, safe from them, reserved, as it afterwards proved, for the more terrible vengeance of God.

"On the night of our discussion, Stanborough, when to my surprise you refused to share with me the most precious thing in the world, it had been my intention to drink with you from the Elixir. No, you need not start. Rose is well aware of my immortality. That night was the night on which I should have taken my accustomed physic. I have already overpassed the time, and am older than it is pleasant to feel."

I looked at him. He certainly seemed much older than I had yet seen him.

"Yes," he said, "you are counting my wrinkles. But to-night I shall drink and be again scarcely older than yourself. I am glad that you will have an opportunity of seeing for yourself how potent, how miraculous in its effect, is the thing you have refused."

Just then his features were sharply moved, seemingly by a spasm of pain.

"Indeed," he said, "I feel already the pains of old age. The more delightful will be my swift return to the freshness of my youth."

"There is some pain attendant on that transition, is there not?" said I, and could have choked myself for saying those words. He turned upon me sharply.

"Who told you that?" he asked. "There is a slight discomfort."

"No one told me," I replied, "but you yourself asked me if I had remarked that you were younger on the day after our arrival here than when we met in the inn parlour, and in that night . . . a cry . . . it seemed to me."

"It is a small price to pay," he said; "it cannot be the fear of that slight pain that kept you from accepting my offer."

"No, it was not that."

"Well, well, Stanborough we will not talk of that, unless you have changed your mind. . . ."

"I have not."

"It will merely be a satisfaction to me to . . ."

He did not finish his sentence. A spasm of pain again crossed his face. He turned round and walked swiftly back towards the house. I watched him with surprise, and noticed that from behind he seemed indeed very much older than before. His shoulders were bent, and he walked with that odd jerk of the knee peculiar to old men. Rose had left us, almost as soon as he began to talk.

I walked to and fro in the garden, trying with an aching head to see a clear path before me in this puzzling labyrinth. I thought that perhaps Rose would come out to me again, now that Killigrew had gone. I was tired, and sat on the stone seat. There was a pain in my thigh which was eased a little when my leg was stretched straight before me. I sat there trying to set before myself a clear account of what had happened in the past twenty-four hours, and to foresee what would happen presently, for I felt certain that the equilibrium of our relations had been destroyed by my refusal, and that Killigrew would not stop at the murder of Michael. It was a strange and horrible position, for it seemed to me that I could do nothing except wait for Killigrew to declare his further intentions, and it was more than probable that he would declare them by some action which would either accomplish them or make it impossible to thwart them. It was rather like waiting to be blown up in order to learn if a petard has been set. Yet I could not fly without Rose, and Rose was somehow tied to this very petard for whose explosion I impotently waited. Unless, indeed, she had been freed by the murder of Michael. She had not said so, but perhaps she would have said so, if Killigrew had not interrupted her. I was not to ask for her. What did that mean? She knew now that Michael had been her father. Had he laid commands upon her? The pedlar at the gate? Anyhow, she had told me clearly enough what I was to do, but it was not so easy to remain still, and do nothing, which, for the moment, was all that was required of me.

I suppose I sat there in the garden for a couple of hours or more. Then, as neither Rose nor Killigrew returned to me, I thought I might at least go into the house. I walked round the garden, and, instead of entering my room through the garden door, went through the gate in that trellis beside the house. For a moment I thought I saw Rose's white dress, flitting through the trees, a quarter of a mile away across the park. I checked myself in my wish to follow her, if indeed it was she whom I had seen, and went in by the great door. I stopped for a moment with my hand on the latch of my room, as I heard Killigrew hurrying with uneven steps to and fro in the room next to mine. There was no other sound in the house.

The sunlight was falling slantwise from my narrow window. On the table in the room were the roses that Mistress Killigrew had that morning gathered, and beside them, on a white napkin, was bread, cheese, a plateful of cold roast beef, and a flagon of clear water. Rose had prepared this meal for me herself. The tears came to my eyes at the thought of the sweet practicality of her forethought for me even on that morning of evil omen. I told myself that I could not eat, but I was young, and hungry; and presently, meaning to take a mouthful, I finished the beef, and tasting the cheese soon made an end of that also. And indeed Rose's wisdom was justified, for I doubt if after my experience of the day before I could have supported the events that followed if I had been called upon to endure them with an empty stomach.

I think it was about this time, or perhaps a little before, that Killigrew discovered the loss of the Elixir.

I had scarcely finished eating, when I heard my name called, loudly, "Stanborough, Stanborough." I ran hurriedly from my room and upstairs to the library, where Killigrew was hurriedly pulling folios and quartos from the shelves.

"What is it?" I asked, a little breathless from the stairs.

He looked at me narrowly, as if to watch the expression of my face. His own was troubled as I had never seen it, and older, visibly older, than it had been when I had seen him in the garden. He spoke in a very calm voice, as if of something that did not matter in the least.

"I have lost a small case containing one of the drugs I need for my experiments," he said. Remember, he had never described the Elixir to me, nor shown it me. I think he wished to learn if Michael had told me of it.

"It was a rare drug, and one that I should find difficult to replace," he said. "I wonder if you will help me to look for it."

I was glad of this excuse to be with him, as when with him I could at least be sure that he was not engaged upon any evil of which I should be ignorant. At least, while I was with him, Rose was safe. So I fancy he must have been puzzled by the expression on my face, if he then suspected me of having stolen the Elixir. For I have ever been a poor hand at disguising my emotions, and his request, which doubtless he thought would wake in me either fear or a look of mere innocence, produced only an obvious relief.

"With all my heart," I said. "Was it one of the drugs we have used together?" It did not occur to me until later what it was that he had really lost.

"No," he replied, "we have not used it together. It was a phial of glass, in a wooden case. A little black wooden case. It was not kept here, but in the hut in the garden, which I use for certain of my experiments. . . ."

I fancied I knew for what experiments he used that hut, and my supposition was confirmed when he continued:

"It was there two days ago. Only Michael and I have had the key to the hut. And he brought it back to me yesterday."

He suddenly went to the door of the room, and called out: "Michael!" and again "Michael!"

I knew that he was well aware that he was calling to a dead man. He turned back, scanning my face.

"If he had brought the drug in with him it would be here, with these others, in the cupboard behind the books. I used once to keep it here."

He pointed to a series of small doors in the panelling behind the bookshelves, which he had exposed by the removal of the big, brown leather volumes. One of these doors was already open, and he opened the others, showing a number of flasks and phials with different coloured drugs, and many small instruments of alchemy, for the most part very old.

I began to search with him, though I believe he had already assured himself that the case he sought was not in the library and only wished my help in order to have an opportunity of observing my face and forming an opinion as to whether or not I was responsible for his loss. It was a strange feeling, to be there in that room, with a man I had seen in the very act of murder, helping him indeed, and conscious all the time that he was watching me as I have seen a cat watch a mouse, lamed, helpless, which the cat has loosed to whet its appetite, by seeing it apparently free to escape, and yet waiting with bristling fur, ready at any moment to recapture it with a swift, cruel stretching forward of its velvet paw.

Killigrew could not make up his mind as to the meaning of my obvious innocence. Perhaps he attributed to me some of his own cunning, and then swept it away with a gust of the contempt which I am persuaded he commonly felt for me, only to let it return again a moment later, hardening his eyes and narrowing his lips.

Suddenly his face was blurred with a spasm of pain, for the third time that I had noticed. He put his hand to his throat, as if there were something there that he would have torn away. For a moment he sat still in his chair, bowed forward. He groaned. Then, springing up, he said, "We must have an end to this," and going to the door of the library called "Rose."

There was no answer.

I did not trust myself to ask him where was Michael without betraying that I knew.

"Rose," he called again.

The house was as silent as a vault. Only against one of the tall narrow windows of the hall a bumble-bee was beating itself with a continuous angry drone.

"Have you seen my sister?" he asked me.

"Not since you were talking with us in the garden," I replied.

He ran down the staircase, and I followed him. We went to the kitchens. They were empty. The kennel where the servants slept was in disorder. The servants had gone.

An angry spot of red burned in Killigrew's pale forehead.

"Perhaps the stables," I suggested.

We went out and crossed the yard. The horses had been fed and watered, but there was no sign in the yard or in the stables or barns of any other living thing.

He set off running back to the house, through the kitchens, and I ran after him, though I found it hard enough to keep up with him. The front door stood open and he ran through it, stood a moment on the steps, sweeping the pack with his eyes, and then ran on, round the corner of the house into the rose-garden, down the narrow path. He burst through the wicket-gate in the trellis, and ran like a man possessed along the path under the trees to the little stone hut. As he ran he looked away to the right, towards the scene of Michael's murder, but he did not slacken his speed, and, when I reached the stone hut, he was already inside, feverishly searching behind boxes and in open cupboards.

Inside the hut was a small room, neatly enough furnished, with a tall chair and table of dark wood. There was a small fireplace, with a stone hood over it built out from the wall. There was scarcely room for two persons in the hut, and it was very feebly lighted, except from the open door. There was an empty glass on the table. Killigrew looked at it, and as he looked his face contorted again with a pain the manifestation of which was horrible to behold. He picked up the glass and examined it, and then set it down on the table so violently as to break its stem, though that was fairly stout. The glass rolled, and would have fallen off the table. I caught it. There were marks scratched with a diamond on its side, as if for measuring.

Killigrew collapsed into that tall chair, rather than sat down in it, and, with groans, directed my search, indicating boxes to be moved, cupboards to be opened, and so on. The hut was small enough, but, by the time we had done, I could hardly believe that so much rubbish could have been stowed in it. At the end of half an hour the table was piled with bottles and boxes, the floor was a waste of straw packing, and the air was grey with the fine dust which had, no doubt, lain long enough before this strange disturbance. Killigrew's pain seemed to grow worse and worse, and he seemed less able to control himself. Little as I liked him, I could hardly bear to see the torture that was in his face. Suddenly, it seemed, the bout came to an end.

"Enough," he cried, "the thing is not here," and jumping up made for the door. The idea came swiftly to my mind that he meant to shut me in, and I was as quick as he, and we jostled together in the doorway. He neither apologized nor waited for an apology from me, but set off running, and presently, breaking through the brambles, turned from the path and ran like a madman into the wood. I knew whither he was going, and, without thinking of the consequences, ran after him.

As we squeezed together through that narrow doorway, I had given violent pressure to the worst of my bruises of the day before. For a moment, I could hardly move, and when, suppressing my pain, I set off after him, he had a considerable advantage of me.

I, too, left the path, and ran as fast as I could, though the brambles were continuously entangling my legs and tearing at my calves. I ran towards the place whither he had led Michael, and, though I had lost sight of Killigrew, I presently knew that my instinct had been exact. When I saw Killigrew again, he was kneeling on the ground, over those clothes and bones that had been Michael. He seized first one and then another scrap, tearing the clothes to pieces, throwing the bones from him, as I have seen a raven pick the carcase of a sheep. It was then, for the first time, that I knew what it was that he had lost. He suspected that Michael had removed the Elixir as well as betraying his wickedness to Rose, and now he was tearing to pieces those grim, wretched remains, to find if the Elixir had been concealed on the person of his victim.

I do not know whether he saw me or not. He suddenly leapt up, flinging aside the last remnants of poor old Michael's brown clothes, and, with a loud, raucous groan, his pain I suppose coming upon him again, ran off towards the house.

I followed as best I might.

I went upstairs to the library, thinking he had returned there. The room was as we had left it. I was on my way downstairs when I heard groans from the room beside my own. I went to the door, and knocked upon it. The groans continued. I tried the door. It was fast. I waited a little while, and then went into my own room. The room was full of the scent of the roses on the table. It is curious to observe what strange, in-essential circumstances a man remembers.

I sat down in my chair, and in sitting pressed something hard that was in my pocket against my bruised thigh. I put my hand into my pocket, and pulled out the little vellum-covered book that had been given me in so strange a manner, and been instantly driven from my head by my talk with Killigrew, by my accident, and to-day, after learning something of its significance, by these swift harassing events.

I closed my door carefully, found that it would not lock, and then, seeking to drive my impatience and anxiety from me, sat down to read.

CHAPTER XIII

Imitatio Satana: Killigrew's Confessions

There are things written in that parchment-covered book which I dare not even copy with my pen. As I read them, I kept involuntarily glancing over my shoulder, as if I were afraid that the mere reading set me in the power of the devil, who might come up and seize me from behind. Such thoughts were let loose by the written words, that it seemed to me, though I did not then put my feeling into shape, that the room must be full of evil spirits, freed from their chains by the mere fact that a man was reading those terrible blasphemous sentences. I have kept the book all these years, for the purpose to which I shall put it to-day. But, when that is accomplished, and I have copied enough from it to show what manner of man Killigrew was, and what the loathsome miracle that was the secret of his life, I shall be glad to commit it to the flames, that, even now crackling in the hearth, are ready to receive it.

It is written almost entirely in the Latin language, with which, thanks to my father's request and my uncle's scrupulous fulfilment of it, I was very fairly familiar. The script varied slightly throughout the book, but it seems probable to me that Killigrew purposely preserved the ancient mannerisms of his handwriting when adding to a document which he had already begun. The first entry, the longest, is dated 1515 *anno Domini,* though it refers to events of twenty years before, and the last in August of the year 1716, only a day or two before the book came into my possession.

A number of pages before the first autobiographical entry are filled with an assortment of chemical formulas, recipes, lists of the names and properties of certain drugs, and a number of such signs as were common among the Cabalists. Several of these I recognized. They are well known. Others however were then and are still entirely strange to me. In particular the sign that, if you will remember, Killigrew showed me on his signet ring, the ring which appears in that row of portraits, whose abnormal likeness is now sufficiently explained: this sign recurs again and again, set in varying patterns. There are the names of a few drugs with, beside them, the signs of constellations, and simple diagrams of the changes of the moon. These, I take it, illustrate, or would illustrate to one conversant with such things, the influence on the drugs of astronomical conditions. Perhaps they only exert some peculiar property when there is some such conjunction of heavenly phenomena as is illustrated by the little diagrams. No doubt these pages would be of great interest to a chemist. I had, indeed, thought of sending them for the enlightenment and study of our Royal Society. But I reflected that it is possible that among those signs and recipes there is the secret of that devilish fluid, and that some rash ambitious man, disregarding the warning that to my mind is written in fiery characters in the pages I am about to copy, would once more compound it, and, drinking it, be, like Killigrew, prisoned in wickedness, and, like him, doomed for God knows how long to be the active servant of the devil upon earth. Not the least terrible impression that is given by the book is that Killigrew himself was at first not wicked, but became the servant of the baleful drug which he had hoped, in innocence, would make him master of the knowledge of this world. But let me proceed to my task of copying and of translation. I shall not attempt to translate the whole book, but only such passages as seem to me to pertain immediately to my story, the passages which best set forth the secret, muffled history of Killigrew, those which touch on the strange relations between Rose, Michael, and the pedlar, and lastly those few sentences which throw a somewhat mocking light on Killigrew's attitude towards myself. These passages and sentences are done with such small skill as I possess out of the Latin into our own tongue.

The first passage I have translated is the very opening of Killigrew's autobiographical confession. It is clear that it was written while he still believed that he had strength to release himself from his service to the Elixir, and while he still wished to bring that bondage to an end. Its remorseful tone is very different from the scornful indifference with which in later years he chronicled the crimes which, in order to preserve that bondage, he freely and willingly committed.

"*The month of August, 1515. He who reads these lines will learn that the secret sought by all the philosophers has been found. He will also learn why it has been destroyed, and why no philosopher should ever seek for it again. I shall here set down my reasons for what I am about to do, and, lest any should think me worse than I am, the circumstances in which I was cheated by false hopes into the loss of all happiness in this world, and the certainty of eternal torment in the world to come.*

"*The learned doctor Valerius Philodoxius, whose pupil I became when, pursuing knowledge, I left the home of my fathers in Huntingdon, and crossed the seas* (he was then, no doubt; the clear-faced youth whose portrait I had seen in the gallery), *was neglected by the doctors of Paris. I was, indeed, his only pupil. Yet this old man had learnt the secret which from the earliest times had baffled the wisdom of the world. He had long sought the Elixir of Life. As nearly as he could remember, it was on his 87th birthday that he discovered it. He did not then know that he had found it, but contin-*

ued his experiments. It might, indeed, have happily passed unnoticed from the world, if he had not accidentally preserved the fluid which, compound as it was of rare drugs, inspired with non-corporeal essence prepared under those sidereal influences which he deemed most favourable, he yet believed to have failed. He kept it, and when ten years later, at the age of 97, he lay sick, all the efforts of the physicians being unavailing, he bethought himself of this physic, which, though it had not succeeded in restoring youth, might, none the less, quicken the flagging heart of one about to die (cor morituri). He sipped, and knew at once that that experiment, now ten years old, had been no failure. He knew that he had discovered the Elixir. For he became, not a young man, but a man with the vigour he had possessed at 87, old in form, but, for all that, with ten years to live.

"This much he told me. 'If,' he said, 'I had first drunk the Elixir at the age at which you are now, I should, no doubt, be able to return to that age on drinking it again. At least,' he added, 'we will ascertain if this be so or not.' He asked me to drink a little of his fluid, and to continue my studies for a few years, and then to return to him and drink again, when we might thus confirm, by a parallel experiment, his supposition as to the properties of the Elixir. I readily and with eagerness agreed. I drank, from a phial, a little of the liquid. It was neither transparent nor opaque, but a liquid of much the appearance of the inner coating of the oyster, in which scarlet, blue, green, and pale violet tints mingled together. I was then 25 years of age. I saluted my master with reverence, feeling that I was fortunate above all the students of Europe in sharing the experiment of one whom I believed the greatest doctor in the world. Although I accepted what my eyes told me, namely, that the learned man had been rejuvenated by ten years, I did not think that he had made me a present of perpetual youth. I only thought with pride that he had chosen me to test the properties of a fluid whose crowning effect, I supposed, would only be exemplified in himself.

"I studied with him in Paris, where we lived in the street of Saint Jacques, and were much disturbed by the riotous clamour of the worser class of students, who sing and make merry when they should be at their books. Presently I left Philodoxius, and went to Leyden, where was rumour of learning, and then to other universities. During these travels that befell me which happens to many young men, but was in my case to have a particular influence on my life. I quarrelled with a youth, one of my own age, and killed him in a fight with swords, a pastime at which I was better skilled than he. The thought of this murder, for it was nothing else, lay heavy on my mind. I was a student, not a soldier, and the memory of that young man's death made me older than my years. At the age of thirty-five, when I returned to Paris, there were many grey hairs in my head. As soon as I reached Paris, that murder, now a memory of some years before, took to itself a sudden new significance.

"The learned doctor received me gladly, and while reviving the sting of my conscience, increased my admiration for his powers, by consulting some notes, and asking me at once: 'You killed some one or something between such and such a date?' He was right. My quarrel had been about midway between the dates he named. I asked him why and how he had learnt this, but he was impatient for me to drink again from his Elixir, and see if on me it would have the same marvellous effect that it had on its inventor. He offered it to me. It had changed in colour. It was now red. At least, the many colours that blend in the pearl were now distinctly under the dominance of red. I drank, and experienced a violent short pain, much like the shock caused by the touching of certain eels, but felt throughout my entire system. The learned doctor, with an air of profound gratification, asked me to look into a mirror. I looked and saw myself at the age of 25. There was not a grey hair on my head. Nothing was old in my face except my eyes, and the knowledge that showed in them. I had lost nothing of my experience in thus taking a step back into my youth.

"I was still contemplating the change that had been worked in myself, when the doctor told me how he had guessed my misfortune, and been able to set it between certain dates. His words filled me with profound disgust for the infernal liquid I had shared with him. He said: 'On the first of those dates, I drank from the Elixir, and there was no change in me. I believed that its power had evaporated, or that I had mistaken the effects of a stimulant for something of deeper import. On the second of those dates I looked at the Elixir again, and saw that it had changed colour. I drank, and was once more, now for the third time, a man of 87, or thereabouts.' I did not understand him, and he then explained, as he had not explained before, the horrible nature of the Elixir.

"The principle of the Elixir is so simple that I wonder at the centuries that have passed over the world without witnessing its discovery. Men have vainly sought to disturb the economy of the universe by making a drug which should restore life to those who had but little left. They dreamed of a perpetual youth, like the youth of the Gods in the Latin poets. I, too, had dreamed of a perpetual youth, in which I should conquer all the secrets that are hidden from man. My desires were pure. I did not ask for youth that I might garland my head with flowers and gorge myself with sin. I cared for knowledge only, and for that end alone I hoped for eternal life. Be it noticed, that I, like all the alchemists, except the learned Philodoxius, envisaged the Elixir in my youthful dreams as a draught that should give me more life than would naturally fall to my share, a youth, a prime, prolonged beyond that which it is the general lot of man to enjoy.

"BUT LIFE IS LIMITED, AND IN THE CLOSED GARDEN OF THIS WORLD WE CAN CULTIVATE ONE FLOWER ONLY AT THE EXPENSE OF ANOTHER.

"Those are the words of my master Philodoxius. The idea there expressed is that which made his discovery possible. He perceived that life could only be bought by life: and so, during the thirty years in which he ceaselessly devised and experimented, the object of his search was not merely a magical drug which should perform the impossible, but a drug which, duly prepared with regard to many and several influences, should be fed on death in order to give out life. His great discovery was that it was necessary to make death itself an ingredient in the Elixir of Life. His difficulty was to find those circumstances which made possible the fusion of physical and spiritual. When he had prepared all, he killed a child. He told me how difficult this was for him, already an old man. He found the child playing in the street, and carried it away with him, hiding it in his gown. . . . He did not tell me all the details of the preparation, perhaps because he feared to lose his mastery over his disciple. Since then, I have myself deduced what I believe to be the more important elements of the formula, and from the data he told me, I have learned, within a certain latitude of error, what were the astronomical conditions which made his experiment a success. All astrologers would admit that at that time the heavens were particularly favourable to all phenomena of the combination of essences of the spiritual and physical world.

"That first time, he drank, as I have said, without results. Drinking again, he became as young as at his first draught. From this he learnt that his drug did not make its drinker indefinitely young, and that it sets a period in his life to which he can return again. He had not learnt the worst. When, me absent, he drank again without result, he concluded that the drug could but once produce its effect. He laid it aside, until a passionate desire for life made him once more examine it, without hope, and find that it had changed its colour. He drank and it acted as before. He was again a hale old man of 87, instead of one already faltering to the grave.

"At first he could not explain the fact of the drug at one time having no effect, and later recovering its original power. He had not touched the drug. It had suffered no very remarkable changes of temperature. Some time, however, before my return, in reviewing all its ingredients, it occurred to him that there was one which might be renewed without physical contact, a spiritual ingredient which might, even at a distance, be strengthened or replaced. He thought of death. He knew that he had killed no one himself. He reminded himself that I also had drunk of the Elixir. He therefore said to himself that it was possible that I had caused a death, and that the Elixir, no merely physical compound, had been affected by that death. He formed no decision, but noted the dates, and, as I have said, asked me that question, and received an answer which confirmed his monstrous supposition.

"The learned Philodoxius was at first only interested in the exactness of his deduction. It had not occurred to him to look at the matter from another point. His greed began later. On the other hand, I was filled with the most terrible remorse and horror. I had regretted the death of the student I had killed. I had had masses sung for his soul. My hair had turned grey with sorrow at being a shedder of blood—I who cared for nothing but science and philosophy. I knew now that I was enjoying my youth a second time through the death of that young man. I thought of myself as a vampire. For two days and nights I knelt on the steps of the porch of Our Lady of Paris, but she did not succour me. I was half mad with misery, and saw that man's face in mine when I looked in a mirror and realized that I had indeed returned to youth. I resolved to spend this new life that had been so terribly bought in pursuit of such knowledge as might repay the world for the evil I had done in it.

"Ten years passed. More than once the learned Philodoxius refreshed himself at that horrible fountain. The liquid in his phial was growing low. The red tints in it had faded, and its prevailing colours were a shimmer of blue and green as if in a solution of milk. He began, indirectly at first, and then openly, and at last with abuse and scorn of my reluctance, to press me to commit another murder. 'What,' said he, 'is the life of a man in comparison with the greatest benefit that has yet been discovered by mankind?' I steadfastly refused to satisfy him. But there came a day when he seemed about to die. He drank the Elixir in vain. When I saw this, when I suspected that even if I wished there was for me also no return to youth, my scruples weakened, and I became afraid. I, too, drank, and felt no shock, nor any change. We had between us exhausted the life of that murdered student on which we had been feeding.

"Then, suddenly, I realized how selfish had been my virtuous resolve. I saw that I had only refrained from adding another murdered life to the malign vitality of the Elixir, because I felt no need of it myself. I had merely resolved to do no murder for the sake of Philodoxius. Knowledge that the Elixir was exhausted, and that I, too, could never drink it again, worked a horrible miracle in my heart. Scarcely knowing what did, I went out into the street of Saint Jacques. And there, at the corner of a dark alley, I waited like a hired assassin, and, with cool decision, drove my poniard between the shoulders of a chance foot-passenger. I do not know who he was, who was the first deliberately murdered victim of the Elixir. I did not trouble to look at his face. My blow had been carefully aimed. I knew that he was dead, and, with a strange elation of spirit, returned to the house where lodged the learned Philodoxius and myself.

"I had left Philodoxius at the point of death, cursing me in a weak voice with all the more terrible curses known to those who have long dealt in spiritual things. When I returned, he fell upon my neck with tears, praised me as his preserver, and pointed to the Elixir, which, in its transparent phial, glowing like a ruby, and increased in bulk, was now almost overflowing the neck *of the vessel. I disengaged myself roughly from my master's embrace, seized the phial greedily, and drank. I groaned aloud. A second time I experienced that violent shock, and with its pains distributed through my body, and sharper than on the first occasion. I had in a moment shaken off half a score of years, and was again a youth of twenty-five.*

"My remorse was so poignant that I could hardly support my life. I seemed to stifle with heaviness of soul at every breath I drew. For, whereas, before, I had killed a man in a quarrel, in hot blood, without guilt except in so far as I had allowed myself to act without thought and to use my superior skill, this last was a deliberate foul murder, planned and carried out with no other purpose than that of gain, and gain of a most horrible kind. I was still further horrified to find that Philodoxius, my master, in no way shared these feelings of natural humanity. On the contrary, he exulted in the nature of the Elixir, spent long hours in contemplating it, invented nicknames for it of affectionate and loathsome significance. . . .

"In the end I killed Philodoxius. But I did not kill him with any worthy motive. So far had the desire for the Elixir depraved me, that, as my remorse passed from me, my learned master appeared to me to be no more than a greedy, childish old man. I resented his sharing in the wonderful evil thing he had invented. He was for ever begging for fresh murders, was petulant when I refused, and punished me by drinking the Elixir freely before my eyes. He seemed to grow old again with ever-increasing speed after each draught that lessened his age. Each time he drank, the ruby of the liquid paled, and he would show it to me, and prophesy that when I needed it, it would already be bloodless and without power. I told him I would not drink again, but I desired to drink, if only I could do so without murder. So I killed Philodoxius, with the poisonous fumes of one of his experiments. His death did not affect the colour of the Elixir, because, but for its drinking, he would have been dead before, and so had no natural life to lose. His body was putrescent at the very moment of his death. I killed him without remorse, but buried him with respect, because, though his success had been greater than his self-control, yet of all the alchemists and astrologers he alone had reached the goal. I even kept his ring, brought by him from some place of wisdom in the Eastern parts of Europe, where he had studied in his youth."* (I believe this ring to be that which Killigrew showed me, telling me it had belonged to Paracelsus, the ring which was painted in five of those portraits in the library. It is now in my possession. R. S.) *"I drank from the Elixir, and woke my remorse in all its violence. The Elixir is now as pale as moonlight. I shall not drink from it again. I am young for the last time. I shall return to my father's house in Huntingdon, which I left twenty years ago, and, having touched the secret for which all the world has sought, having learnt that it is evil beyond all human wickedness, live and die in the effort to expiate the sins into which* *it has led me, and those into which I have eagerly fallen. . . . Before I die, I shall destroy the Elixir."*

Would that he had done so. Many innocent lives would have been saved, if the remorse which followed the drinking of the fluid had not died and given place at last to a furious eagerness to drink again. The next paragraph that I shall translate from Killigrew's book is not dated, but must have been written some years later, when the wretched man was already fallen deeper into its power.

"I am ashamed at the strong fetters that are about my hands when I would do good, at the swift wings lent to my feet when they run to accomplish evil. I returned to England, to my father's house. I brought the Elixir with me, telling myself that I did but postpone the moment of its destruction. There were rejoicings at my return, and much wonder at the way in which my features had preserved their youth. My father was an old man. He alone was not surprised at my appearance, for to his father a son is always but a boy. Now and then, growing rapidly older, I had a fierce desire to drink. Many times I restrained myself, and strengthened my resolve with prayer. At last I did indeed drink, but only to find, what I had already suspected, that the Elixir had lost its power. It was starved for want of death. So firmly was I resolved not to drink from it that I was glad at this proof that I should drink in vain. I grew older. I could think of nothing else but the Elixir, but I held to my purpose, until . . . My father was dying. They called on me to use my doctor's skill. He was an old man, and the pallor of the Elixir, that I never forgot, was like a perpetual moonlight in my brain. I prepared a subtle poison, and gave it to him with a kiss, and then went away into my chamber to watch the Elixir. . . . Two hours later there was a sudden flush of pale rose in its horrible whiteness. A few minutes after that the servants called me to my father's bedside. He was dead. When I returned to the Elixir, it was already white once more. I knew that my father had been very near his death when I killed him. I had robbed him of no more than an hour or so, and made myself a parricide for nothing.

"I raged, and my transports of anger were mistaken for those of grief. My remorse was gone, for ever. I perceived that the Elixir and its welfare were more to me than the death of a father whom I had revered. My mind would think of nothing else. I looked this way and that to find a victim for it. It had begun to be for me something personal. I felt that it might be offended, hurt, vindictive. . . . I became a devil. . . . Soon after my father's burial, a pestilence broke out in the house. My mother was already dead. There was none in the house but the servants and I. The servants sickened swiftly and died, and I was myself slightly affected. None but the Elixir and I knew the immensity of that crime. No doctor in England knew as much of the secret properties of certain drugs as was known by the pupil of Philodoxius. Night by night, in exultation, I watched the

Elixir, luminous in its phial, blushing in deeper and yet deeper waves of ruby, creeping up the phial's narrow neck, as each servant, man or maid, died in the torments of the fever with which I had afflicted them. They have called the house where my ancestors lived an honourable life the House of Death. It is that, indeed. But it is also the House of Life, where in a small Venetian phial is stored the lives of all those murdered souls."

After that for many pages there is little in the book which would repay in interest for the labour of translation. He notes the shifts to which he came to be put in hiding his immortality, as that became more noticeable. It seems that he moved from place to place, out of England, in Italy, in France. He learned the business of an attorney, to enable him the more easily to arrange his own succession to himself, for he returned always as the heir to the Killigrew property in Huntingdon, lived in the Old Hall until such time as his youth would have become remarkable, and then went off again. During these foreign intervals he seems to have had regular places of abode in Florence, in Paris, and more than once he revisited Leyden, the scene of that student's fight which at the time caused him a regret far deeper than any qualm he later felt about the growing mass of his crimes. Here and there are sinister little lists of names, which may or may not be the names of his victims. A number of dates, with shorter and shorter intervals between them, show, I think, that as he lived longer he had more frequently to supplement his youth from the Elixir. I now translate a scornful comment on the remorse he had ceased to feel, a comment which shows how completely his better nature had been subdued by the needs of his artificially prolonged existence. It is dated 1601:

"I read, laughing, my confessions of regret, the expression of my ridiculous resolve. It is difficult for me to believe that I ever truly thought I could destroy the Elixir. It is humiliating and still more difficult for me to believe that I ever wished to destroy it."

And on the next page, undated:

"I know now that I am singled out from men, and I pursue my immortality with exultation. I have made myself, with so many years of practice and unimpaired physical strength, a master with the French rapier, and sometimes I kill my victims with honour. Not often, for a mishap may befall even the most skilled, and I am losing, as the years go by, any pleasure in risking my existence. I am already far over the brink of natural life. I think that fact has altered my behaviour towards the Elixir and towards myself. Formerly I was a man kept young by a wonderful drug. Without it I should merely have been old. But now the time of my death is long past, and, on the power of the Elixir, like a mountebank on a tight-rope, I step warily above annihilation."

The passages I am now about to translate are concerned with the curious relations between Michael and the pedlar and Rose. They explain much that had puzzled me before I read them, and confirm from another side much of the strange, muddled tale which had been told me by the pedlar at the gate. I translate them in full, separating them from their contexts, which are irrelevant, and omitting the name of the family concerned, with whom, though she might do so, Rose would not wish to claim relationship. To do so would be to revive by a thousand impertinent questions the whole sinister story from which, though she cannot forget it, she has at least escaped.

"(a) 1666. *The great plague and the fire in London have driven many into the country. Accident brought the brothers Michael and Egerton —— to ask refuge from me. The elder is a man of 36. The younger, of a foolish religious turn, is 25. I have conceived the idea of letting the elder drink from the Elixir, and so, since the time will come when it will be in my power to keep him alive or to bring his life to an end, of making him my slave for ever. . . . The man scoffed and drank. They have gone, but when he feels age coming upon him, he will remember and come back, hoping even against hope that he was wrong to scoff, and that the draught at which he jeered will give him another year or two of youth.*

"(b) 1694. *The brothers —— have visited me again, the younger unable to hide his wonder at his brother's wish to come, both doubting whether or no I am the same man. They are old men now of fifty and sixty. The elder is very feeble. I have been amused to observe their senile courtship of Madeleine, who laughs at them.*" (I have searched the book in vain for further knowledge of Rose's mother. R. S.) "*The elder, clumsily, speaks to me of the Elixir. I affect not to understand him.*

"(c) 1695. *Egerton —— has gone away, because his suit is not acceptable to Madeleine, walking out on the high road, I believe, like a vagabond. So great is the power of passion on a narrow fanatic mind. When he was gone I offered, upon conditions, Madeleine and the Elixir to the elder brother, the dotard, Michael. . . . He has agreed, has drunken, and henceforth is mine. Madeleine, wholly unsuspecting, is yielding to the new impetuosity of the youth that I have given him.*

"(d) 1696. *The ridiculous Madeleine, duly married to Michael, has borne him a daughter.*

"(e) Paris 1696. *Egerton —— in the fantastical clothes of a pedlar came back to the Old Hall, recognized Michael, and, in a frenzy of jealousy, denounced him. Madeleine is dead. The child is put to nurse. Michael is a strange, feeble spirit, snivels at his memories, regrets the happiness I gave him, and yet, frightened to die, is a dog at my heels, and will be, world without end, for I find him a good servant. The episode of Madeleine is over. Egerton ——, however, may stir up flames for my feet. His extraordinary passion for*

Madeleine made him perceive the identity of Michael. He watched our depar-
ture. Foolishly I tried to kill him. The only pistol-shots I have missed in a
hundred years. It is, perhaps, well, for he will die without my killing him. . . ."

These entries are taken in the order in which they occur in the
book, but they are separated there by much that I do not choose to
translate. They make it fairly clear to my mind that Rose was the
daughter of Michael and this Madeleine, whose origin is unexplained. It
seems that Michael drank from the Elixir for the first time at the age of
35, and that, before marrying Madeleine, when 63, already an old, fail-
ing man, he drank again, and so recovered his youth. From that time I
imagine that he had been growing steadily older, perhaps faster than if
he had never drunk. He must actually have lived well over ninety years
when he drank the Elixir again, and this time, without the desire, the
passion, that had blunted any remorse he may have felt the first time,
been moved to tell something of the truth to Rose, and in giving me
this book to do his best to save me from falling like himself into the
power of Killigrew. He had paid the penalty for this defection from his
master, and, at the moment of his murder, must already have been
some years older than the term of his natural life. That, I think, is
proved by the instantaneous decay of his murdered body. At the time of
the events in which I shared, the pedlar must have been seventy-five.
The only sign I find in the book that Killigrew gave another thought to
the existence of this man was a long Latin curse, originally applied to
fraudulent pilgrims, which Killigrew had copied out, altering it here and
there to apply to travelling hawkers and wanderers on the roads, an example of that odd childishness which I more than once noticed in him,
as a strange contrast to his philosophy.

It is curious to observe what sordid mathematical intricacy is in-
volved in this tampering with man's mortal destiny. When I worked out
the real age of Michael, I omitted one factor from my calculation. It is
clear that Killigrew found that he grew old with increasing rapidity after
each return to youth. That does not mean in years, but in age, in weakness, in nearness to the sensations of death. It would be unreasonable to
suppose that this did not also happen to Michael, though as he drank
less often, its effect would be less marked. In the case of Killigrew, I
have reason to believe that the longest interval he could allow himself
without imminent risk of the death he had so long avoided was, at the
time of my story, scarcely over two months, whereas at the beginning it
was as much as ten years. As for Michael, he would be older than
ninety-six when he died, though he had lived only ninety-six years, and
though, when he was killed, he had but the day before given himself the
appearance of the thirties.

After the series I have translated, there are other references to Michael, all expressing an increasing contempt for one whom, even at the beginning of their acquaintanceship, Killigrew had only regarded as promising to make a useful menial. Killigrew more than once compares his new partner in the Elixir to Philodoxius, adding on one occasion "*but he* (the alchemist), *though a greedy old man, was the finest philosopher of Europe, whereas Michael is not only dull, but even has touches of piety, fears the pit, and regrets the privilege he undeservedly shares.*" Killigrew must have come, during the twenty years they lived together, after Rose's birth, to regard Michael as nothing but an elderly fool, and in his own folly not to have perceived that these touches of religion might come to be the means of his own disaster, and that the remorse which survived Michael's passion might, unrestrained by the eager gratification of a desire, burst out unchecked when he should drink from the Elixir again.

I come now to an entry which helped me to understand something that had always puzzled me, the cry of agony in the wood that I had heard on the night of my arrival. It seems that as the intervals between Killigrew's rejuvenations decreased the penalties he had to pay for them grew greater.

"1698. *Would that I could devise some means of assuaging pain. Poppy and hellebore, known to the ancients, do not help me. As remorse left me, so with successive renaissances has the physical pain of rebirth increased, until now, when I am warned by the sickening anguish of decay that I must have recourse to the Elixir, I am torn between the fear of death and the horrible knowledge of the torture that is the price of life. This pain is frightful, unimaginable. It is no longer a simple shock, or even a pain limited to peculiar organs of the body. It spreads through the whole texture of my frame. It is as if my body were, in its elder state, composed of frozen streams, which, in the moment of my rebirth, melt and swell, and force their turbulent passage through my limbs, with the violence of rivers loosed in Spring, with the dreadful heat of the red-hot streams that pour from the burning mountains of Sicily. I put off from day to day the moment of the draught, until, feeling the imminent approach of death itself, I face the terrible but lesser evil, and submit myself to the agony of resurrection.*"

About 1700 occur the first references to solitude and to a desire for companionship. It seems that he had become a little weary of his isolation, or that the experiment of sharing the Elixir with Michael has suggested to him that it might be possible to obtain better than a mere servant in exchange for the gift of immortality. But his heart had been too far destroyed to harbour so innocent a wish as that for friendship, and the following passage suggests a far more sinister reason for Killigrew's desire to entrap another into sharing Michael's position.

"*My companion shall be young. He shall drink for the first time in early youth, so as to return again to the age of strong desires and vigorous health, ever at variance with slothful virtue. He will the more readily tame his first remorse, lose his compunction in feeding the Elixir with the deaths of others, and, moreover, be better able to accomplish this task. Why should I risk my life in murders? Better will it be if some young man keep the Elixir red with power for us both. Lately I have feared detection, but, if this young man should be the sacrificing priest, none would believe his tale if he were caught, and I should but have profited even by the clumsiest of his killings.*"

That is dated 1705, eleven years before Killigrew actually carried his plan so far as to attempt to supply himself with a companion, a whipping boy who should risk the penalty of detection, while Killigrew should himself profit without peril at the cost of that young man's soul. Not until the autumn of the year before I met him, does he seem to have made any serious attempt, and then there is a long account of his difficulties in choosing this companion, of a stay in Paris, of an acquaintanceship with a student at the university which ended in nothing "*because I found the young man incurably religious.*" Then the idea seems to have come to him to use Rose as a bait for his snare. "*What Madeleine was for Michael so may Rose be for a more useful slave.*"

Lastly there are passages written in that very summer of 1716, some of which, affronting to my self-conceit, I copy with a certain pleasure in my humiliation. I set them down, just as they stand, a strange contrast to the flattery with which Killigrew had loaded me during my stay with him. My cheeks burned as I read them, and remembered the pride I had taken in his apparent friendship for me.

"*Accident, after so many disappointments, has provided me with the precise material I was seeking. Michael and I were almost despairing, and were indeed on our way to the Old Hall without the companion we had set out to find when we left Paris, when this youth walked into our arms.*" (It is clear that when he wrote this he had not perceived Michael's disaffection. Even in my humiliation it was a salve to my pride to notice this instance of Killigrew's obtuseness. R. S.) "*A youth, Stanborough, of a north-country family, far enough away, gifted with a sort of light cleverness, wholly ignorant and inexperienced, but of pleasant appearance, and accomplished in the empty manners of this age, which I can conveniently learn from him. His ignorance, his inexperience, his blind conceit, expose him to flattery, of which he is greedy. These qualities are also those which will best serve my purpose, for I may make him what I will before his own boyish character is sufficiently formed to resist the impress of the mould. In two months, I fancy, he will be all that I need. He shall then drink, and so through all the centuries, unless at last I find him useless, will return continually to this callow age of twenty-*

one. He is already so vain, so puffed with his scraps of learning, that he will be readily persuaded of his right to live on the deaths of other men without his futile knowledge. Perhaps he will at first wish to be assured that his victims are duller than himself I fancy he will be easily assured."

There are several entries in which he notes sarcastically the progress of his ascendancy over me. Then, the last entries in the book:

"*The youth has fallen readily into my plans. When the time comes, I have him in my power, for he and Rose think of nothing but each other. Any goodness in him, any ridiculous reluctance to feed the Elixir as it should be fed, will be destroyed if his passion for Rose continues, and she, too, drinks of the Elixir. He will hide the truth from her and feed her secretly with death with the same exalted feelings in his foolish heart as those with which, now, he presents her with a bunch of wild flowers.*"

Then, I fancy after a day on which I had listened eagerly to a long lecture from him on the philosophy of the ancients, he writes:

"*The cleverness of this boy, for with all his folly he has a sort of liveliness, promises that when I have lessened his ignorance he will be more than a mere sword in the Elixir's service. I find it pleasant to talk with him, for, unlike Michael, he does seem indeed to come near understanding what I say. Michael will become unnecessary to me and shall be destroyed.*"

Then, perhaps the next day:

"*What a fool this boy, Stanborough, is . . . what an incredible fool! Was I so foolish when I first became the pupil of Philodoxius, more than two hundred years ago?*"

Then, the last entry in the book:

"*Michael is nearing dissolution. He has begged for the Elixir. I shall let him suffer till to-morrow, so that he shall value it, and then give him the key. I shall need him another twenty years, till Stanborough feels the thirst of youth, and takes his place.*"

*　　　*　　　*

The little book, that record of a soul's swift progress towards damnation, is now burning in my hearth, its yellow parchment cover curling in the flames. And I sit here, and try to remember that strange night of long ago when, with its author separated from me by a single wall, I read it and learned how dreadful was the fate I had escaped. This, then, was the thing I had, almost unwillingly, refused at Rose's bidding. This was the secret that had lain behind Killigrew's offer of immortality, this the explanation of his anger at my refusal. This, then, was the Elixir of Life. A better name for it, I thought, would be the Elixir of Death. I saw Killigrew's life suddenly as a long plodding forward over the brittle skulls of better men. I knew now how true had been the instinct that told me Killigrew was hiding something from me, that night in the library when with his false, smooth frankness of manner he had seemed to be telling me all. This was what he had offered me with the appearance of generosity, a life like his, a long throttling in the cords of mortal sin, growing ever tighter and tighter, to lose in life all that was sweet and fair and honest in exchange for the power to go on living and sinking deeper and deeper into the quicksand of iniquity. You may imagine with what relief I considered my freedom from the slavery into which Killigrew had been determined to entice me. You may imagine how I looked on my unsuspecting intercourse with this man from whose soul, as I now saw, the last scrap of goodness had been swept by the imperious desire of life, or, perhaps, even less honourably, by the little quick besoms of the fear of death. And I had so narrowly escaped. I had been so ready, but for Rose, to place myself, body and soul, in his unscrupulous hands.

But for Rose: and then with dreadful clarity I saw once more the image of Michael standing there in the wood, waiting to be killed for having told something of the truth to Rose, in an effort to save me and to free her from Killigrew's dominion, an effort to expiate the crime of his fatherhood. I saw, of course, that he had meant me to read that book before the interview with Killigrew from which, thanks to Rose's note, I had escaped unsnared. Michael had paid with his life. Once, already, Killigrew had tried to murder me, whose presence on earth with the knowledge of his secret he could not suffer. And Rose also knew. Michael was gone. Were Rose and I, standing between Killigrew and the secrecy he had so long preserved, likely to have any better fate? And Rose? Had he already struck? I did not think so. I reminded myself over and over again of her whispered words in the garden. I could, in obedience to her, wait in my room, but, not even at her bidding, could I stay the alarms of my heart. I had trusted her once, in refusing Killigrew's offer, and I now knew she had been more than right. Yet, I had read that book, and knew Killigrew for what he was, knew that what I had seen that morning in the wood was but the last of a long series of dark evil deeds stretching back into the past. If Rose were dead, then I cared not what became of me. If she lived, then together, knowing our enemy, we might yet win free from that labyrinth of deceit and death. I prayed, and, upon my knees, felt that she lived, only a moment later to forget even the God to Whom I prayed, as I was blown this way and that by fierce gusts of foreboding, and of almost tearful anger at my impotence.

CHAPTER XIV
I Watch My Own Assassination

It was already night when I came to the last entries in that book, and slipped it back into my pocket. I flung myself wretchedly on my bed, and lay there miserable and angry. I thought of the pedlar, and wondered whether the doom that he had said was coming on the house would come before the falling of that more imminent doom which I felt hung over Rose and myself. Did Killigrew know that I had read his terrible confession? Where was Rose? There is no more unhappy state for a young man to be in than this of knowing that she he loves is in danger which might be averted by some swift, prompt action, and to know that action of any kind is impossible to him, and that he must wait, hands folded, for the reading of fate. I had blown out my candle, but, wilfully, had not undressed, and was tossing impatiently on my bed, when I heard a noise outside the little door leading into the rose-garden, a noise of stones being moved, a noise for which I could not at all account. Then I heard that little door open slowly.

I made sure at once that it was Killigrew, and that he had come to kill me. I supposed that he had already made away with Rose, and that it was his plan to kill us all, and go, to reappear again, when the Elixir had been re-fed on the deaths of murdered men. Believing Rose to be dead, I had no wish to live myself, but there came into my heart a fierce desire to be myself the executioner of Killigrew. I accordingly drew my sword noiselessly from its sheath, and sat on the edge of my bed, leaning forward, with the sword in my hand outstretched towards the little door. In that way, I thought, in my folly, my murderer will have no difficulty in finding me, and as he springs upon me, God will use my sword, toy as it is, for his transfixion. You see, I hoped that the murderer would succeed in his purpose. I did not wish to survive my vengeance, and remain in the world in which Rose was no longer, but I had at the same time a very proper repugnance to suicide, and more than that, a wish to join Rose in heaven, and not be cast alone into unhallowed ground, and be for ever in hell, in the company of Killigrew.

I could hear that whoever had opened that little door was now slowly crossing the room before me. I braced myself, and held my breath. Suddenly I felt something touch the point of my sword. The moment had come. In accordance with my plan, I should have drawn the sword back, but my instinct was too strong, and I thrust forward.

There was a stifled cry in the dark, and the next instant I had dropped my sword and was holding Rose in my arms.

"My darling, my darling," I said. "Forgive me."

"That little sword of yours," she said, "it will be the death of me yet. That is your second effort on my life. But oh, my dear, how glad I am you are alive!"

"Where are you hurt?"

"You put your sword through the palm of my hand," she said. "It is nothing, nothing at all. And you are alive. I was so dreadfully afraid I was too late. There is no time to lose now. Strike your tinder, and light the fire that lies ready in the hearth."

I did so, and presently the ruddy firelight was dancing on the walls of the room.

"Quick, quick," said Rose, "and now, come with me."

I followed her through the low doorway into the garden. The light was very dim, stars only, and no moon. Rose pointed to something that lay on the ground at our feet.

"As I came back," said she, "I came through the garden, and, you need not be too proud, sir, but I thought of you, and stayed a moment in the path here, and saw those."

I bent and examined more closely what she had pointed out to me. There were two big stones, plucked no doubt from some rotting corner of the ancient house.

"They lay there, close against the door, and I knew that they had been put there to prevent you from opening the door from the inside. Whoever put them there meant to keep you in your room this night, and, Dick, dear, I am terribly afraid."

The stones were heavy, and square, and it would have been quite impossible for me to open the door if they lay against the bottom of it, on the farther side.

"And you moved them away," I said, and caught her hand. My own was instantly wet.

"You are bleeding. Oh, Rose, what have I done?"

"It is nothing. Tie it with your kerchief. So. But now, look, look."

I looked where she was pointing, and saw that there was a faint light in the window next to mine.

"There is a ladder close by the trellis here," she said, "the little ladder the old pedlar used for tying the climbing roses."

I fetched it noiselessly, and was for setting it up at that other window.

"No, no," she said, "here. What does it matter to us what is done in that room? It was against your door that the stones were laid. And, before anything else, put the stones back."

I replaced the stones so as to prevent egress from my room and then set the ladder up against the wall under my window. Rose climbed it, using but one hand, poor girl, since I had hurt the other. I climbed after her, and stood on the step below, supporting her with my arm. We could both see into my room, which, as she had wisely planned, was lit by the leaping flames of the wood fire.

The flames lit up the whole room with an irregular, wavering light, and it was perhaps owing to this that, when I felt Rose stiffen in my arms, and saw that she was looking with a face of utter horror at my bed, it was a moment or two before I perceived what it was that caused her emotion.

The bed was one of ancient pattern, with a heavy canopy, supported on four pillars. I stared at it, through the narrow window, and, when, by chance, the flames steadied for a second into a dull red light, I saw that the canopy was slowly descending. Very slowly it sank between the pillars, and we could presently see that it was supported by four cords which passed over pulley-wheels through two holes in the wall into the room where we had seen the light. The canopy sank, lower and lower, until it was half way from the top of the pillars. Then, when, as I perceived in thinking it over afterwards, there was but slight fear of its jamming and so being held up before the conclusion of its descent, it fell suddenly, with a heavy, muffled thud, distinctly audible to us outside the window. It lay a foot and a half thick, fitting exactly over the bed where ten minutes before I had lain, and where, with the completest trust, I had slept during every night of my stay in the house.

I felt Rose shudder violently.

"If I had come home the other way," she said. "If I had been ten minutes later. If I had not loved you, and stopped just here in the path. Oh, thank God. Thank God."

I have often thanked Him since, for this as well as for many other of His manifold mercies, but I had hardly realized my escape, and was still staring stupidly at the closed trap in which I might so easily have been lying at that moment panting for breath, vainly struggling, a man buried alive in a padded coffin, when the door from the hall was flung violently open, and Killigrew danced into the room. I cannot otherwise describe the grotesque triumph of his entry.

He came in with a swaying, mincing step, and bowed towards the bed. Then he began, horrible as it is to relate, he began to dance, violently, earnestly, grimacing as he twirled and twisted in the firelight. I had already noticed that he had aged during these latter days of my stay in his house, but now, suddenly, old age seemed to have leapt on his shoulders, and shrivelled the skin of his cheeks, and bent his back, and thinned his arms and legs, until as they flung about they made him look like a skeleton elegantly dressed. His face was like a skull, and yet it was his face, unmistakably, even when, with grimaces so frightful that one felt instinctively that they cost him physical pain, he peered about, and put out his tongue like some insane devil escaped from the nethermost pit.

Suddenly he became serious, and once more solemnly bowed towards the bed.

"Good evening to you, Mr. Stanborough," he said in a thin shrill voice that was the more frightful to hear because by the fact of hearing it through the glass we knew that it must be pitched at the level of an uncontrolled scream.

He bowed, and waited, leaning forward, with a smile of mocking politeness on his shrunken face, as if he would not lose a syllable of the reply that the dead man, the man he supposed that he had murdered, would give him from under that canopy of death.

"Good evening, Mr. Stanborough, he screamed again. "You are a little deaf, my friend. It is dark in there, perhaps, and you cannot see that your admired instructor is waiting to converse with you."

Rose and I were frozen where we stood on the ladder, and could not stir if we had wished.

The thin shrill screeching voice went on, accompanied by exaggerated gestures.

"You can hear me in there, where better men have stifled before you. You can hear me. I know you blush for your enforced rudeness. You struggle, ah, you struggle, only to be able to reply to my civility.

"I will excuse you. You are tired, no doubt, thief, scoundrel, traitor, empty, grasping fool. So you are tired, after reading my *Imitatio Satana.* You are tired. Well, rest, my friend. We were such friends, were we not, Mr. Stanborough?

"You understand me now, Mr. Stanborough. You have read that book. You know that you are food for the Elixir you were too proud to share. That was your plan. You would refuse it when I offered it to you. You would talk of love. You would thank me. You would pretend doubt. And then, secretly, you steal it and plan to let me starve into old age and death. You and the pedlar's niece. The Adam and Eve of the new immortals. That was your idea."

"It is quite true," whispered Rose. "I am Michael's daughter, and the pedlar was his brother."

"I know," I whispered, and pressed her to me in the darkness.

"Then," screamed Killigrew, "you read my book. You learnt that you would have to pay for your immortality with your soul, and, pious youth, you hesitated. You learnt of the greed of the Elixir, and you were afraid. You a philosopher. You a student of Paracelsus.

"Ha, ha, ha," he broke into fantastic laughter. "I lose the pleasure of your companionship. But you would have been a poor companion. Sickly and serious. You have taught me more than I you, the manners of your generation, the fashionable tricks, and modern love. Ha, ha, ha. Do you remember, my sweet, stifling, thieving friend? . . . 'Oh Rose, if you will not have me, there is nothing in the world for me.'" He knelt for a moment, in absurd caricature of my attitude in the rose-garden, as I had seen him practising before the mirror.

I felt Rose shudder in my arms, and for one dreadful moment it occurred to me that she might think I had told him. But she set my mind at peace by finding my hand where it held the ladder and laying her own upon it.

"Well, my friend, Rose will not have you, and so I am very much afraid there is nothing in the world for you. Rose will not have you, and now that Michael is gone, and you also . . . you have yourself to thank if you taught me to make love. . . ."

He jumped up, and nodded at the bed, with an affectation of grave concern.

"Yes," he screamed, "it is with your own life that the pale fluid in the phial you stole is now glowing red. It is your life that will presently throb in my veins. Ah, I thirst, I thirst. My hands are wrinkled. My skin is dry. Because you, stealing the Elixir, have kept me from it too long. Another twelve hours and it would be too late. But now, my sweet friend, you lie there, and I have only to search your room, and to drink the Elixir that your death has enriched, and I . . . my throat . . . my throat . . . this thirst."

I was puzzled beyond measure by his evident belief that I had obtained possession of his Elixir. I did not even know what it was like. I was about to whisper to Rose, when with a sudden frenzy of hate, or, perhaps, pain, he leapt upon the bed itself, pranced there, like a maniac, grimacing frightfully, and with a shrill echoing laugh, plunged his long sword clean through the heavy cushioned canopy. He chose the spot with gleeful precision, and drove the sword straight downwards, like a man spearing eels. In spite of myself, in spite of the knowledge that I was really outside the window, on a ladder, with Rose, I felt that sword pass cold between my shoulders, and rasp against my backbone.

He leapt from the bed, leaving the sword sticking in it, buried almost to the hilt. The idea came into my mind that the sword hilt, quivering there on the thin stem of the sword, was a crucifix, and the man in the red firelight a devil. I remembered a picture I had somewhere seen.

Killigrew began to search the room. He looked first for my clothes, and found a quantity in a wardrobe, which he pulled out and hurriedly felt through, clawing at every morsel of lining or lappet, like one of those monkeys that have been lately brought from Africa. He continued his search, with movements made grotesque by their very speed, and by the fact that it was impossible to foresee them. He seized a chair, and, as if in a single movement, placed it beside the wardrobe and leapt upon it. He looked on the top of the wardrobe, and perhaps finding the flickering fire gave an insufficient light, he sprang down, grabbed the candle from my table, thrust it in the flames, and drew it out, dripping wax, and flaring like a torch.

With this in his hand, he sprang again to the chair, and examined the top of the wardrobe. Then, kicking the chair aside, he jumped down, and began ransacking the drawers of the writing table. He pulled the drawers clean out, and threw everything in them on the floor after each thing had passed through his fingers. He felt even the handkerchiefs, pressing them, to make sure that nothing was hidden between them. I knew that he was looking for the book.

Suddenly, when he was going through the third drawer, he gave a squeal of odious triumph.

"The Elixir," he screamed, and pulled out a folded cream-coloured shirt in which something was evidently wrapped. He undid it with swift convulsive movements and the face of a greedy child.

Suddenly he howled with rage, pulling from it a small square book, which I recognized at once as a little foolscap copy of the Gospels which had belonged to my nurse, Mistress Barber. She, dear soul, had doubtless slipped it in with the clothes I had asked her to send. I remembered the Yorkshire cake, and, even in that strange moment, smiled to think of my dear old Babkins, and her present of a cake and the Gospels, which I knew she prized, although she could not read them.

Killigrew in his anger half tore off the cover of the book, in opening it, and, when he saw what it was, he thrust it deep into the fire, so deep that he must have scorched his hand in doing so, and had a foretaste of hell. I noticed that he did not seem to feel it, and wondered if he would be equally callous in the hereafter.

Then he returned to the drawers, and went on with his search. He began now to lose his air of insolent, fiendish delight. He began to search more wildly, sometimes plunging his hands into the heap on the floor, as if he thought there was something there which had escaped his notice.

Suddenly an idea came to him. He jumped up, and I saw that he was looking for my shoes. Of course he could not find them. His face became baffled, and even more hideous, and he rushed at the little door into the garden.

I thanked God for Rose's foresight in making me replace those stones where she had found them, against the foot of the door. He tried the door and, satisfied that I had not gone out, returned again to his search. No doubt he would have heard me had I gone out by the other door, if indeed he had not locked it from without, which I begin to think probable.

He looked, for the first time irresolutely, at the bed.

"Ah, Mr. Stanborough," he said, in a voice only a little higher than was ordinary to him, so that it was more difficult for me to hear what he was saying. "Ah, Mr. Stanborough, so even in death you are my enemy. You have read my book, and learnt that after all these years I do not like to touch the dead.* No doubt you thought of that when you lay down to die with the Elixir, and the book, beneath your pillow."

Then he laughed.

"I had forgotten," he cackled, "you did not know that you lay down to die. I must acquit you of that. You had the insolence to suppose I would not kill you, even for the sake of the very fount of life. Poor fool. Since you were so mad, it may yet be that, the things are hidden in the room, and that I shall not have to soil my hands and sully my eyes by searching your body, by seeing you lie as I shall never lie. For ever and ever, world without end, in saecula saeculorum, vivat Iohannes."

His voice broke, and he set himself again to search the room. He held up my riding boots and shook them. He dived with his hand into the ewer. He began to hesitate, and stood in the middle of the room, grimacing with what seemed like fright. I thought he was about to break into hysterical weeping.

He turned towards the bed, and began whispering, rapidly. I could see his lips working, but, of course, could not hear a sound.

Then he rushed suddenly out of the room.

We had not time to wonder what he was about to do, when that question was answered for us. The ropes by which the canopy had been sustained, which were now hanging loosely above it, suddenly tightened. The canopy, after a moment's hesitation, began to rise again, very slowly, lifting the sword with it.

At this moment Rose pressed her fingers tightly on my hand. "Take me away," she whispered, "take me away."

---

*This is a reference to a very disgusting passage in the confession which I have preferred not to translate.

The spell laid on me by the horror of the scene we had just wit-nessed was broken, and I knew that in a few minutes Killigrew would know that he had failed in his attempted murder, and that I had es-caped with, in my possession, the book that was filled with his own evi-dence against himself. I thought of going into the house and fighting with him then and there, but I reflected that if by any chance he should kill or even wound me, without dying himself, Rose would be at his mercy. There was no question that it was politic to remove Rose as soon as possible to a place of safety, from which I could return to settle my account with Killigrew. Looking back now, from a distance, on the whole of that extraordinary adventure, I find nothing more strange in it than this readiness on my part to assume that I could on equal terms stand up against that man, who, I knew, had proved himself more than man and worse than man in the long course of his horrible career. In the excitement of the moment I was blind to a sort of towering great-ness that there was in him, even in his madness, even in his villainy. It may seem odd that I should talk of reverence in connection with such a scoundrel. But there was that in him which only my extreme youth, confirmed in its confidence by the love of the sweetest of women, could have disregarded.

As silently as possible, I descended from the ladder, and received Rose in my arms, and lowered her to the ground. Her wounded hand had been bleeding through my kerchief, and, though she had not no-ticed it while we had both been fascinated by the sight of Killigrew, now that we were preparing to escape from him, she felt the weakness caused by the loss of blood. I feared that she would faint. I supported her as well as I could, and we went out of the rose-garden and to the stable.

We had scarcely reached the stable-yard, when the silence of the autumn night was broken by a series of screams so loud, so hoarse with anger and fear, that I felt the skin of my face quiver on my cheekbones.

Rose recovered herself quicker than I.

"He knows that you are not dead," she whispered, and, with fren-zied haste, I unfastened the latch of the stable-door.

CHAPTER XV

The Last of the Old Hall

We had no sooner opened the stable-door than we became aware of the completeness of Killigrew's preparations. I had expected to find three horses sleeping in the darkness. Instead there was a lantern lit and hanging from a beam and, tied to a ring, finishing a bucket of oats, was the big black horse, saddled and ready for the road. The mare and the other horse were nowhere to be seen. It was clear to me that Killigrew had meant that night to bring to an end his habitation of the hall, and, destroying the witnesses of his past, to ride off again into the world. He had killed old Michael. We had just seen him murder me, as he supposed. He would then have taken the Elixir, which he evidently believed that I had stolen, and ridden off, to reappear in some distant place as a young man of twenty-five with considerable charm of manner and a profound knowledge of philosophy. And Rose? There was but the black horse saddled. Was Rose not to have ridden with him? What had he meant to do with her? I secretly shuddered. Was she, like myself, to have been food for his horrible Elixir? Had Killigrew intended to grow young not only on my death but also on hers?

"He had meant to ride away?" said Rose, wondering.

"Yes. Alone," I replied, and began unfastening the horse.

"But where are the other horses?"

"I am sorry for the black," I said, "but this is no time for looking for horses in the dark. We must do the best we can with what Killigrew meant for himself."

"Quick, quick," she said, "I can hear steps."

Well, I had the horse outside in a moment, patted his neck, told him that I had great faith in him, and was trusting him with what I valued most on earth, and then, lifting Rose to the top of the mounting-steps that were against the stable wall, I sprang to the saddle, gathered her into my arms, and freeing my right hand for the reins, touched the horse with my heels, and rode out of the yard into the darkness of the park.

I was anxious to get as soon as possible to the road leading to the great gateway, and so away, for I did not know how long it would take me, without moonlight, to find my way through the glades and woodland paths which I commonly used. I therefore turned to the left out of the yard, and keeping some distance from the house, moved slowly, lest galloping hoofs should betray us to Killigrew, who, for all I knew, was already on his way to the stable.

It was very dark, and I put down the noises of wheels on grass, and tramping feet, and whispering voices to my own fancy, stirred and disordered by the events of the last two days, until, suddenly, I perceived that there were dull torches moving in the darkness, here and there. Whichever way I looked I seemed to see faint moving lights. I told myself vehemently that they were no business of mine, and that I need think of nothing but of getting Rose to a place of safety, anywhere outside the Killigrew grounds, anywhere in the world of reality. I suddenly banged the horse's sides with my heels. The big beast sprang forward, and I was almost thrown from the saddle, with my precious burden, when the bridle was grasped by a man, and the horse brought to a sudden standstill in the very moment of its forward leap.

"The wizard! The wizard! Help there, some of you! Trying to make off. The devil in the form of a great horse. Help me there!"

There was a sudden rush of men over the grass, a torch appeared as if from nowhere, and was thrust flaming up into our faces.

The black horse reared tremendously, but there were three men now at his head. A man tried to seize Rose, and drag her from my arms. I struck downwards, and drove my fist into his face. He recoiled, but from that position my blow could be but weak, and he sprang at me again, crying, "Kill them! Kill them! Wizard and witch! Kill them!"

He grabbed my leg, and began pulling me from the saddle. At the same moment, just as I was striking at him again (I could not get at my sword), I felt that another had seized Rose from the other side.

I do not know what would have happened, if at that moment the mob about us had not been suddenly quieted by the sound of a voice, which I recognized at once as that of the pedlar at the gate.

"Now, men," the voice came out of the darkness, old, strange, but unmistakably the voice of one who would be obeyed, "whom have you got there?"

"The wizard and the witch," cried the man at my leg.

I struck him again, and called out:

"Master pedlar, I beg you bid these men let us go."

In another second I saw the pedlar. He stood like a prophet, surrounded by a mob of fanatic believers. Torches waved. He stood there, very tall, with his long hair, his eyes flashing in the fitful light. I saw that most of his followers were carrying great bundles of straw. A little way off was a cart, piled with straw, moving slowly through the dark towards the house.

"Fools," he said to his men, "did I not tell you to lay hands on none save Killigrew himself? These are neither wizard nor witch, but children flying from the devil. Not them, but the devil, it is our business to slay."

Then he came close up to the horse.

"Young man," he said, "you are taking my advice and saving alive your soul and hers. To-night the end is accomplished. To-night is the vengeance of the Lord. To-night this house of iniquity will rise in flames, a burnt sacrifice welcome to the Lord. And I am the instrument of God."

I had no time to answer him. He suddenly changed his voice, which became that of an old, old man, no longer fired with prophecy. He pulled from a pocket in the skirts of his long coat a bundle and a leather bag tied together.

"Take these," he said, "with an old man's blessing, who sees that there may yet be happiness in the world. The bundle is Rose's dowry, and in the bag is money for your journey, and I beg you for your own sakes to put as great a distance as you may between yourselves and this place. God knows what will happen here to-night. Go far, and, if you can, forget all that you leave behind. You are children, and the world is before you. Young man, you need not quarrel with me because I give you money for your travelling." (I had said nothing, but the pedlar seemed to know my thoughts.) "It is a wedding present, and you will need it, if only for Rose. And now," he said, "God have you in His keeping, for ever and ever. Amen."

Those were the last words we heard him say. He turned from us towards the house. A torch was waved. Instantly other torches answered from all sides, and a ring of flaming torches closed about the house. We waited there on the great black horse, watching the torches, which showed that a great number of men were about the house. Inside the house a light moved rapidly about, and then disappeared. Before the door many torches gathered, and it seemed to me that I saw the tall figure of the pedlar standing there, a head and shoulders above the crowd, his arms outstretched, prophesying. Suddenly the door opened. The hall was full of light. Whether Killigrew had himself set fire to the house from within to help his own escape I do not know, but the opened door showed like a great square of light in the darkness of the house, beyond the torches. I could see nothing in that square, nothing, that is, inside the door. But on that square of light the tall gaunt figure of the pedlar stood out like a crucifix.

Suddenly two pistol-shots rang out, one after the other in close succession, and the door swung to, leaving the whole face of the house black as before. There was a movement among the torches, and I could no longer see the pedlar.

"The pedlar is dead!" whispered Rose.

"I know," I answered, and indeed I not only knew that the pedlar was dead, but that he had himself known that he was going to die. His work was done. The pistol-shots had scarcely sounded before a great flame flared up behind the house, a thin, light flame, climbing up above the house into the sky, and dying down again.

Flames sprang up all round the house, close under the walls. Some of them we could see. Others showed themselves only as a sudden lightening of the sky. In the light of the flames were men running, with great bundles of straw and faggots on their backs.

"The pedlar could not have had a happier end," I said.

Just then a flame shot out from the side of the house, and travelled swiftly towards the wood. It was a moment before I realized that the trellis of the rose-garden was on fire.

"Poor old man," whispered Rose, and I felt like weeping myself. But I choked down that weakness and replied:

"No. All these years he has waited for this day. All the years that he spent among those roses there were flames in his head. He has thought of nothing but the end of this house. And the end has come, and he has lived to see it and to bring it about."

And with that I turned the horse upon the grass-grown road, and he presently broke into a canter. The darkness before us was made the deeper by the ruddy light which leapt up again and again behind us, throwing forward the shadow of the great horse as he carried us away from the hall that had been the witness of so strange, so intricate a story. As we galloped, I thought of the innumerable dead who had been sacrificed to that man's life, and wondered if the rustle in the woods, the rising wind, were the ghosts of the Elixir's victims, hurrying to see the end of their executioner.

We passed here and there men and women, running towards the house always in twos and threes, and, I noticed, holding each other's hands, less, I thought, because of the darkness than because of the fear that had hung about the house for nearly two hundred years. They were like children bravely running into a wolf's den, when the wolf is dead, and, for all that, frightened by their memory of the dread in which they held him when alive. Here and there was a torch, and each face I saw was lit by the same expression, of fear, of vengeance, of fanaticism, The faces were horrible, and I shielded Rose from seeing them.

A strange noise made me, in spite of my eagerness to be gone and to carry Rose to a place where she might forget all this, tighten the reins of the horse. He slackened his pace, to a trot, to a walk. The men and women in the park were singing. They were singing a hymn, even while the flames licked up the ivy, and plucked at the boarded windows of the house that stood in those desolate grounds, like an evil thing threatening the simple life of man. I turned and looked back. There were woods between me and the house, but when, suddenly, the singing broke into a great, terrible shout, I saw a huge sheet of flame leap up above the trees, lighting, as it seemed, the whole world. It seemed to me that burning beams were blown up to heaven in that monstrous flame. Then there was a slow, rumbling crash, and the flame sank suddenly and rose again not so high, although the sky seemed now to be red with blood from its zenith to where its horizon lay below the trees.

"I think that is the end of the old hall," I said, and sent the black forward again. In a few minutes we were at the gate.

There was a crowd of women at the gate, and I had once more to rein in the horse. They were holding torches, and staring at something in the midst of them. At the sound of the horse's hoofs they separated a little, though still blocking the road, and I saw, lit by their torches, that same old woman whom Killigrew had addressed on the occasion of the race which so very nearly ended my life. You will remember how he spoke to her, and how she, on seeing who he was, had fallen into a fury of fear and hate. She was kneeling on the ground by the fallen griffon. Her hands were raised above her head, her skinny arms showing through her rags. Her face was distorted by the violence of the denunciation she was shrieking at the sky. I remembered what the pedlar had told me of the little girl, and I thought that here was another of the crimes of the Elixir risen from the past to call down vengeance upon Killigrew.

Suddenly she saw us, and recognized the black horse.

She rose, screaming, to her feet.

"The black horse," she shrieked, "the black horse. Accursed! Accursed!"

The women who were with her closed in round us like a brood of furies.

I did not know what to do. I could hardly ride over them, and, if I did not, and they once laid hands on us, it would certainly go hard with us. I have never seen such faces.

Rose saved us. She looked fearlessly towards the women, and cried out, "Let us go, good people, for the pedlar sent us, and . . . let us go, good people, for the pedlar is dead."

She broke into weeping there in my arms.

But the women hesitated, and made way, and the great horse, answering my heel, passed swiftly through them, and broke into a gallop on the road, as behind us the silence which, on Rose's words, had succeeded the angry threats of the women, was wrung with a terrible lamentation.

Through all these latter years, I supposed, the pedlar, fanning the distrust of the villagers, promising them at last a vengeance for their dead, had seemed to stand between them and the great house with its walled park. He alone was not afraid. They did not know that the house was burning, and that the day of vengeance had indeed come. They knew that their sons, their brothers, their husbands had gone in there, led by the pedlar, and strong in his presence and in their faith, to fulfil what they believed to be the will of God. And then, the pedlar dead, their faith was taken from them, and they were like lost souls. They did not know, I thought, that the vengeance was accomplished, and Killigrew dead, as well as the pedlar.

And then the knowledge came to me, as clearly as if I had at that moment seen him at my side with a smile upon his mocking lips, that the vengeance of God was not fulfilled, and that Killigrew was still alive. Not only that, but I remembered his face as I had seen it through the window of my room. I remembered his words. I knew that he believed that I had stolen the Elixir, and that therefore there was nothing possible to man or devil that he would leave undone in order to recapture us, and, as he supposed, obtain possession of the loathsome means to continue his horrible career.

I said nothing of this to Rose, but pressed the sides of the black horse, and considered in my mind what we should do. Supposing he should catch us up, I thought, and demand that I should give up Rose, what proof had I that she was not his ward? Her protestations would merely convince any magistrate before whom he caused us to be taken of the justice of his claim. As for the book, he would say I had written it myself. I knew very well that he would shrink from nothing to accomplish his end, and, the more I considered our position, the more precarious it seemed. There were only two places in England where I could feel that Rose would be safe, and those two places were Bigland Hall away in the north country and my uncle's house in London. London was much the nearer. Killigrew would, I thought, suppose that we should take the London road. I resolved accordingly to make for that inn where I had first met him, and then, instead of turning southwards to London, turn northwards to Yorkshire and the hills—two hundred and fifty miles of road.

The village, as we galloped through it, was a village of the dead. I have ridden through many a village by night, and there is always a strange, lonely feeling about such a ride. The noise of the hooves on the road, when there is no other sound, and all the windows are dark and blind, and not one soul calls out to speed your going, and you know that your galloping hooves are merely making a noise in the dreams of sleeping folk—there is a strange, queer feeling in that, but it is very different from the feeling of that night as we rode on the great black horse that had so often carried Killigrew through this village, where all was dark, but not one man or woman asleep. I heard a door bang and a child cry. I knew that in one of those houses all the children of the village must be gathered, perhaps with an old crone to guard them, while the rest of the villagers were gone to the grim business of ending the terror that had lain on them all so long. The houses were dark and empty. We had seen the dwellers in those cottages in the park, those men mad with fear and fanaticism, those old women at the gate. They were singing hymns about the burning of the old house, and I thought how they would come back, their minds scorched by that deed of vengeance, expecting at last to live with joy and freedom, and finding the memory of the past still too strong for them. It will be a hundred years yet, I thought, before the children in this village will grow up with no worse terrors than naughty Puck or Lob-lie-by-the-fire. And then I wondered how long it would be before Rose would forget the horror of the villainy with which Killigrew had surrounded her childhood, and I wondered how much of it she had perceived. Perhaps she did not know all. God grant she did not, I thought, as I encouraged the big horse, and we left that empty shell of a village behind us on the road.

I knew we had a fair start of Killigrew, even if he had escaped, and I had no intention of putting ourselves at his mercy, by riding the horse to a standstill. Presently I made him walk.

"Where are we going?" Rose asked, and I was glad of the sound of her voice.

"We are going home," said I.

"Home?"

"Ay, home, to the north."

"And Mistress Barber?"

"Ay," said I. "Babkins will be there I hope, and if not, she soon will be, and she shall look after you for me, until . . ." And then I stopped, for I was not quite sure if I dared say what was in my mind.

"Until?" asked Rose.

I dropped the reins on the neck of the black horse, and gave her my answer in a kiss. That was bolder than the words, but, somehow, it was easier. And Rose kissed me back, and suddenly clung to me and broke into a passion of weeping.

I kissed her again and again, and now a torrent of words came to my lips, for the most part quite meaningless, such words as one would use to a frightened child.

We rode on.

I think we must have left the village some fifteen miles behind us when, after slowly climbing a long rise, we looked back over the broad country below us, and saw, far away on the horizon, the glow of a great fire. There were low hills between us and the old hall, so that we could not see the fire itself. This glow in the sky, a broad wavering glimmer of red in the night, was the last we saw of that strange, desolate place, that grim house, where I had turned from boyhood to manhood, and in doing so had found the only thing on earth that is more precious than philosophy.

As we turned and rode round a clump of trees, and began the descent on the farther side, I think we both felt that we were riding out of one life into another. On the horizon behind us, we had left that crimson, angry glow. On the horizon before us were the first pale lights of the coming dawn.

CHAPTER XVI

We Decide to Remain Mortal

At the bottom of that slope was a long stretch of level road, and for some time we galloped, and for that reason alone could not talk. My mind played continually over the last time I had ridden through this country, in my fine black clothes, with Killigrew and poor old Michael, full of exuberant delight in Killigrew's discourse on philosophy, and, at the same time, puzzling over the warning that had been given me by the old servant. There was much in it that I did not yet understand, although a good deal had been explained by the odious confessions in the brown book, which I could feel bobbing in my pocket.

When at last we came to another upward pitch, I thought it well to let the black walk. I dismounted, and set Rose in the saddle, and walked beside her as we slowly climbed the hill together. She sat there with her wonderful hair in disarray, her eyes like a sleepy child's, what with her tears and the fatigue of the night, and I walked beside her, exulting in her presence, and in the morning, and in the new life that opened before me, enjoying a sort of triumph with every step I took. I set my feet down firmly on the ground, and won a sort of ecstasy from that. I felt I could have walked a hundred miles. I felt it was really a miracle that I could keep my feet to the ground.

I looked up at Rose and saw that she was smiling at me.

"You will always be a child, Dick," she said; "always younger than I."

I did not answer this directly, but brought out what was in my mind.

"Why was it that you did not wish me to come?"

"Because I did not think that things would turn out as they have. Because I feared Killigrew. Because I thought that he could make me do what I least wished to do. Because . . . I knew what was waiting for you in that house, and I did not know . . . much that I know now."

"Tell me."

"I did not know that I should love you, for one thing."

I kissed her hand, and she went on:

"But even if I had known that, I think . . . I think I should still more have wished you not to come."

"But why, Rose?"

"For your own sake. I knew that Mr. Killigrew wished you to share his life, and be like him. And that was dreadful. Ever since I can remember I have lived with him, fearing him and knowing that he was bad, oh, and cruel. And old Michael must have feared him never to tell me the truth about himself. I cannot think of old Michael even now as my father. He was always the other one that was afraid of Mr. Killigrew. And Killigrew . . . my brother . . . I remember nothing but fear. And the secret. That was like a cloud shutting us all in together. Old Michael, and that man, and I."

"You knew his secret?"

"Ever since I was a little child. . . . I never was a little child."

"My dear," I said, "if you never were, you will be as soon as you meet Mistress Babkins."

"Ever since I can remember I knew that he had a terrible physic which made him live longer than men, and grow young every time he drank it. Lately he would have me near him when he drank it. And I knew that it was an agony to him to drink it, and nearly always, after he drank it, we had to move on somewhere else. And I knew that if ever other people knew of this it would be ill for all of us. I saw that old Michael himself was afraid of other people knowing."

"You know that old Michael begged me not to come, and that was why I came."

"Yes," she said. "When first Killigrew said that we were coming to that house, and that he was going to let some young man share our life, old Michael quarrelled with him. They sent me from the room, and when I came back I knew that old Michael had been crying."

"Poor old Michael." I reflected that probably he felt he was sealing the warrant of his own damnation in letting Killigrew beguile another into the service of the terrible Elixir. I privately hoped that she did not know the full horror of that mystery, and that the man who was her father had himself drunk from it. That, of course, she knew, but to this day her step is the lighter, her eye the clearer, for the fact that she has never learnt that the power of the Elixir came from the deaths of other men. That she has never known, nor will she ever.

"Poor old Michael," she said. "I think of him so. I cannot think of him any other way. He was the only one I could trust, till you came, and I could not always trust him against Killigrew. Dear Dick, I feel I have no right to come into your life, with such a cloud of wretched memories. Oh, thank God that it is all over."

I wondered secretly if it was all over, but was too glad to see her hope of happiness to say so, and instead asked a question which I had long wished to ask.

"It was not Killigrew who taught you to thank God?"

"No, that was old Michael. Killigrew did not like it."

I thought of old Michael, giving his daughter faith in the God he knew he had grievously offended, teaching her the simple sweet rites of the religion from which he had cut himself off by service of Killigrew and the Elixir, and comforting himself as a damned soul by the thought of the child he loved but dared not own, kneeling at her prayers.

Suddenly my mind shot back to that terrible scene of the night when Killigrew had searched in my room for the lost Elixir. I saw his haggard face, insane with desire, and I said to Rose:

"You know Killigrew was wrong last night in thinking that I had stolen the Elixir. I have not the smallest idea as to where it is."

For a moment she looked at me with indecision. Then with a smile of grave but childish trustfulness, she said:

"I know. Michael gave it to me, to destroy."

She put her hand into the bosom of her dress, and brought out a small black case of carved wood, and gave it to me, as I walked there by her side. It was a little black wooden tube. At either end of it was carved the emblem that I had seen on Killigrew's ring, a wheel, with a snake encircling it, holding its tail in its mouth. Round the body of the case were also snakes carved, curling round it in such a way that it was impossible to find a beginning or an end. The little case was strangely heavy for its size.

I begin now to believe that the devil had indeed some hand in the making of that accursed thing, for, as I held it in my hand, the Elixir that I had refused when Killigrew offered it, I felt an elation for which I could not account. There it was in my hands, the wish of all the world. I had read that terrible book in which Killigrew confessed the wickedness that, at the bidding of that thing, had sprung and flourished in his soul. Even two minutes before I had been thanking God that I was taking Rose away from the dark life that had been due to it, away from those grim shadows to the sunlight of the simple world that lives and grumbles and dies and makes its peace with mortality. And yet, with that little wooden box in my hand, I felt cunning creep into my eyes, I knew that my lips smiled with a joy that was not one I could tell even to myself. I felt that I was already hiding something, and greedily looking forward to the time when I should have more to hide. A glorious dawn was spreading in the east before us. Birds were singing, and beside me on the tired black horse sat Rose, yet my fingers tingled about that little black case, and I looked with blind eyes at the sunrise, and listened with deaf ears to the birds, and was conscious of Rose, for a moment, only as of one from whom I had a secret to keep.

"Dick, Dick, I beg you not to look like that. Oh, Dick, did I do wrong to keep it? Michael told me to destroy it, because he could not. And I . . . I thought . . . Oh, Dick!"

"You did very right," I said, in a voice that was not my own, holding the little box tightly in my hand.

"No. No. I did wrong. I knew that I did wrong, for I could not tell the pedlar that I had not destroyed it. When I went to him—was it only yesterday?—I told him Michael was dead, and I meant to tell him all. But I could not. And now, Dick, Dick! Oh, Dick, I wish I had destroyed it then."

"No," I said, and still my voice did not seem to be mine. "You did very right. Do you know that here is that which will let us live for ever as young as we are now? We can live for ever, and be lovers always, while the world grows old about us, and houses crumble into dust, and trees grow old and die, and philosophies spring up and are forgotten."

And even while I said this, I remembered the dreadful cost of the Elixir, and knew that if we were to drink it, I should have to feed it with murder, and wither my soul with sin.

"Remember Killigrew," said Rose. "Remember Michael. They got little joy from it."

"We are different."

I knew she did not know the whole truth, and yet, so horribly had that accursed thing worked on my mind, that I wished her to agree, so that I might agree also, and tell myself that I did so for her sake. I wished to be able to tell myself that I damned my soul for her sake even while I well knew that I was led to wish this by nothing but my own iniquitous desire.

"We are different," I urged. "We are lovers, and the Elixir has been put into our hands because ours is a love that should endure through all the ages, a lantern lit by Heaven in the world." Thus I blasphemed.

"Dick," said Rose, "let me tell you why it is here."

"I listen."

"Michael had given it me in the garden. He was crying then, because he had not been able to destroy it. And I, I took it with me, when I went to give his message to the pedlar. I meant to throw it away. My dear, dear Dick, I understand you, because, when I wished to throw it away, I could not. I was mad. I wanted to keep it for ever. I remembered how it had been a dreadful shadow over us all. I remembered everything. But, with it there . . . in my hands . . . I could not. And then I prayed there in the woods. And I was free. I could have destroyed it then. I was happy and came home, thanking God, who had saved me . . . and when I saw the stones at your door, and knew that a few min-

utes later would have left me alone with it and without you, I knew that
He had forgiven me. . . .

"Dear, in the wood, I could have destroyed it, but I kept it, for your
sake. It came to me that if I were to do that, I should be taking the
choice out of your hands. Dear, don't you see, you are taking me from
all that darkness, and I wanted you, too, to be able to throw away the
thing which, in Killigrew and Michael, has been a shadow over my life. I
wanted to put it in your hands, and see you take it, and destroy it, so
that there should be one less source of evil in the world, and so that we
could start on our life together, knowing that there was nothing left
which could pull us back from the sunshine into the shadow. Oh, Dick
you must understand. I took it because for the sake of our life, I wanted
you to be the one to throw it away."

I could not answer her. My mind was twisting this way and that in
effort to find a way of justifying my keeping the Elixir. In the library,
when Killigrew had offered it me, and had urged me to it with such elo-
quence as he possessed, the written word of Rose had been enough to
make me definitely refuse it. But now, when Rose herself was urging me
against it, when I could see in her eyes her fear for the whole future of
our happiness, I held that thing in my hand, and against its horrible
power the sweetness and wisdom of the wisest and sweetest of women
were powerless as a daffodil to stop the wind. I knew that she was suffering, but the touch of that carven ebony case in my hand had made me
cruel as Killigrew. I thought of nothing but the gaining of my end. Everything that should have held me went for naught. I did not forget the
grim story in Killigrew's book, nor the agony of his cry in the night, nor
the fact that Rose too would have to bear such pain if I persuaded her. I
forgot none of these things, but I walked by the side of the horse, not
looking at Rose, glancing this way and that with furtive, unseeing eyes.

Suddenly Rose slipped down from the saddle and flung her arms
about my neck.

"Dick," she said, "I can ride no farther into a new life, until we have
made up our minds and know whether or no we are going to regret the
old. Let us have this talk out. I am willing to listen to all you have to
say, and I have something also for your ears."

We had reached the top of the hill. Before us in the morning
sunlight lay the broad rolling country of middle England, woods and
farms and fields where the corn had been cut, and the scarlet poppies
had sprung up again among the stubble. Behind us, the hill we had
climbed threw all in the shadow. At the side of the road was a low
bank, and the opening of a lane into a wood, already gold with autumn.
The bank was dry, and we sat down there, with our feet in the road, for

all the world like a couple of gipsies, while the tired black horse cropped the long grass at the roadside, and presently made his way up the bank, and set to the enjoyment of the less dusty grass that grew about the opening of the path into the wood.

"Now Dick," said rose, "tell me all that is in your mind. You trusted me before, when I asked you to refuse Killigrew when he offered you the thing that you hold in your hand. Tell me why it is that you do not trust me now."

I shame myself in writing down this dialogue in which my part was so unworthy, but, perhaps, that shame will in some small measure expiate my weakness. I felt like a schoolboy asked a question in the Latin grammar, who, having once said he does not know the answer, holds sullenly to his ignorance, and sets a mask of stupidity upon his face. For I could not tell Rose all that was in my mind. Against my own judgment, despite my knowledge, I wished to overrule her wiser instinct. Knowing all that I did, I yet deliberately closed my mind to that knowledge, and told myself over and over again, as if I were likely to forget it, that I held immortality there in my hand, and might be for ever freed from the fear of death. I thought of all the cold unpleasing circumstances of human decease, of the odour of the dead, of the damp churchyard bed, of the weight of earth above the body. I saw myself dead, under the earth, in a rotting coffin, a putrid body, with the vilest of worms crawling slowly through the sockets of my eyes, exploring the recesses of my brain. And then I turned to Rose, and spoke of deathless love, and of how we two might live for ever, young, joyful, with the strength of our limbs and the light of youth in our eyes! I spoke as if I were moved by hope, when, in reality, I was moved by craven fear.

And Rose sat there beside me, listening, with tears in her eyes.

I would not let myself look at her, as she sat there, with the sunlight making a glory of her hair. I turned over in the grass, and lay on my belly, playing with the little black carven box.

And then I opened the box.

Within it was a small phial of thin glass, such glass as the Venetians blow, very delicate in shape, ornamented with a glass snake, which, curling round the body of the phial, twisted up at last, so that its narrow neck and head became the phial's mouth, so fine, and thin, that the liquid within would pour out slowly, a drop at a time. The divided tongue of the snake made the stopper, and the Elixir, when the tongue was removed, would trickle out from the hideous little head of the reptile.

As I pulled it out from its black case, Rose uttered a little cry of horror.

"It has turned to blood," she said. "I looked at it before, and it was as pale as thin milk, and now . . . is it the sunlight?"

The liquid in the phial was like melted rubies. I shaded it with my hand, and knew that it was not the sunlight that made it gleam as if there were a fire burning within it. I knew whence came that fire. I knew it came from the life of murdered men. We had heard those pistol-shots, but the death of the old pedlar could hardly have loosed so much life for the feeding of the Elixir. No. Killigrew had had other victims. I knew now, for sure, that he had escaped, and wondered what had happened away there in the dark about the burning house, and how many of those frightened fanatic villagers had paid with their lives for their attempt to lift the fear of death from their children and their children's children. I saw Killigrew in a frenzy of rage, rushing here and there in the darkness, killing and killing, an invisible death swift moving among those who had come with hymns and with the hatred of long years to put an end to him, and to destroy the house that had been an outpost of the powers of hell, walled in, brooding beside the village where they had lived, and seen first one and then another die mysteriously, or disappear for ever within that high wall, that ring of ominous great trees. Then the thought came to me that the redness of the Elixir promised life to me, that I should not have to pay for in murder. Already in that phial were lives waiting to flow into my veins when I should have need of them. My only wish now was to keep the Elixir for myself and Rose, my only fear lest Killigrew should overtake us and demand his share in it.

I was just springing up, to proceed upon our way. For an instant, I left the Elixir on the ground, lest I should break it as I scrambled to my feet, when Rose put out her hand and took it. She did not snatch it. She just put out her hand and took it, as if unconscious of my jealous wish not to lose possession of it, even to her.

For a moment, such was the madness which the touch of that thing had roused in me, I felt a sort of rage. I would have seized it from her, even struck her, Rose, whom I loved.

But she looked at me gravely, and said, "You need not fear, Dick, I will give it back to you," and I stood in front of her utterly abashed.

The madness of the last few minutes passed from me like a blown cloud, when I no longer held the phial in my hands. I was shaken, weak, as if I had had a fever, and I heard Rose talking like a voice a long way off, heard in a dream.

"Do you think," she was saying, "that because he has so fierce a wish to live his life is really desirable? Are you sure that he does not live on only because he dreads the end, and the awakening and the reckoning before God? Dear Dick, do you not think that perhaps it is well that

men and women do not live too long, for they sin, in spite of themselves, and perhaps death saves them from sinning beyond forgiveness?
I do not know how long Killigrew has lived, but I know he has lived far
beyond the natural life of man, and there is nothing in his life that I
would envy for your sake. Do you not see that this is what I dreaded
when I wished that you might not come to us, when I feared for you,
when I feared lest any other human being should be tricked into living
as Killigrew has lived? I have never seen him happy. And now, dear
Dick, you would make it of no use that we have escaped. And listen,
Dick. Ever since I loved you and thought of us, together, in that house
where life was eternal, I have dreamed of a different life for us. I have
thought of us, young together, as we are now, but not young with a
dead youth that would last for ever; just young, and growing older,
making memories for ourselves. Of what use are memories to Killigrew?
I have thought of us growing older, side by side, hand in hand. I have
thought of us not as immortals, but as an old man and an old woman
who have shared their lives together and trusted each other, and with
that trust are not afraid of the end, when it should come, and we should
part, only for a little time. Dick, I have thought of you with white hair,
and not so tall as you are now, and I thought I too should be old, and
that we, together, should find a sweetness even in old age, and then, at
last, leave the world before it grew too strange for us. . . . No, Dick, I do
not want you to be unhappy. . . ."

I had thrown myself on the ground, and with my face in my hands
sobbed, in spite of myself, with weakness, though there were no tears in
my burning eyes.

At last, still keeping my face from her, I begged in a low voice:

"Rose, destroy it, before I see it again."

She answered gravely, "No, Dick, for if I destroy it you will still be
its slave, as if you had drunk it. I want you to destroy it, you yourself,
and of your own free will. If I destroy it, it will always be between us."

I knew that she stood up, with the Elixir in her hand. I stood up,
swaying, so that I could hardly stand. I tried to see her eyes, without
seeing that horrible crimson phial that she held in her hands.

"I will destroy it," I said.

She gave me the phial.

For one instant I felt that madness coming back upon me like a
great wave of blood, towering above my head, and then, with desperate
haste, I lifted the phial and flung it down into the road. There was a
faint thin splintering sound as it struck a stone in the road, and the
thing had disappeared for ever. The fine glass powdered, the crimson
fluid lay for an instant like a splash of blood, and then was gone.

I staggered like a man drunk. I felt as if I had been holding my breath for a long time. Then sanity came back to me and I heard myself laughing incredulously, Rose was in my arms, weeping as if her heart would break.

"Oh, Dick," she whispered, "we are alone in the real world at last!"

We stood there for a long time in the sunlight, and, though we did not kneel, I do not think our thanksgiving was for that the less sincere.

Suddenly the black horse, cropping the grass above us, lifted its head and whinnied. There was the faint noise of galloping hooves, a small noise, but sharp and clear in that early morning, when there was nothing else upon the road. I do not know which of us first guessed what it meant. We stood there listening, looking back along the road to the gold woods on the farther slope.

CHAPTER XVII
The End of John Killigrew

We guessed the meaning of that sound, long before the little figure of a man on a galloping horse, at that distance like an ant, showed just where the road left the woods, and, a curling white ribbon, began to cross the valley.

"We have yet to reckon with Mr. Killigrew," I said.

"And you have only that sword, that very little sword," said Rose, and, for a moment, looked towards the woodland path close behind us, and then at the big black horse, who seemed to know as much about it as we, for his ears were cocked in the direction of the distant noise, and he was listening with obvious excitement and uneasiness.

"No," I said, "if we run away from him on the horse, he will only catch us up a few miles farther on, for the black, well as he has carried us, is heavily over-weighted. Better to meet him here. Also, I cannot send you to seek for help, for the help when it came would probably be given to Killigrew and not to us. We might hide in the woods and trust that he will ride past, but the black horse has left so clear a set of prints when he climbed the bank that unless Killigrew is riding with both his eyes closed he cannot fail to perceive that we have stopped here, and, further, to guess whither we have gone."

"I will do what you think best," said Rose, "but you must not send me away."

I kissed her, and as I did so forgot Killigrew and all else, except that now, come what might, the shadow of the Elixir had been destroyed, and that if we were to die we should at least die without that sinister barrier between us which had been there only a few minutes ago.

"Remember that I am younger and stronger than he," I said to Rose, trying to comfort her, and also trying to comfort myself, for the thing I feared in Killigrew had little to do with youth or strength. There is no man alive who does not prefer to fight with a sane man instead of with a lunatic. And the thing that I feared in Killigrew was something worse than lunacy, which merely makes a man's actions incalculable, and therefore hard to forestall. It was a spiritual thing, something that separated him from men, and left no man a match for him.

The noise of the hooves grew louder. There was a strange irregularity in their sound, which seemed to disquiet the black in an extraordinary manner. Horses no doubt know more about each other than we know of them, and I think the black knew that these approaching hoof-beats were those of a wounded horse long before I had fitted that explanation to them.

For the greater part of the way across the broad valley the road was invisible, and, when we next saw the horseman, he was near enough for us to recognize him. He was at the foot of the long slope we had climbed. It was Killigrew, bent almost double on the back of the brown mare, flogging her wildly with the scabbard of his sword. The thought flashed through my mind that at least I had not to reckon with his superior swordsmanship, and that he would presently pay for his attempt to murder me. I remembered that the sword was probably still stuck through the raised canopy of the bed, or lying among the ashes of that ingenious instrument of death.

The brown mare was laboring terribly. There was a fog of steam about her nostrils. Her head hung loosely, jerking with Killigrew's efforts, and suddenly I perceived that she was bleeding from a wound in her chest, perhaps from one of the pitchforks of the yokels. She thundered weakly up the slope, stumbled, gathered herself, and, suddenly, not thirty yards from us, her legs crumpled under her, and she fell. Killigrew was out of the saddle as she dropped, and pulled frantically at her bridle. She rolled over. One hind-leg straightened suddenly in the air, and remained there, motionless. The brown mare was dead. There was a dreadful little noise from the black horse, who stood with dilated nostrils. Then, suddenly, he leapt forward, and charged down the slope. Killigrew looked up, and saw him coming, slipped round to the farther side of the dead mare, drew a pistol, and, taking swift aim, fired. The black horse, shot in the head, fell within two yards of him, almost on the body of the mare he had been rushing to avenge. It was over in a moment. A moment later I knew that the black horse had saved one of our lives at least.

Killigrew looked up the road, and saw us, waiting there. He bent to take his powder-flask, and reload the pistol. The lid of the powder-flask must have been shaken open by that furious ride, and the powder escaped. I saw Killigrew shake the flask upside down, and, with a gesture of anger, toss powder-flask and pistol into the bracken at the roadside. The black horse had taken his last shot.

Killigrew walked to where the scabbard with which he had been flailing the dead mare had fallen in the road. He picked it up, and broke it between his fingers. To the very end the man had such strength in his muscles as could only have been given him by the devil. Then, leisurely, he sauntered up the road towards us.

He stopped when about five yards away, I suppose at seeing the look in my eyes, and the readiness of my sword. He stopped, made us a low bow, and smiled. Rose turned her face away. She could not bear to look at that countenance on which, in spite of his manner, was written in unmistakable characters the truth, the horrible, the loathsome truth, that lay in that man's soul. He had seemed old when I had seen him through the window of my room, dancing before the bed, making ironic speeches, as he supposed, to the body of a murdered man. He had seemed older when with feverish, quick gestures he had searched my room for the Elixir which was not there. But now, in the sunlight of the morning, he seemed infinitely older, the oldest, the wickedest thing on earth. His skin had contracted about his face, so that his cheek-bones glistened in the sun. Between his cheek-bones and his nose were parallel deep wrinkles. His lips, always thin, had now entirely disappeared. His mouth was just a narrow opening in his face, as if it had been cut with a knife, and cut carelessly. It was crooked, and it smiled, a horrid, narrow, smiling hole. His eyes had fallen deeper in his head, and were so shadowed by his brows that he stared unblinkingly into the sunlight, and, when he looked at me, it was as if in place of eyes there were two sparks of fire in the sockets of a skull.

He bowed, I say, and smiled with that dreadful slit that was his mouth.

"So we meet again, Mr. Stanborough. I had feared that you had died in the fire from which only with difficulty I escaped. I am happy to greet you as a survivor. And Rose too, she also has escaped. I congratulate the two of you on your remarkable foresight."

It was impossible to tell whether or no he expected me to take him seriously. I am not sure to this day whether or no he was trying to find out how much we knew. Perhaps, if he had found that we knew nothing, he would have taken a different tone in the ensuing conversation.

I did not at first answer him.

He went on:

"You are a little impolite, Mr. Stanborough. You fled yourself, taking Mistress Killigrew with you. It seems you did not spare a thought for my plight in the hands of those fanatic ruffians. And now, when by my presence I show you that I am still alive, your joy at your friend's escape is shown chiefly by a somewhat nervous silence, and by play, almost threatening play, with the hilt of your sword. And you, Rose, are you, too, silent?"

He waited, as if for us to answer him.

"Your foresight extended even to taking with you the Elixir. It is true, Mr. Stanborough, that I had offered it you, but, if I remember rightly, you refused it. I was the more surprised and grateful to you when I found that you had rescued, for me, what you did not wish for yourself."

"Mr. Killigrew," I said, suddenly, surprising even myself, "set an end to this theatrical business. We shall talk to better purpose if you know that both Mistress Rose and myself were witnesses of your attempt to murder me in my bed, nay more, that I saw you murder Michael, and am not ignorant of the reason."

Killigrew opened his mouth a little wider. It seemed to move upwards and sidewise in his cheek, and he laughed.

"Stale news," he said, "but given me with good intention. I thank you."

"Well," I said, "have done with your sneers, and tell me what you wish from us."

"You have not yet told me what you are doing with my ward."

"Mistress Killigrew will presently be my wife, and, as you well know, she is not answerable to you."

"So you know you are marrying Michael's daughter."

"I know I am marrying the daughter of a man who, unlike you, repented before it was too late, and had the courage to die for his conscience' sake."

"A pretty death he made of it," said Killigrew.

"He was an unarmed man, and he neither ran nor asked for mercy," I replied.

"And you, Mr. Stanborough, you have no particular objection to fighting unarmed men. I see your hand has never left the hilt of your sword, and it seems to me that if the moment should prove favourable to you you would run that sword through me with as little compunction as I felt in punishing an unfaithful servant. You have seen me throw away my pistol, and my sword . . ."

"Is struck in the bed in which you plunged it, believing that you plunged it into my prisoned body. Pah," I said, and stung by his words, just as he had wished, I threw my sword from me. It fell on the road behind us.

I had no sooner thrown it away, than I regretted the action, and, indeed, it was very foolish. I trusted Killigrew less than any man in the world and feared him more, and now I had thrown away the only advantage I had over him, and that small enough, in the little sword which had aroused my uncle's jeers.

He moved a step nearer.

"You are near enough, Mr. Killigrew, I said.

"I entreat your pardon." He bowed ironically. "I am tired, and had thought of sitting on the bank at the roadside."

"I think we can finish our conversation standing," I replied, "since the talking will be entirely on your side. I have said all that I wish to say, which is, to ask you to go your way and leave us to go ours."

"A very pleasant arrangement, no doubt," said Killigrew, "but, my generous friend, you forget that you are in possession of my Elixir."

"You are mistaken," I replied; "you will no longer by its help continue the infamous existence of which, as perhaps you are unaware, I have the fullest knowledge. The lives of others will no longer be food for your own."

More than that I did not wish to say, for I hoped to keep Rose in ignorance of the darkest side of the secret she had innocently shared.

"Ah, Mr. Stanborough," said Killigrew. "You know so much. You know indeed so very much that you will not wish to sully your spotless conscience with so infamous a means of living. You will not wish yourself to share what you consider, in your childish narrowness, villainy in me. We can therefore strike an equitable bargain."

"I know of no bargain that can be made between us. You sought to trick me into participation in your crimes. You failed. That is enough. Let me be quit of you henceforth, and I ask no more."

"And that, on my side of the bargain, is precisely what I offer you. Give me the Elixir you detest, and I will go my own way, and leave you to go yours. Give me the Elixir, and I will bid you good-day, and go to tread my path alone, my proud path that you have shown to be above your understanding. Refuse to give it me, and . . ."

I interrupted him.

"You think that I would willingly let you go forth into the world to continue through centuries your odious trail of blood. I would not. And, Mr. Killigrew, I am happy to say that I cannot even if I would."

"What do you mean? You have not, idiot though you are, left the Elixir in that burning ruin?" He turned for a moment, and looked back down the road.

"The Elixir is destroyed," I said.

He did not believe me.

"Very clever. But you forget that you are talking to one cleverer than you. Man does not lightly destroy what through all the ages of the world man has desired. It is not in the power of man to throw away the secret of eternal life, the one thing that can keep him from the grave."

I remembered, shamefully, my own weakness. He must have seen my thought flit across my face, which he was watching intently.

"No," he said, "you are more of a coward than I, and I know that it is impossible to throw that thing away."

"You forget Michael."

"Michael?" he laughed. "That was a suicide. He did not wish to live. Moreover, he had just drunk from it, and tasted the remorse to which. I have taught myself to be indifferent. But you stand there, and I do not see in you a wish to die. No, you wish to live. You still believe in love. Rose is for you something more than the silly child . . ."

"I will thank you not to defile her name with your lips," I said.

"Ah, I thought so. She is a Goddess, and you her slave. And you ask me to believe that you do not wish to live with her for ever. I am not such a simpleton. Leave that pretence. Admit frankly that you still possess the Elixir, and discuss the terms on which we are to share it. I tell you, you will not be able to keep it to yourself. Rather than that I will myself bring all the world about your ears."

"Will you be pleased to understand," I said, impatiently, "that there is no Elixir to be shared. The Elixir was destroyed, here, by me, half an hour ago. You are too late."

I saw his face change a little. His mouth closed, lipless, so that it was no more than a crooked, scarcely visible line below his nose. He put his hand into the breast of his coat. I knew in that instant that he was still armed, and that there was a weapon concealed in his hand. I cursed my folly in allowing myself to answer his taunts by throwing away my sword.

He hardly opened his mouth when he spoke again,

"You insist on keeping up this stupid deception?"

"The Elixir has been destroyed."

"Very well then," he said, "your blood will be on your own head," and with that he whisked out an open knife from where it had been hidden in his breast, and, with a swift trick of the wrist, that I suppose he had learnt in Italy, he flung it at me. I saw a long flash in the sunlight, like a silver snake, and at the same time felt a sharp pain at the side of my neck, as if it had been touched with a hot iron. The knife fell on the ground behind me, and the blood, spurting out from a flesh wound in my neck, trickled down into my shirt and fell on my white ruffles.

"You are hurt," cried Rose, and caught my hand.

"It is nothing," I said, and snatching out my kerchief, pressed it to the wound as I stood facing Killigrew. I dared not take my eyes from him for a moment.

When he saw that he had failed, his face contorted horribly, as I had seen it on the previous night. He lost all his confidence. He seemed to shrink into himself, and stood there in front of us, shaking with anger.

The anger suddenly gave place to fear. All disguise fell from him:

"I wished to kill you," he said, "yes, I wished to kill you . . . but you forced me to it. You do not know this thirst. You do not know the pain that is twisting me now, even now. Stanborough, you are cruel. You are more cruel than you know. Give it me now. Give it me, and I will do anything you wish. I will be your servant. I will kill myself, afterwards, when this pain is gone. You do not understand. I am tortured. I cannot wait for it. Do not keep it from me longer than I can bear. You would forgive me if you knew. Give it me. Give it me. You cannot have destroyed it. No. No. Not even you would be so mad. It is there. It is red with life. It waits for me. Three of them I killed last night, perhaps four. It must be sparkling with blood. Stanborough, Stanborough, you cannot have destroyed it."

I could say nothing. I stood there holding my kerchief to that wound in my neck, which was indeed no more than a scratch, and presently stopped bleeding. It had none the less made me feel faint, and I was already weak from the spiritual struggle that had so lately ended. I had no more strength than was enough to keep me standing in front of him, with my eyes on his face.

"Rose," he went on, "you have lived with me all your life. You would not see me tortured now. Rose, beg him for it, make him give it me. Have I ever been unkind to you?"

"Twenty years ago you were the cause of my mother's death," said Rose, "and yesterday you killed my father to whom you had done worse. I would not, even if I could, give you the means to live and work such wickedness on others. But I cannot. Mr. Stanborough has told you the truth. The Elixir has been destroyed, and for that I thank God."

"No, no, no," he screamed. "Rose, Stanborough, think of what that means. You will be beginning your immortality to-day, but if you do not let me share it, you will be wasting all the years that I have lived."

All the greatness of his wickedness was gone from him, all that which had made me respect him, reverence him, even while I feared him. He was like one of those devils in the old paintings, cringing wretchedly before the Judge on the Last Day, thin, twisted creatures, out of which the evil has been wrung by terror.

"I cannot die," he whined; "you must not let me die . . . not now . . . not after all that . . ."

"Rose," said I, not turning my head, "on the ground just behind you is the little black case of the Elixir. Please put it in my hand."

She looked on the ground and put it in my hand. I held it up.

"See," I said. "Will this make you believe? Is this or is it not the case in which you kept that accursed drug? You see that it is empty."

With that I tossed it to him. He tried to catch it, but his hands were too eager, too greedy, and it fell to the ground. He picked it up, murmuring over it and fondling it with his fingers. It was as if his fingers would not obey him when he wished to open it. Or perhaps he already began to believe, and he was afraid. He stood, crouching over it, as he held it in his hands. At last he opened it, and saw that it was indeed empty. His long thin fingers ran about over it. He poked them into it, felt it all over, like a monkey playing with an empty nut that a squirrel has picked.

"Yes. It is empty," he said, "but you have taken the phial, the little snake . . . scarlet in the glass. You have taken it out. You were about to drink. It is on the bank behind you. It is in your coat. Be careful with it. It would break so easily. Be careful with it. Rose has it in her kerchief. Give it to me. I will be more careful than you. You should have kept it in its case."

Just then the sunlight glinted on something small in the road between us.

"Mr. Killigrew," I said, "you may make one step forward. Now look at the ground at your feet."

He stooped and picked up the little glass snake's head that had been the mouth of the phial. For one second he bent over it, motionless. Then with a shriek as dreadful as that which I had heard in the June night in the rose-garden, he threw himself at my throat.

I cannot explain what happened. I think that it was already long past the time at which he should have refreshed his life with that iniquitous drug. Perhaps he had only kept alive during these last hours since he first noticed the loss of the Elixir by virtue of the superhuman will which had made him the devil he was. It seems to me that I braced myself against the shock. There was no shock. He must have died in the very act of his last murderous onslaught. There sprang at me that man, terrible even in his agony. But empty clothes fell against my chest. The air was filled with a light grey dust. That was all. It was if some one had thrown some empty clothes at me. I cannot describe it in any other way. Empty clothes, that flapped against my chest and fell loosely at my feet, and then that little cloud of grey dust, that died in the road, like the dust after a horse has gone by. There was a faint smell.

Then I understood.

"Good Lord," I said, I hope without irreverence, "Good Lord, the man has been dead two hundred years."

CHAPTER XVIII

My Uncle in Another Mood, and
How, When One Story Ends, Another Begins

I heard a little low cry behind me, and turned, just in time to catch Rose as she fell. The sight of that horrible end to a life, for I find it difficult to describe it as a death, had been more than her tired nerves, overwrought by the events of the night, could bear, and nature, like a mother, preserved her child from too full a realization of what had passed. I lifted Rose in my arms, carried her a few yards along the road, round a bend, so that the bank and the trees should hide from her the scene of the destruction of the Elixir and of Killigrew's end. I laid her on the bank in the sunshine, so that when she returned to consciousness she should be looking not on those dead horses, or on anything that should immediately remind her of what had happened, but on the broad spreading landscape, where the sun shone, and here and there among the fields thin streams of blue smoke poured up from human dwellings into the quiet air. Then I set myself to revive her, slapping her unwounded hand, as I had seen Mrs. Barber do to the hands of a fainting maid, though, I admit, I found it hard to do violence to that little hand of hers.

She came to herself at last, asking where she was, and whispering my name. I took both her hands, and comforted them for the slapping. I kissed them. I kissed her brow, her eyes. It may seem foolish to you now, but I remember that at that moment it was as if she had returned from the farther side of death. And indeed I had myself a curious lightness in the throat, and a readiness to weep, though I did not actually shed tears.

Suddenly she came back to the full memory of what had passed. "Is he dead?" she asked.

"He died long ago," I replied; "my dear, we need not think of him again."

"Let us go on," she begged; "I can walk." She tried to rise, but I would not let her, and made her rest for a moment.

"We will go on at once," I said, "but rest while I recover my sword."

"Your sword," she said, "that little sword," and with those words I saw a faint smile come about her lips.

I left her there on the bank, while I ran back along the road. I had no difficulty in finding my sword. I slipped it back into its pretty scabbard, and then, in spite of myself, turned to look once more at those empty blue clothes that had been Killigrew, or, at least, were all that was left of the man who had held the secret of the world's desire, and, by two hundred years of miserable, sinful life, had proved it worthless. As I looked at them, stirring them, disgustfully, with my foot, as a boy stirs a dead rat, I saw that the clothes were not all that was left. Close by one of the sleeves on the ground lay that gold ring which Killigrew had taken from the fingers of that old alchemist who had found the secret of the Elixir. It glittered there, gold in the green grass. The dust that had been bone and flesh had blown away from about it. There were no dead fingers to revolt me. Killigrew had, as it were, been cleaned off the face of the earth, and, with but slight compunction, I picked up the ring and looked at it curiously. I had already picked it up before thinking that, though nothing had been visible, Killigrew had never taken it off, and so, though it had lain loose in the grass, I had really plucked it from his hand. It lay in mine, a plain gold ring, with the wheel and the serpent about it, and I thought wonderingly how many strange and terrible things it had witnessed in the course of the long, horrible existence of its last owner. I thought of that row of portraits. I thought of the crowded life that I in my twenty years of boyhood seemed to have experienced, and then I thought of that long, sinuous career of sin, a trail in life, like that of a hideous snail over the petals of a flower.

I decided to keep the ring, as a reminder of evil, as a reminder of my earnest resolve to keep our own lives, the life that henceforth we were to share between us, free from such smudges. I also picked up the little ebony case that had held the phial of the Elixir. This I wished to keep, for another reason, to prevent me from forgetting the urgent need for that part of the Lord's Prayer at which I had always sneered in my heart—"Lead us not into temptation." Time had been when with the callow confidence of boyhood I had felt that a sound philosophy was proof against temptation. Henceforward the sight of that little box of black wood would remind me of those dreadful minutes when, overwhelmed by the sinister power of the Elixir, its mere touch had separated me from Rose and from all that is sweet on earth or precious in the sight of Heaven. That ring and the box are on the table before me as I write. I have even now felt a shudder pass over the skin of my cheeks as I touched them, and I have comforted myself by looking through the window into the garden, where Rose and our youngest child, children together, are telling the time of day by blowing the down from a flower of the dandelion.

But I will not make my history too long. I went back to Rose, and together we set to walking down the hill into that broad open country. We were not far now from the great North Road and the inn where I had met

Killigrew after my quarrel with my uncle. When I saw it lying below us, we turned aside to the north into a field path that led us out upon the great road just beyond the crest of hill where, at midnight in June, I had found myself suddenly alone with the noise of departing carriage wheels. There we rested by the roadside. We had met a farm lass in the fields, coming from milking, and she had given us a drink of fresh milk. But we had had no other food, and I did not think it wise to go to that same inn, lest I should be known, and questions asked, and we again be drawn into the end of Killigrew. I knew not if the tale of the burnt house and the murdered peasants would carry so far, but I had an earnest desire to keep Rose henceforth free, utterly free from that odious past. We rested there in the road, and planned what we would do. We had money from the pedlar. It was only a question of getting farther north along the road. It was four o'clock in the afternoon when Rose fell asleep.

I sat there on the bank beside her, watching her, and feeling a great desire to sleep myself. I suppose about an hour had gone by, when, fighting my sleepiness, I stood up and decided to walk to and fro in the road, just so far from her as not to wake her with my steps. I had not taken two turns in the road, when I heard the sound of wheels and horses trotting. For a moment I was full of regret that the sound came from the north, so that we could not ask the driver to give us a lift on our way; and then my regret was changed into incredulous hope.

A fat grey horse, with a fat servant upon it, a long gun swinging at his back; a broad, swinging, dusty carriage, drawn by two more greys, and a boy riding a fourth horse some little way behind the equipage. It could not be, I thought, and yet it was, that same old coach in which my uncle periodically journeyed to London from the north and back again, the coach in which I had played as a child, the coach from which I had been so unceremoniously ejected—projected rather—into the midst of my adventure. It was no such miracle as at that moment I was inclined to suppose, for if my uncle were travelling on any road, that would be the road. But it was perhaps more than a fortunate chance that he had not started a day earlier.

"Brocklebank," I shouted to the old coachman.

He looked at me with his round red face, and pulled up the horses. "Praise be to God, Master Dick," said he.

My uncle's head shot furiously out of the window.

"Why, in the name of . . . are you stopping? Get on, man, get on." And then, as he saw me, his face changed, and, just as I might have known he would, he asked me, as if there was nothing unusual in our meeting:

"Well, Richard, have you been sitting here ever since we parted?"

"Uncle," said I, "I owe you an apology."

"Rot your apology," said he; "let me have a grip of your hand." Behind my uncle in the coach I saw Mrs. Barber in a stupendous bonnet. She almost pulled my uncle from the window, and embraced me.

"Didn't I tell you, Master Dick," she said, and then, "Eh, the bairn, what have you done to that neck?"

"Into the coach with you, Dick," says my uncle, "you have saved me the rest of the journey; for to tell you truth, boy, I was uneasy about you, and what with Mistress Barber for ever snivelling about you, I was coming to see if we could not lay hands on you again. Turn the coach, Brocklebank," he cried, "we'll be tempting that trout in the long dub inside of a week."

"Yes, sir," said old Brocklebank, who was as keen an angler as my uncle.

"Uncle," said I, "I am not alone."

"Not alone?"

"I have a lady with me."

"You always were a fool, and always will be," said my uncle. "I've half a mind to quarrel with you again. And did you find her in the road?"

"I did not," I said, "but I was bringing her to Bigland, and she is very tired. And the sooner she is in Mrs. Barber's care the better. I will tell you the story later, when we are on the road, for the sooner we are away from this country the better it may be."

The door at the other side of the coach flew open, and Mistress Barber squeezed out, her great bonnet flapping round her face.

"And where is she? Eh, Master Dick, have you no better sense?"

My uncle simply stared at me with open mouth.

"You'll be telling me next you're married. And is she a gipsy?"

"I shall be married at Bigland, I hope, sir, and with your leave, and I would remind you, sir, that I said I was accompanied by a lady."

"Hoity-toity," said my uncle, "and here we are quarrelling again. I will not have it, sir; I tell you, I will not have it. You may, sir, stare at me like a turkey, as much as you will, but devil a quarrel you'll get for your pains. You don't know, my dear Dick, what I've had to bear from old Babkins."

Just then Mistress Barber came back to the carriage.

"The prettiest bairn that ever was," she said, "and you, Master Dick, and Mr. Stanborough, you must turn the boys off the horses and ride, while she and I have the coach to ourselves. 'T will do you good, Mr. Stanborough, after that bottle at midday."

My uncle made a wry face, but tumbled out of the carriage, and made the boys, who were aged about fifty and sixty, dismount from the fat grey and the other horse, a roan, also too fat to be fast, and climb up beside Brocklebank. The carriage was turned round. I carried Rose to it, still half asleep. She was tired out, poor girl, and when she woke she was there in that old coach with Mistress Barber scolding and fondling her, like a hen with one chick. As for my uncle and me, we mounted the riding horses, he on the grey and I on the roan, and trotted solemnly before the coach on that long straight road that leads over hill and dale to the grey fells and green valleys of the north.

As we rode, I told him something of the story I have here written down; not all, for he was an incredulous old man.

"And do you expect me to believe all this?" he asked.

"I cannot say that I do," I replied, "but my wounded neck is one proof of it, and here are two more."

I rode close beside him, and put into his hand first the ring and then the case.

He felt them and handed them back, as if he did not wish to touch them.

"They seem to me to be real," he said, "but the young woman? Who is she?"

I told him the name of Michael's family, which I do not intend to write here, and he was comforted.

"For all that 'tis a strange tale," he said, "and there are not two uncles in England who would not quarrel with you over it. But let be. I have not seen the maid."

"You will be proud of your niece when you know her," I said, and just then Mistress Barber called to us from the carriage window.

"Not bite nor sup they've had since yesterday," she cried to my uncle, "so I've taken the cold chicken from the hamper, and routed half the coach out for a corkscrew, forgetting I put it back in the pocket of that coat."

In a few minutes we were sitting, my uncle and I on Sinai, Rose and Mistress Barber on Ararat, with an open bottle wedged between my uncle's knees, and Babkins dexterously cutting up a chicken. I think it was the happiest meal that ever I remember.

Neither Rose nor I said much. We were too tired, and we had no need, for my uncle and Mistress Barber talked ceaselessly, so that before she had been acquainted with them half a dozen hours, Rose must have known almost all that there was to be known of Bigland. With Mistress Barber it was the maids and the men, the gossip of the countryside, how James Newby had married again, and Mistress Swainson been brought to bed of twins. With my uncle it was the dogs, every one of whom he knew by name, and expected me to know. And then it was the fishing. "Dick," my lad, he said, "now you are getting married, you'd best mend your ways and take up a rod . . ."

"For shame, Mr. Stanborough," cried Mistress Babkins with abounding indignation.

My uncle was taken aback for a moment.

"Nay, Babkins," he said at last, "not for that, I warrant there'll be no need. But a rod for fishing, and he must let me show him a cast or two, and how to tie a fly, and then they'll be the happiest married couple between York Minster and Skiddaw."

There was much more of such talk, simple, honest talk, that was to our ears like a gentle breeze after one of those hurricanes that blow your hair about your eyes and your knees from under you. It was restful to listen to it, and the more so, that with every mile in that old coach we were farther from the scenes in which we had been so torn with doubt and fear, and overshadowed with the mysterious gloom of the Elixir.

Evening fell, and it was dark in the carriage. There was one stout candle in a horn lantern, hanging from the roof. I think I slept. Anyhow it was with a feeling as if of waking that I opened my eyes and was aware of Rose sleeping with her head pillowed on Mistress Barber's motherly bosom. Mistress Barber was also asleep. I looked sideways at my uncle and saw that he was awake. He was looking at Rose, and I perceived that, perhaps unknown to himself, he had a bit of my coat in his hand. There was a look of extraordinary kindness on his old, rugged face, and to my astonishment I saw that a tear, an incredible tear, was slowly trickling down his cheek. He turned his head towards me, but fortunately I was in time to close my eyes. He never knew until he died that I had been a witness of this proof of the softness of his quarrelsome old heart.

*   *   *

That really is the end of my story. It is an old story now, the story of twenty years ago. Rose and I were married at Bigland, and lived there with my uncle and Mistress Barber. My uncle died some six years later, thanking God that his illness had come upon him at the end of the trout season, instead of at the beginning. He had had the satisfaction of making a fisherman of me, and of fastening a bent pin on the end of a thread, and seeing his first great-nephew catch a minnow. I believe he never caught a salmon himself with greater pride. I took again to my philosophers, but left the alchemists alone, and found that even the ingenuities of Bishop Berkeley somehow lose in interest in comparison with the sayings of one's children. Rose, as I had prophesied, enjoyed her first childhood under the care of Mistress Barber, so that she be-came, as it were, contemporary with her own children. The Elixir could never have made her so young. But to tell of our life here in the old house at the foot of the fells is to begin a new story instead of putting an end to an old. And already I have, perhaps, spent too much time on this history, which may be of interest only to my children, and possibly not to them. All through the bright days of this summer of 1736 I have sat here at my window, and written, and looked out upon the garden, and, with a strength of mind that I had not in my boyhood, resisted the sweet noise of the bees and the laughter of my children, that sought to draw me from my labour. And now I may write the word "Finis," and go out to them with the satisfaction of having earned my freedom, to sit with Rose in the arbour beyond the hollyhocks, and, when she leaves me at twilight to see the younger bairns to bed, to hesitate between Lu-cretius and Vergil, and not knowing whether to take the philosopher or the poet from my pocket, to sit there in the dusk reading neither, and listening to the owls calling in the low wood under the fell.